HAUNTING MISS TRENTWOOD

BOOK 1 OF THE HESITANT MEDIUMS

BELINDA KROLL

Bright
Bird Press

BRIGHT BIRD PRESS

This is a work of historical fantasy, and therefore a work of fiction. The appearance or mention of certain historical figures may be inevitable. Names, characters, organizations, places, events, and incidents are the product of the author's imagination or are used fictitiously. Any resemblance to actual events, locales, or persons, living or dead, is coincidental or historically-inspired. Eerie happenings during Victorian séances are to be expected, do try not to be too alarmed.

BELINDA KROLL

FATHER KNOWS BEST,
EVEN AFTER DEATH

HAUNTING
MISS TRENTWOOD

A HESITANT MEDIUMS NOVEL

ONE

COMPTON BEAUCHAMP, FEBRUARY 1887

THREE DAYS' RIDE WEST OF LONDON

AT TWO IN THE afternoon the coffin of Mary Trentwood's father was lowered to its grave. The sun shone unseasonably bright. Mary squinted through burning eyes. She heard the wooden box hit the bottom of the hole. She heard the whispers of her servants and father's friends behind her. However quietly they thought they were speaking, Mary heard every word. The whispers grew louder and moved closer, crowding her ears.

"Right barmy, that's what she is."

"I heard she hasn't any feeling at all."

"Certainly would explain the lack of tears."

"Making us stand here and watch the digging of the grave, it's indecent, that's what it is."

"Well, I certainly don't know how you can expect any better from hermits, they're not fit to be gentry, I say."

Mary didn't know who they were, these people whispering about her as she stood a mere four feet in front of them. She didn't care. They weren't there for her, they—whoever they were for she hadn't invited them, no, that had been the workings of her aunt Mrs. Durham—only cared about their gossip mongering. The local farmers and tenants would never treat her thus. But the funeral guests were certain to spread their hissing rumors across the countryside. Mary hated that unnamed mass of huddled, whispering heads standing behind her. She hated her father for dying, for making this entire ordeal necessary in the first place.

The vicar finished his sermon and snapped his Bible shut.

Mary hunched her shoulders as the mourners filed past. She gritted her teeth, but allowed the men to solemnly brush their lips against her gloved fingers. Her jaw all but shattered in her effort to not scream at the women making tut-tutting noises.

And then Mary was alone, her black netted veil scratching her pale cheek as the wind blew. She stared at that father-sized hole. She stepped closer. How close to the edge did she dare tread? How soon before her nerves, strained to their last, snapped, rendering her as lifeless as her dear father at the bottom of that dark pit?

Mary jumped when Mrs. Durham's hand touched her arm.

Mrs. Durham was a squat woman, with soft features that hinted at great beauty, once. Once upon a time, a very long time ago, Mary figured. Mrs. Durham had been her mother's twin, fraternally speaking. Mary was glad she didn't resemble her aunt in the slightest. Mrs. Durham's cheeks arched upward—reaching, straining, pushing—trying to touch the topmost curve of her eye sockets. Truly an appalling sight; Mary decided her aunt should never squint, if she could help it.

"Come away," Mrs. Durham murmured, "let the men folk do their job." She shifted so Mary's view of the gravediggers filling the grave was blocked. She began pushing Mary back to the manor house, where a light luncheon waited for them.

Whatever suggestive power Mrs. Durham had on Mary could not prevent the horrifying vision of a man, muddy and coughing, clawing his way from the grave site. He hung from the edge of the hole into which Trentwood's coffin had descended, his elbows digging into the dirt as he wriggled his way out.

Mary stared open-mouthed.

He was dismayingly flexible, able to swing a leg over the edge and roll onto the disturbed ground. He stood, brushing himself off almost apologetically though no dirt clung to his clothing. He gave Mary time to study his determined chin, firm mouth, and snappish eyes. He combed his sandy hair back from his forehead while clearing his throat, revealing streaks of gray running from temple to crown. The overall effect was chilling familiarity.

Mary wrenched free of Mrs. Durham. "Father?" she said, her voice hoarse from not speaking the week since his death. "Papa?"

Mary sat upright, kicking her bed sheets away from sweat-soaked legs. A lock of her dark hair was plastered to her cheek. Her head ached from the bobby pins still shoved into her scalp. She lifted her hand to pull the bobby pins out and noticed she was wearing black crepe sleeves, the same she wore in her nightmare.

Her hands shook. She hadn't been dreaming. Mary knew she hadn't been dreaming. She had buried her father, and he had crawled from his grave right before her eyes.

Her bedroom door opened to reveal Mrs. Durham with a tray of tea. "Oh good," Mrs. Durham said with false cheer, "you're finally awake."

"Finally?" Mary said. Her voice was no more than an awkward croak, but it seemed Mrs. Durham understood her.

"You've been sleeping for three days."

Mary shook her head. She gasped. Three days? Had it been three days since she had buried her father? Panting, she unbuttoned her dress to her collar bone, unable to inhale with the neck buttoned to her chin. She felt so hot. Why hadn't anyone undressed her? Right, that's right, she had dismissed her maid after her father died to alleviate costs.

Mary shook her head again as Mrs. Durham placed the tea tray on the little table beside her bed. Everything felt fuzzy.

Mrs. Durham sat in the vanity chair that had been dragged to the bedside while Mary slept. Her black dress rustled sweetly as she moved, the fabric shining in the gray sunlight. "You fainted dead away after the coffin went down."

Mary sighed. "Yes, I just—I thought I saw Papa."

"But you did, my dear."

Mary's hazel eyes narrowed to slits. "I did?"

"Well, do forgive my callousness, but I'm not certain who else you think we buried."

Mary felt a retort forming, but she held her tongue. She had to remember her aunt had lost her dear husband only four months ago, and was still out of sorts. She took the time to study Mrs. Durham shiny black earrings, the way her hands folded in her lap, the perfection of her graying hair pulled into a tight chignon topped with white lace.

Do I tell her? Do I admit I saw Father crawl from his grave? No, Mrs. Durham was not one for believing such "folderol" as she called it when Mary confided her nightmares or shared folklore and haunting stories with the servants.

Mary looked at the bedroom door, not hearing the raucous laughter of the funeral guests. "Where is everyone?" Mary asked instead, accepting a lukewarm cup of tea.

"Ah, I sent them home. Well," Mrs. Durham chuckled, "they left fairly quickly on their own. They were quite startled when you announced you wanted everyone to follow the coffin to its grave. What in the world made you do such a thing? It simply isn't done."

No, it wasn't done, but then, there were a great many things that Mary had done to satisfy Society, and she had decided that Society, in turn, could grant her this one aberration. Mary swallowed the last of the tea and placed the cup on the tray. "I'm rather tired."

Mrs. Durham frowned, hearing the finality in Mary's tone. "Of course," she replied, standing. "I trust you will send for me should you need me?" At Mary's silent nod, she took her leave, looking none too pleased.

As soon as the door was shut, Mary threw her hands to her face. "I did not see my father's ghost." She shivered despite being drenched with sweat. "I must be mad."

"A bit dramatic, I suppose, but mad? Would I allow you to run my household if you were mad?"

Mary screamed. She grabbed her skirts and scrambled atop her headboard.

At the foot of her bed stood her father. At least, she thought it was her father. It certainly looked just like him. Trentwood stood as he always had when lecturing her, hands clasped behind his back with a stern look on his face. "So you didn't see me, eh?"

TWO

IN WHICH A FATHER RETURNS

MARY REMAINED WHERE SHE was, clinging to her headboard and staring at Trentwood. She shook her mind free of the memories from that horrible night over a year ago. There was nothing to be done about that now. Steele had never called, and she hadn't the time for courting anyway, not with her father so ill. And now that her father had died—and his ghost was standing at the foot of her bed—well, that didn't make her future chances at courtship seem any brighter.

Practically speaking, of course.

Mary's mouth wavered between hysterical laughter and another scream. Her father was dead, and she wanted—needed—to mourn him. She wanted to remember him fondly and cry herself to sleep over her loss. She did not want to be crawling away, terrified of this vision that was her father.

It wasn't right or decent, this horror replacing sorrow.

She swallowed, biding her time, waiting for words to come. Did ghosts need to sit? Or was it merely the principle of the matter? Her father had been, if nothing else, concerned with the principle of the matter. Did such things carry over into the afterlife?

"Aren't you growing rather tired of hanging from that headboard as if you were some primate?" Trentwood said.

Mary dropped to her knees. She landed with little grace in the jumble of sheets piled atop her bed. She couldn't take her eyes from Trentwood. His fingers were grimy, most likely from his unearthly climb. He smelled of earth and age and disease, spiced with a hint of peppermints—his favorite treat.

"There now, isn't that better?" Trentwood looked as he had in his life but for his eyes, the irises particularly. They had lost almost all pigmentation, so that the dark hazel she had inherited looked an insipid beige.

She scowled. A knock at the door startled her from responding.

"Miss Trentwood?" It was Pomeroy, Trentwood's valet-cum-butler. His voice was gentle, but firm, as he said, "I happened to be in the hallway just a moment ago and had the oddest idea I heard you scream. Might I come in and inquire?"

Mary cleared her throat and dragged her gaze from Trentwood. "No, thank you," she said, raising her voice so Pomeroy could hear her. "I thought I saw... er, there was—"

As Mary scanned the room looking for an excuse for screaming, she caught sight of Trentwood looking rather smug while he waited for her reason. She pressed her lips together. He was having fun with this! She crawled from her bed and backed to the door. Her chin jutted out, and she glanced at Trentwood, noting the way his brows rose.

It was easier to breathe by the door, Mary couldn't smell Trentwood. She pressed her cheek to the carved wooden door that kept Pomeroy from entering. She breathed the warm smell of old wood, relishing in its solidity. She needed to convince herself she was grounded, sane, normal.

"I had a nightmare," Mary said, "and frightened myself awake. Please don't concern yourself, it was very silly."

She heard Pomeroy clear his throat and imagined him shifting his weight from one foot to the next as he searched for the most proper way to voice his thoughts.

"Shall I ask Mrs. Durham to keep you company?"

Mary closed her eyes. "No, thank you."

"Shall I keep you company, Miss?"

Now that was an interesting thought, to allow Pomeroy enter. Especially with Trentwood standing there as if he hadn't died a week earlier. If Pomeroy saw Trentwood, then Mary would know she wasn't entirely mad, or certainly not delusional. *Of course, the danger in ushering Pomeroy inside would be the realization that I am, in fact, losing my wits.* Mary bit her lip.

"Why not let the poor man in, make certain you haven't done harm to yourself?" Trentwood suggested. He had moved to the vanity, taking the seat Mary had not offered to him. He watched her archly, radiating his displeasure with his stiff carriage and the way he picked at the dirt beneath his fingernails.

If I answer him, I acknowledge his existence, and then I'll know I'm mad. If I don't answer him, I don't know either way. Decision made, Mary threw open the door. "Just for a moment, yes, I'd like your company. I find my… thoughts disturb when I'm alone."

Pomeroy was as tall and lanky as Trentwood, and as old as him, if not older. Mary had no idea, in fact, how old Pomeroy was. She knew only that he had always been her father's valet, he never had a hair or piece of clothing out of place, and he worried about her as if she were his daughter. And that he was a prize pugilist who was more than happy to teach her a thing or two.

Pomeroy's hair was completely white and had been so since he turned twenty—something about the shock of losing his sister in a fire. Mary never knew the details and knew better than to ask.

"Thoughts are one's own enemy at a time like this," Pomeroy murmured, entering the room.

"Would you care to have a…" Mary's voice trailed off. Trentwood sat in the only available chair in the room and didn't look as though he was about to give it up to anyone, especially not his valet. Thankfully, Pomeroy had no plans to sit.

"I've only come to say, and do pardon my impudence, that I'm worried about you. We both are, Mrs. Beeton and me. You've had a rough year, taking care of your father and your aunt besides."

Mary nodded once. She crossed her arms over her chest. It rankled, the awkward sounds of kindness about her loss. She hadn't decided if she was prepared to accept such words yet. Having her dead father in the room didn't help matters.

Pomeroy continued, stammering a little as Mary stepped away from him. "It was decided I should tell you we will handle the running of the house, to—to ease your burden."

Trentwood scoffed from his corner. "A lovely sentiment, I'm sure, but what are you to do with yourself if he takes away your one occupation, hmm?"

Mary squared her shoulders. She anticipated Pomeroy to shout, scream, blanch, faint, or all of the above. He did none. He waited for her response, giving no indication that he had heard Trentwood speak, nor revealing any suspicion that anyone but Mary was in the room with him.

This does not bode well for my sanity.

"I must admit the offer is tempting, and so very generous. I am, of course, touched and overwhelmed by your kindness," Mary whispered, "but I must keep myself busy."

Pomeroy bowed. "I find it's best to stay busy, Miss, and be certain to not be alone for too very long."

Mary risked a sidelong look at Trentwood, who grinned. "Depend upon it; I don't think I shall be alone often."

THREE

IN WHICH HARTWELL ARRIVES

SWINDON, MARCH 1887

MR. HARTWELL WAS JOLTED awake, his arms flailing, when the train from London pulled into Swindon. His low-brimmed hat, which he had pulled down to shade his face while he slept, fell to his lap. He heard the snickers of the little boy sitting in the aisle across from him. He knew he should resist the temptation, but he looked at the boy and scowled.

The boy gasped and pointed at Hartwell's face. "Mama," he cried, "what's happened to him?"

The boy's mother looked at Hartwell, blanched, and slapped her son's hand. "Don't point, dearest, it's rude." She turned to Hartwell, though he noted she avoided meeting his gaze. "Please forgive him. He's the most mischievous terror of all my children."

Hartwell nodded and gathered his things, but not before making a face at the boy for good measure. He couldn't help it. The boy was a brat, his mother knew it, and Hartwell was in no mood to be someone's entertainment, child or otherwise. He slapped his hat onto his dark hair, threw his coat over his shoulders, and stomped from the train.

The station was far quieter than the London one he had left that morning. There were still children crying, paperboys shouting, train attendants ushering, and far too many people milling about as if they had no idea where they were going. Well, Hartwell knew where he was going. At least where he needed to get to, and damned if he was about to tarry simply because someone wasn't sure just which car they wanted to sit in and happened to be making that decision in the middle of his path.

"You there," Hartwell said to a dirty boy playing by the tracks, "where might I find the manor house at Compton Beauchamp?"

"At Compton Beauchamp, methinks," was the reply.

Hartwell clamped his jaw. "And where, pray tell, is Compton Beauchamp, exactly?"

"Me Pa can drive you there, if you like," the boy said, jumping to his feet.

Hartwell stepped back so the upset coal dust didn't touch his suit. "Take me to your father, and be quick about it. I need to catch the evening train back to London." He followed the boy, who he discovered was named Peter, to a wagon full of animals. Pigs, of all things, and geese, and sheep. "Oh no."

Peter bounded to his father's side and tugged the hem of his frayed jacket. "Gent here'd like a lift to Compton Beauchamp, Pa."

Hartwell shook his head when Peter's father squinted at him from beneath his straw hat. "Forgive the intrusion, I thought your son was taking me to the stables."

"You've a pretty way with words, son." Peter's father had a voice of gravel. It sounded smooth, yet Hartwell could hear ball bearings tumbling over one another in the undertones. "What are you doing trying to get to Compton Beauchamp?"

"I've business with Mrs. Durham," Hartwell admitted, "and the sooner I get there, the sooner I can return home."

Peter's father chuckled and tightened the harness on his farm horse. "I'll be the only one heading that direction. No one goes to Compton Beauchamp unless they live there."

Hartwell's shoulders sank. "Really?" he said, his voice flat.

"Aye, and you'll be having a trial of getting to Mrs. Durham, what with the goings on at the manor house."

One of the geese looked at Hartwell and honked loudly at him, finding some offense. Hartwell rubbed his forehead. "What has been going on at the manor house?"

"Well, the young miss lost her father a month ago, and the house is in mourning."

"Ah, I see." That certainly posed a problem; they would be in mourning for a year, and Hartwell simply didn't have that sort of time. He shook his head. "Sorry, I must have misunderstood you. Young miss? Mrs. Durham is forty-five if she's a day, as I understand it."

Peter's father chuckled. "Not her, but her niece by way of her twin, Miss Trentwood. Mrs. Durham's doing her duty and watching after the girl. Though she's going through her own mourning."

"How very noble of her," Hartwell said through clenched teeth. Well, he had come this far for answers. Certainly he could come and go quickly without disturbing their period of mourning too much. "I should be much obliged then, if I could ride with you to the manor house."

Peter cheered and scrambled up the large wheel to sit on the wagon's wooden bench that would seat the three of them.

"I'm Frank Brown," Peter's father said, holding his hand out for Hartwell to shake.

Hartwell glanced at the weathered hand, seeing years of dirt encrusted in its folds. He shook Frank Brown's hand with a tentative smile. "Alexander Hartwell."

The ride to Compton Beauchamp was, Hartwell found with no little surprise, pleasant. Frank Brown was by no means chatty, but he answered all of Hartwell's questions amiably enough.

The countryside was the sort of tame green beauty he remembered from his childhood, and Peter, when Hartwell had removed his hat to enjoy the warmth of the sun's rays on his head, made no mention of his scarred face, which he appreciated.

Even the noisy animals crowded in the back of the wagon seemed to Hartwell a happy respite from the drudgery of London life. It was charming to hear the pigs snort as if scoffing at something the geese said, or the sheep's low murmuring when the wagon swayed over a bump in the road.

Hartwell marveled at The Great White Horse, an ancient carving in the chalky ground on the hills just outside of Compton Beauchamp. The Browns humored him and drove the wagon up the hill so he could study the horse closely. He shared their packed luncheon of generously cut bread and cured meat while listening to Frank Brown's folktale that the horse was actually the bones of the horse belonging to none else but William the Conqueror.

In fact, by the time he was dropped off at the pale lane just outside the manor house, Hartwell was so totally enamored with his new friends that he almost forgot why he had come to Compton Beauchamp in the first place. He waved to the Browns as they ambled away, and chuckled at the sight of the pigs, sheep, and geese watching him forlornly from their rocking, wooden cage.

When the wagon was out of eyesight, Hartwell sighed and turned to the high wrought iron gate that provided the only opening to the brick wall surrounding the manor house. The gate was propped open by a sizable rock, so he slipped inside. He squared his shoulders. Better get this over with, Hartwell thought, shrugging to adjust his shoulder cape.

Hartwell walked along the gravel path that was wide enough to usher carriages to the portico that sheltered the front door. The manor house, it seemed, had seen better days.

Far better days, by the looks of it.

The house had a Palladian façade that spoke of modest grandeur. The yellow limestone of the façade was laid in an irregular pattern and was accented by smooth ashlar dressings smartly jointed together. Red brick archways decorated the windows, pulling the eye up to the roof, which sorely needed repairing.

Hartwell tugged the embroidered bell pull hanging just right of the door and waited. And continued to wait, hearing neither a bell, nor anyone coming to open the door.

He yanked the bell pull again. This time it snapped in pieces into his hand.

His mouth dropped open. Frowning at the portico and seeing finger-sized cracks in the plaster, Hartwell lost confidence, what with the remnants of the bell pull dangling from his fingers. He rapped his knuckles against the front door and jumped away just in case the portico decided to fall on his head.

Finally, Hartwell thought he heard someone approach the door. He heard concerned mumblings. Whoever was behind the door continued to mumble for a full five minutes. He tapped his leg with the bell pull impatiently. "Oh, for heaven's sake, will you open this door?"

The voices fell silent.

He hadn't expected them to hear him.

The door creaked open to reveal a tall, lanky man with a shock of white hair and a woman with a cap of white lace atop her graying hair. They both wore black, reminding Hartwell that the house was in mourning. Their solemnity seemed out of place with the fine weather tickling the hairs on the back of his head. *I ought to have sent a letter ahead.*

The two persons stared at him, and Hartwell realized they wanted him to explain himself. He reddened. "I'm Alexander Hartwell, and—."

The woman lost all color and slammed the door in his face. She, he assumed, was Mrs. Durham.

He knocked on the door again, relieved this time when the man opened the door, the woman was nowhere in sight.

"Do come in, sir," the man said. "I believe Mrs. Durham has fled to her room. If you would wait in the library, I will send for my mistress."

"Then Mrs. Durham is not the lady of the house?" Hartwell asked as he entered with a small frown.

"No indeed."

"Excellent."

"Yes indeed." The man smiled at Hartwell's apparent surprise. "I'm Pomeroy, the butler and valet to Mr. Trentwood that was. If you'd be so kind as to wait in the library, I shall send for Miss Trentwood and have a pot of tea sent to you."

Hartwell allowed Pomeroy to take his hat, coat, and satchel, relieved to be rid of the carried weight. He ignored the way Pomeroy started at the sight of his face, already building up his tolerances as he followed Pomeroy to the little library just off the main hall. *I've been so used to being with people who are used to me,* he thought with a disgruntled sigh.

"Miss Trentwood will be in shortly," Pomeroy said.

Hartwell nodded, and handed Pomeroy the bell pull. "Er… do apologize in advance to Miss Trentwood for me?"

Pomeroy stared at the bell pull in his hand, and his face tightened as if he was trying not to laugh. He cleared his throat. "We haven't had visitors in quite some time, sir."

"I never would have guessed," Hartwell replied.

Four

In which Pomeroy deflects

WHEN A GIRL LOSES her father, no matter her age, whether in the school house, married, or a spinster like Mary, she wants to mourn. She wants to take time to remember the most influential man in her life, if she has been blessed enough to have the influence of her father, if she has been blessed enough to have a father who cares enough to have an influence on her.

She wants to look back on times of laughter with fondness, and times of punishment with sheepishness. She wants to give credit where it is due, and take the time to put his dearest possessions away for moments of tearful reminiscence.

Admittedly, Mary had not been looking forward to life after her father—especially when faced with the unfortunate truth that she would have to face it with her aunt, of all people. For all her disappointment regarding Steele, Mary had been glad to read to Trentwood every night and guarantee that he had eaten enough during their meals.

Despite his sometime pigheadedness, Trentwood had been a generous and encouraging father.

He hadn't liked to read, but he had indulged Mary's obsession with books precisely because her mother had done the same. He had preferred to ride rather than walk, and Mary the reverse, so, rather than shuffle the duty to Pomeroy or a footman, Trentwood had joined Mary on her walks to Wayland's Smithy, the collection of sarsen stones at the edge of Compton Beauchamp.

Life with her aunt would not be so easy.

The sound of slamming doors roused Mary. She had been staring through her bedroom window in the direction of the family plot where her father, supposedly, had been laid to rest.

She shifted her focus to her reflection, not liking the sight of her bloodshot eyes and the bags beneath them, or the hollows in her cheeks. She tucked a stray strand of hair behind her ear and sighed. "What would Steele think of me now?"

"You're still on about that chap?" Trentwood said.

She jumped from the window because she couldn't see Trentwood well enough. She had yet to respond to him, though he had haunted her a month. She had hoped, futilely, that he would leave her alone if she ignored him long enough.

"You aren't mourning me at all, are you? You're mourning that fop, aren't you?"

I can't take this for much longer, Mary thought, clenching her hands into fists at her side.

"I trust someday you'll see the sense in what I did."

Mary glared at Trentwood, or his ghost, rather, and strode to her bedroom door. Better to investigate the mysterious slamming doors than answer him and confirm her fears of insanity.

Mary threw the door open and yelped. Pomeroy stood there, silent as ever, his hand raised to knock.

"Sorry to disturb, Miss, but—"

"What is that?" Mary said, pointing at Pomeroy's hand.

"The bell pull, miss."

Mary swallowed. Her mother had embroidered that bell pull; it was the last thing she had completed before her death. "I see that, I was wondering what it was doing in your hand."

"It seems to have fallen apart, miss." Mary could feel her face fall, and so wasn't surprised when Pomeroy continued in a conciliatory tone, "It is rather old, miss. Almost twelve years."

Mary nodded, taking it from him. "Very well. I'll begin work on a new one immediately." She glanced down the hall. "Was that Mrs. Durham's door I heard slam? Don't tell me she didn't get her tea on time this morning."

"Mrs. Durham, it seems, is hiding from the person who ruined the bell pull."

Mary shook her head. "You aren't making sense."

"I don't know much more, Miss, I've asked the gentleman to wait in the library."

Mary stopped mid-nod. She looked at the decimated bell pull in her hand. "You mean someone destroyed the bell pull, and you sent him to the library? My library? And that my aunt is hiding from said person?" She lifted her black skirts and rushed down the hallway. "Pomeroy! What if he does something to my books?"

"I don't think that's Mr. Hartwell's intention," Pomeroy said, his voice suspiciously even-toned as he followed her.

Mary stopped halfway down the staircase. "Hartwell?"

"I took the liberty of looking through the late master's correspondence book," he said, slowly, "and found no mention of him. Whoever Mr. Hartwell is, he's known to Mrs. Durham alone."

Frowning, Mary tapped her lower lip and pondered a moment. "And he asked for me?"

"No, Miss, he asked if Mrs. Durham was mistress. When informed otherwise, he seemed most pleased."

Mary groaned softly. "It must be a representative of father's solicitor. I was written he would arrive soon."

She peered around the stair banister at the library door at the end of the first floor. They had kept their voices low, so the mysterious Mr. Hartwell probably hadn't heard them. She wrinkled her nose. Mary didn't like to think of herself as cowardly, but she just couldn't stand the idea of speaking with her father's solicitor, not knowing if or when Trentwood's ghost might appear.

She nodded, her mind made up. "Make my apologies. Give him a scone or something." Mary ran up the stairs she had recently scurried down.

"And what should I tell him?" Pomeroy said, trailing her, irritation deepening his voice.

"That I've a headache. It always worked for mother." Mary darted into her bedroom, threw her dolman around her shoulders, snatched her hat and some hat pins, and smiled an apology at Pomeroy. He watched her with a frown.

"I suppose my telling you that your father would disapprove will do nothing," Pomeroy grumbled.

Mary kissed his cheek. "Not a thing."

"Or we haven't the resources to send a footman with you?"

"I'm twenty-seven, Pomeroy, I don't need a chaperone."

"A chaperone, no. Protection, yes." Pomeroy flushed and ducked his head. He knew better than to argue with Mary when she was in this mood. "Be careful out there; Mrs. Beeton says a storm is coming."

Mary pinned her hat to her head and pulled the veil made of black netting down past her chin. "I'll just have to get to Wayland's Smithy before the clouds open then, won't I?"

With that, Mary slipped out the back staircase, startling Mrs. Beeton and her dilapidated kitchen in her escape.

Clouds, dark and thick, descended over Mary as she crept along the manor house wall beneath the library window, hoping she did so unseen. She waited until she was out of earshot before dashing down the gravel drive to the high wrought iron gate. Her black skirts swirled around her ankles. She slipped through the gate, looked back at the manor house, and sighed.

"Not really what it used to be, eh?"

Mary yelped for the second time that day and jumped away from the voice. She grimaced, having scraped her back against the brick wall enclosing the Trentwood property. Hand at her bosom, she snapped, "Will you stop doing that?"

Trentwood stepped through the wall and gave her a half-hearted shrug. "So now you've decided I'm real?"

"I've decided no such thing, I'm simply tired of being caught unawares," Mary retorted.

Trentwood grunted. Whether real or not, his mimicry of the man was uncanny. "Where are you off to?"

Mary spun on her heel, turning her back to Trentwood as she walked down the pale English lane, where the very last remnants of autumn's leaves spun and danced with an eddy. Unable to hear footsteps, Mary glanced behind to be certain Trentwood was (or was not) following her.

He was. Mary stumbled through the hedgerow, heading southeast of Compton Beauchamp proper. Brambles clung to her skirt and she yanked it free.

Mary's breathing became labored—she had halted her walks during Trentwood's illness and so was a year out of shape. It was a cold day for March, and her breath left little white cloud bursts in the air. She glanced behind her. Trentwood persisted.

"At least he's being visible about it," Mary muttered. She stomped across the farmer's field to the copse of trees shading the sarsen stones—much like Stonehenge—stacked together to make the ancient tomb known as Wayland's Smithy.

She stumbled to the front step of the yawning opening in the ground. She sat though the step was covered with lichen and moss. Mary had been coming here for years, but she had never once worked up enough courage to venture inside the tomb. It was something Trentwood never failed to—.

"Still don't have the courage to step inside, eh?"

"If you aren't my father, you are eerily similar."

Trentwood chuckled and sat beside her. He never made a noise when he moved. That was the worst of this whole business, Mary decided. She could handle the smell and liked that it alerted her to his presence. His low, serious voice, something else Mary had inherited from him, had remained as she had remembered it. And he looked as he had at his peak, which brought a certain sort of comfort… once she had gotten past the idea that he was supposed to be dead.

"Do you think you could… erm, wear a bell?" Mary said, kicking her legs out before her and smoothing her skirts. She avoided looking at Trentwood.

His eyes—she couldn't abide his eyes.

"You would have me wear a bell, like a dog?"

Mary scowled at his indignant tone. She should have known better. He was supposed to be her father, after all. "Of course not, you're right, how silly of me."

They sat together in an awkward silence, the wind blowing Mary's veil across her face. The wind did not affect Trentwood in the slightest.

"So you aren't going to ask why I'm here?" Trentwood said, breaking the silence after ten minutes or so.

Mary lifted her veil with great reluctance to meet him, eye-to-clouded-eye. "No."

"You aren't the least bit curious?" Trentwood prodded.

"Oh, I am," Mary admitted ruefully, "just not enough to ask about it."

A branch snapped, making Mary jump.

"Who are you talking to?"

FIVE

IN WHICH HARTWELL PURSUES

HARTWELL PACED THE LIBRARY for half an hour while waiting for Mary. He kept his hands clasped in a tight fist behind his back. He frowned not because he had been kept waiting, but because he had no idea what he was going to say once Mary entered. Everything had seemed quite simple when he had left London that morning.

He had assured his sister he would return for dinner. That was before he had realized Compton Beauchamp was in the back of beyond, and his quarry was a rude little middle-aged woman.

Well, to be fair, Hartwell had expected the latter. He couldn't think of anything kind to say about Mrs. Durham, though his sister proclaimed fond memories of their school days together.

Never mind all that, back to the task at hand: how was he to explain his presence?

When the library door opened, Hartwell turned in nervous anticipation. He didn't think Mary would look favorably on the fact that he had scared her aunt to some undisclosed location in the manor house. Luckily, it was not Mary but Pomeroy with the tea who entered.

Hartwell's frown deepened, this time with genuine displeasure.

"Miss Trentwood begs your pardon, sir," Pomeroy said as he settled the tray on a side table. "She's been suffering a terrible ache and cannot meet you today."

Hartwell opened his mouth, ready to say a thing or two to Pomeroy about his Miss Trentwood, when a distinctly female-shaped form clad in all black scampered into the periphery of his vision. Brows raised, Hartwell faced the window just in time to watch Mary slip through the front gate, having practically sprinted from the manor house.

Well, then. Hartwell grinned at Pomeroy, who was preparing the tea far too studiously.

"I take it that was Miss Trentwood?" Hartwell bit out.

"Yes, sir."

"And she has a terrible ache, is it?"

"Yes, sir, of the leg."

"An ache of the leg."

"Yes, sir. She ached for a walk."

Hartwell rubbed his forehead. "Oh, for the love of—do you know where she's heading?"

"I couldn't say, sir."

Hartwell waited until Pomeroy met his cold expression. "Hazard a guess." He watched Pomeroy look him over, trying to size up his pugilistic abilities. Doing as any other man had done since his accident, Pomeroy stopped at the sight of the scar on Hartwell's face. Beyond that, Pomeroy looked directly into Hartwell's eyes, long enough for Hartwell to shift his weight in unconscious discomfort.

Whatever Pomeroy saw in Hartwell's face, he must have approved. "If I had to hazard a guess, I would say she's taken a right down the lane, cut across the field, through the hedgerow, toward the gathering of trees southeast of here. If I had to hazard a guess, sir."

Hartwell blinked at Pomeroy, who did the same in return. "Oh. Well. Thank you." He grabbed his hat and coat from the chair where Pomeroy had settled them earlier. A funny expression on his face, Hartwell strode from the library in pursuit of Mary.

"I trust you will ensure her safety given that you have business with her, Mr. Hartwell?" Pomeroy said, following him to the front door. His tone made no mistake about his meaning.

Hartwell bristled. "Yes, of course."

"Very good. I'd hate to have to kill you."

Again, Hartwell blinked at Pomeroy, who again did the same in return. Hartwell swallowed when Pomeroy maintained a steady gaze, while his faltered. "Right," he muttered, slapping his hat to his head.

"Take this," Pomeroy said, handing Hartwell a woolen blanket from behind a hidden door in the hallway, "in case she refuses to return before the storm hits."

Mouth agape, Hartwell accepted the blanket, too surprised to refuse it. "Just how often does she do this?"

Pomeroy opened the door. "Best be going, sir, or you'll not beat the storm."

"You're really sending me out there after your mistress? A complete stranger. With a blanket, of all things?"

Pomeroy's smile chilled Hartwell almost as much as his reply. "No need to worry about her. She's haunted. And her father's more protective than I am."

Mind racing, Hartwell wet his lips with a drying tongue. What was it Frank Brown had said about visiting the manor house? That he would have a trial of it? That the master had recently deceased? "I was brought here by a Frank Brown. He told me Mr. Trentwood had died, of late."

"Frank Brown is correct."

Hartwell narrowed his eyes.

"I suppose one has to be dead, sir, to haunt one's daughter."

Hartwell exhaled. "Do you treat all your guests like this?"

Again, Pomeroy smiled. "You're the first guest we've had in quite some time, sir, excusing the funeral, of course."

Flabbergasted, Hartwell let Pomeroy usher him from the manor house. After the door shut in his face, blanket in hand, he debated chancing a walk back to Swindon, damn the consequences.

Except that wily butler still had his satchel, with all his money and papers.

"Holy hell, Frank Brown was right about this not being easy!"

A timid raindrop splashed on Hartwell's hat brim. He scowled at the gathering clouds. It was most definitely going to rain, and he was most definitely going to be caught in it. Did that butler give him an umbrella? Oh no, that would have been far too sensible, and what did sensible thinking have to do with a house governed by a haunted lady?

Nothing, that's what. Absolutely nothing.

Hartwell felt so exasperated he could have stomped his way down the gravel drive, through the wrought iron gate, and down the English lane to find Mary. But Hartwell was sensible and knew that stomping that distance would exhaust him, let alone take far too long. Hartwell threw the blanket over his shoulder, shaking his head. He knew what he was in Compton Beauchamp for, he just wasn't sure it was worth all this nonsense.

Hartwell had little difficulty following Mary's hasty retreat to the lonely gathering of trees in the middle of an empty pasture. He slowed his pace at the end of the clearing in the middle of the trees, hearing voices.

Rather, not voices, but one low voice, carrying a stilted, one-sided conversation.

Hartwell ducked behind one of the larger beech trees and shivered in the cold. On the front step before an opening that seemed to lead underground sat a woman in all black. She was looking to her left as though listening for something.

To something.

To someone?

She lifted her veil with trembling fingers. Hartwell was too far away to see her face clearly. This was definitely Mary Trentwood, however. He couldn't think why that rascal Pomeroy would lead him elsewhere.

The wind blew, racketing a shudder through Hartwell, who hadn't dressed for chill weather. Had he not been so cold, he might have held onto his exasperation. There was something frightening about the way Mary spoke to herself. It was almost as though she believed she was haunted.

"Oh, I am," she said to nothing and no one. "Just not enough to ask about it."

Hartwell stepped closer to get a better look. He winced when a branch snapped beneath his foot. He swallowed when she swiveled to fix her serious, alarmed, hazel gaze at him. Oh well. Best to satisfy his curiosity and hope the answer would alleviate the queasiness in his stomach.

"Who are you talking to?" he asked, stepping into the clearing.

Mary jumped to her feet. She readjusted her veil so it guarded her face. "Who are you? Are you following me?"

The panic in her voice reminded Hartwell that if she was haunted, then the last thing he wanted to do was raise the ire of her ghostly father. He shook his head. *What am I thinking? There are no such things as ghosts. I'm tired, that's all.*

"My name is Alexander Hartwell. I watched from the library window as you escaped the manor house." He held up the blanket. "Your butler sent me with the message that a storm is coming."

He wasn't sure, what with the veil masking her expression, but Hartwell thought Mary might have allowed a wry smile before a blush crept over her cheeks.

"Well," Mary said, "if Pomeroy sent you, then I suppose I'll have to speak to you, shan't I?" She didn't wait for his response before reclaiming her spot on the stone. She brushed her skirts briskly, arranging them until she was satisfied, and looked at Hartwell expectantly.

Hartwell stepped closer, incredulous. "You want to talk here?"

"What's wrong with here?" Mary looked around the clearing, though what she saw in it, Hartwell had no idea. "It's quiet here."

Hartwell frowned at the sarsen stones, the way they were stacked like a deck of cards to make a shelter, of sorts, but with a flat top. "It looks like a tomb."

Mary shrugged and flicked a speck of dust from her skirt. "I think it is."

"It is what?"

"A tomb."

"And you see no problems with holding a conversation here?"

"Not at all, it's very quiet here, we won't be interrupted."

"That's because it's a tomb," Hartwell exploded. He was going to continue, but the tree boughs swayed overhead. Not a good sign. True to his suspicion, the rain began to pour onto his hat and shoulders. He grunted.

Mary stood, brushing off her backside, and turned to stare at the tomb's opening. If anyone was buried there, they would be nothing but bones. But still she hesitated. The woman had obviously lost her mind, Hartwell figured, or was somehow still in shock over her father's death. Indeed, the latter explained the ghost farce quite nicely.

In any case, Hartwell, having had the misfortune of having to stand through too many rain showers, saw no reason to stand through this one. He threw the woolen blanket over his head and shoulders before dashing to Mary's side. He grabbed her by the arm and dragged her inside the doorway of the tomb.

"For someone who seems quite averse to the idea of tombs, you're rather ready to jump into one," Mary said. She pulled away from Hartwell to crouch as close to the doorway as possible.

There was hardly room for standing in the little cave-like structure, and it smelled of mildew. *Better that than decomposing bodies*, Hartwell thought darkly. He stooped, his shoulders scraping the top sarsen stone. He shuddered to know what his coat would look like after this unforeseen romp.

There was a bed of rotting leaves beneath their feet, adding to the sickly sweet smells assaulting Hartwell. A gust of wind threw a sheet of rain into the tomb, and Hartwell backed away from the opening. Mary, however, remained where she stood.

Hartwell clamped his jaw. "Would you rather stand in the rain and catch your death of cold than stand beside me?"

Mary gave him a steely glare. "I will die eventually, Mr. Hartwell, but it won't be from catching cold, not if I can help it."

Hartwell resisted the urge to scratch his head, puzzled as to why he felt he had royally put his foot far into his mouth. Maybe it was the way Mary's shoulders were hunched. Or the way she was inching as close to the door as possible, and therefore as far away from him as she could get without venturing into the rain. Or maybe it was the way she had said, "Not if I can help it."

He still couldn't see her face very well, what with the veil firmly in place. But then, he didn't need to see her face to talk to her.

"Miss Trentwood, I feel we've started on the wrong foot."

"To say the least," she replied.

She had no reason to be so terse with him, she could have no idea why he was in town. As he mulled over her reactions, he realized he was still holding the blanket over his head.

Mary looked very little standing there, rocking back and forth ever so slightly, shivering as she hugged herself. It must be her mourning weeds that made her so small—she looked nearly his height, and he was tall by anyone's measure. Ashamed by his callous behavior, Hartwell stepped close enough to wrap the blanket around Mary's shoulders gingerly. She stiffened, but when he stepped away, she relaxed. Marginally.

"Well, we won't be going anywhere anytime soon," Mary said. "Why don't we share the blanket and you can tell me why you destroyed my mother's bell pull, frightened my aunt so that she locked herself in her bedroom, and dragged me into this tomb."

Mary looked at him then, her hazel eyes transfixing him. "Whatever it is, it must be very important."

Hartwell coughed. In all his thirty-five years, he had never been as uncomfortable as this moment. He couldn't tell her the real reason. For all he knew, she was part of the plot.

No, he wouldn't tell her the truth, but some approximation of it. Something close enough to the truth that he could remember the details, as he had always been, and probably would continue to be, an awful liar.

"My sister was schoolmates with your aunt, Mrs. Durham," he began.

"What?"

Hartwell repeated himself, unsure why Mary frowned so.

"Then you're not my father's solicitor? Or related to him in any way?" Mary asked, her voice flat.

Hartwell's responding frown wavered, then exploded into an understanding smile that threatened to become a laugh. Hartwell liked to think her voice was flat with embarrassment and a sort of sheepish dismay.

"You thought I was a solicitor?" At Mary's nod he did laugh, a little. "No wonder you ran away."

"I didn't run away, I went for a walk."

"A walk to a tomb."

"It's my favorite spot. No one bothers me here, usually."

Hartwell didn't mistake her meaning. "I've come, Miss Trentwood, at the behest of my sister. She heard of your sorrows, from your aunt, I assume."

Mary stood very still, her neck craned to see him. It was obvious she hadn't noticed his scar yet. She still considered him an annoyance rather than someone to be feared. He had every intention to use this to his advantage, and made sure to stay shadowed as long as possible.

Mary shifted, pulling the blanket closer around her shoulders. "And what does your sister intend for you to do, Mr. Hartwell?"

"My sister has asked me to help in any way I can, being such friends with your aunt. Perhaps," he said, hesitating slightly, "when the real solicitor's representative arrives I can be of service?"

"So you are familiar with solicitors, then?"

"Oh yes, my father was one."

"That only makes you familiar with the person. What does that mean in terms of a solicitor's business? I thank you, but no."

Hartwell inhaled, not expecting such a blast of sharp logic thrown at him. He fought the urge to study her expressions and guess her responses before she had the chance to make them. She was the trial, he realized, that Frank Brown had warned him about. Not the death in the family, not the unwillingness of Mrs. Durham, but Mary Trentwood.

She had a logic that rivaled many of his schoolmates. That rare sort of common sense that cut to the point and left casualties in its wake.

"I am often in the company of solicitors, Miss Trentwood," he began.

"Do you often require their services?"

"Yes," Hartwell snapped, "I do. I'm a barrister, Miss Trentwood. It is my profession to require the services of solicitors."

Mary was quiet far too long for Hartwell's liking. She seemed to be looking behind him, listening intently to something he couldn't discern. Her expression seemed to go slack for a moment, and then tightened as though she had just heard most unpleasant news. When she spoke, finally, Hartwell jumped, bashing his head into the stone ceiling.

"Well," Mary said, pausing for him to shake away the stars from his eyes. "First, you better sit down in case you've hurt yourself." She scooted to the side ruefully, giving him room to plop beside her.

Hartwell hesitated. She had given him space to sit to her right, which would have put his scar in view. For whatever reason, he wanted to postpone the unveiling; he was, he found with great amusement, enjoying her odd manner of speaking. He didn't want to discourage this frank dialogue by startling her. He sidled to her left and waited for her to shift positions to afford him a space to sit. She did so with her brow wrinkled in confusion.

"Second," she continued, the way a prodded child might, "you might as well stay for dinner, since you've come all this way."

Still rubbing his head, Hartwell said, "Thank you. What's the third item?" It sounded as if Mary wasn't quite finished.

"Third, I don't believe your story about your sister, and I don't like you, but we'll have to see what my aunt says, given her supposed history with your family." She glanced at him with a very slight curl in her lip. If Hartwell hadn't been looking, he might have missed it altogether. "Pomeroy saw something in you, though I'm not sure what, so I'll have to give you a chance, I suppose."

Hartwell's mouth dropped open. What a pert mouth on this one! Had it been anyone else, he might have given them the benefit of the doubt and excuse her manners for grief or shock.

But the words and tone came too easily—this was how she was, he suspected dourly.

"Technically," he said, keeping his tone light, "wouldn't those be items three, four, and five? You had conjunctions in there."

Mary narrowed her eyes at him.

"Oh look," she said, "the rain is letting up. Do let us return and show Pomeroy he doesn't get to hurt you."

"Oh yes, let's," Hartwell said sarcastically.

Six

In which Mary is haunted

Mary shoved her hands beneath her dolman, clasping them tightly together. She walked smartly ahead of Hartwell.

It wouldn't do if they arrived together, despite Pomeroy's questionable trust in Hartwell's honor, just in case one of the locals saw.

It was better, really, if he walked a few paces behind her. He was carrying that blanket, after all, and so anyone looking would see a familiar sight: Miss Trentwood walking with her footman.

Mary had been decidedly more pleased with this impromptu plan than Hartwell. Being relegated to a footman was not something Hartwell relished. But when Mary had explained her logic, he had been unable to find fault with it.

Which was probably why he was so annoyed.

Mary glanced behind her when she caught the sound of Hartwell muttering to himself. "Everything all right, Mr. Hartwell?"

His face was shadowed by the rolled brim of his derby hat. "Would you like me to answer honestly, or politely?"

The edge of Mary's mouth trembled in the direction of a smile. "Polite would suffice."

"This is a most charming walk, Miss Trentwood." He sounded so very maudlin that Mary couldn't help but break into a smile.

"Dare I ask what the honest answer would have been?"

Hartwell shifted the heavy blanket to his other arm with a slightly exasperated huff. "This isn't exactly what I thought I'd be doing when I left London this morning."

Mary stopped and waited for him to approach her, noting that he pulled his hat down low over his eyes so she couldn't see his face. There was something off about the man, something he didn't want her to see. It made her want to slap the hat off his head. "What did you expect you would be doing?"

She watched him watch her from the safety of the shadows beneath his hat. She knew what he would see. A tall woman with changing eyes, long features, and limbs all-akimbo. A female creature with a sort of awkward, lanky grace. An exasperated daughter with a father who wouldn't stay dead.

Well, Mary doubted Hartwell thought that last point. But the others, she was fairly certain he thought them. She had heard it often enough from her aunt to see the truth of the matter: she wasn't beautiful. She wasn't even very pretty. Which had never bothered her until now, until this particular man who seemed to always carry laughter behind his voice even when annoyed, wouldn't look her in the eye.

"To be honest," he said after a length, "I hadn't entirely thought it all the way through."

Mary's brows jumped. And there went his opportunity to redeem himself. She spun on her heel and continued her march back to the manor house, muttering to herself. Hartwell followed her after a moment, also muttering to himself.

Hartwell trudged behind Mary wondering why he had agreed to dinner when all he really wanted was to be on the train back to London and sanity.

The simple answer would be to meet Mrs. Durham. The slightly more complex answer was that for some reason, Miss Mary Trentwood was an interesting little duck, and Hartwell's curiosity hadn't been piqued like this in quite some time. It was rare that anyone disliked him, and even rarer for anyone to dislike him in the span of half an hour *and* to say so to his face. He should have felt insulted. And maybe he did, a little.

The pervading emotion, however, was a perverse sort of excitement. Here stood a challenging woman with wit, common sense, and the boldness to use those features to her sometime-best-interest. And she wasn't that bad looking, either.

In fact, when she had pulled the veil from her face and the sun had hit her eyes just right, he couldn't help but let his gaze drop down to her frowning mouth. She had a very nice mouth, in spite of the daggers it threw in the form of words. Her mouth had a natural curve, a sort of subtle plumpness.

Hartwell watched Mary trip over a tree root and steady herself immediately, her shoulders rigid with embarrassment. She moved so self-consciously, so carefully. She wasn't timid, but she seemed almost obsessively aware of where she was in proximity to him.

Hartwell remembered hearing once that the Trentwood family was a line of hermits. Apparently so, if Mary was a prime example.

He expected Mary to slow down when they reached the gravel drive. Instead, she maintained her pace so by the time Hartwell entered the manor house, she had already deposited her wet dolman, hat, and gloves with Pomeroy. She had also taken the time to leave orders that Hartwell dry off in the guest room. As Mary was nowhere to be seen, Hartwell assumed she had disappeared to her bedroom to do the same.

Pomeroy took the sodden blanket from Hartwell with an easy bow. "Looks like you survived, sir. My compliments."

Hartwell bit the inside of his cheek. "The guest room, if you please," he ground out.

"Of course, sir."

Hartwell followed Pomeroy's lead, each step he took making a satisfyingly loud squelching noise on the threadbare rugs running the length of the stairs and hallway.

If Mary was doing what Hartwell suspected, what he was here to investigate, she certainly wasn't putting the rewards back into her home. Now that he thought about it, the library had been rather lackluster, though well-loved.

In fact, the entire manor house had a sort of timeless style, relying on subtle details that culminated in a happy balance of taste and status. No matter the current financial status of the gentry Trentwood family, at one point they had been well off and governed by a mistress gifted with an excellent eye for wallpaper, paintings, and other such knickknacks and furnishings.

Pomeroy was silent as he led Hartwell to the guest bedroom, for which Hartwell was glad. What had been a simple task this morning was quickly spiraling out of his control. The task at hand, then, was to decide his next move. Would he growl in irritation, or step back and laugh? As per his usual inclination, he found himself chuckling over the day's happenings. And it wasn't over yet.

By this point, Pomeroy had ensured there was warm water for Hartwell to splash across his face, and that the fire wasn't too hot. He must have heard Hartwell's laugh, because he stopped at the bedroom door, ready to leave Hartwell to his own devices.

"Sir?"

"Do you really think Miss Trentwood is haunted?" Hartwell surprised himself by asking.

"When one finds one's mistress whispering to herself, one begins to look for reasons."

"So you don't think she's haunted, then."

"I think she's a very interesting subject to watch, Mr. Hartwell."

Hartwell nodded, having thought the same thing. Only… how would Pomeroy have such insight to his thoughts, unless…

"Why you—where is my satchel? You went through my papers, didn't you?" Hartwell, mortified, felt his ears turn red.

Pomeroy smiled. "What kind of butler would I be, if I didn't ensure the safety and reputation of my mistress?"

"You could have chased after the chit yourself, rather than sending some unknown after her, for example."

"But then I couldn't have rifled through your papers to determine why you're really here, Mr. Hartwell."

Hartwell narrowed his eyes.

Pomeroy stepped from the room, adding, "Your drawings are very good. I hope you find our flowers and animals as worthy of your skills."

It took every ounce of control to not slam the door behind Pomeroy. Huffing, Hartwell threw his hat and coat on the chair sitting directly before the fire to dry them out. He hopped around, struggling to extract his wet, swollen feet from his shoes. Once off, he placed them by the fireplace grate, followed by his shirtwaist, shirt, and pants.

Clad only in his undergarments, Hartwell stood before the fire with his hands on his hips. His hair, which he kept cut long to cover the awkwardness of his left eye, fell before his face. The fire snapped, making him jump.

For whatever reason, he had been pondering Mary's eyes. Hazel, Hartwell thought, would best describe their odd combination of green and brown. Far more interesting than his plain brown eyes.

There was something about her eyes that upset him. Something about them made him want to ask her what was wrong.

Hartwell shook his head. He wasn't going to solve the mystery by staring into a fire in his underwear. He heard a door snap shut and the voices of women. Two women, as far as he could tell. Mary and Mrs. Durham. It took him a moment to realize that the guest bedroom was next door to Mary's bedroom. The thought made him feel nude. He tested his clothes, and satisfied that they were dry, gathered them in his arms. He carried the bundle over to the left wall so he could eavesdrop and dress simultaneously. Such small efficiencies always seemed to feel good, for whatever reason.

"Why is he here?" Mrs. Durham asked.

"I'm not sure," Mary answered. Their voices were muffled so it took Hartwell a moment to process what they were saying. "But he seems genuine enough."

"Genuine! What can he be genuine about?"

"He said his sister was a schoolmate of yours."

Silence from Mrs. Durham.

"That would make his sister a schoolmate of Mama's as well. Or am I mistaken?"

"Yes," Mrs. Durham said, her voice strained. "I assume you are giving him the courtesy of drying before asking him to leave?"

A lengthy pause. Hartwell realized he was holding his breath.

"He's staying, dear Aunt." There was nothing tender about Mary's tone. "We have not been the most gracious of hostesses. The least we can do is provide a meal and place to sleep."

Mrs. Durham scoffed.

"He can't go back to Swindon tonight. There is no one to take him. And anyway, you know as well as I do that our walls are very thin, and I've placed him in the guest bedroom. Unless he's plugged his ears, he can hear every word we say."

Hartwell, who had bent to splash his face with water, slipped, dunking his head and shoulders in the basin. He tried to stifle the curse that burst from his lips, to no avail. Though he knew Mary couldn't see him, his ears reddened anyway when he heard the smug smile in her voice when she said, "See?"

Hartwell was seriously beginning to dislike the way Mary could make him feel like a schoolboy again.

SEVEN

IN WHICH MARY HIDES AMONG BOOKS

MARY ESCAPED TO THE library, looking it over with newly-awakened eyes after sending the sullen Mrs. Durham back to bed.

Ever since her father's illness, Mary had lapsed in the care of the library. It was her domain. She had long ago ordered the servants to tend the fireplace and candles only. She, on the other hand, cared for the books. When she entered the library, knowing Hartwell had waited there at least half an hour, she was past feeling dismay—she felt ashamed.

Her books were coated with dust, those on the low bookcases and those stacked on the side tables. The eight buttoned, fringed, and tufted chairs, deep-seated for snuggling beneath a blanket while reading, frayed at the upholstered edges. The mirror running the length of the wall opposite the windows was tarnishing. The windows were gray-green with winter grime. The fireplace was sooty to the point of being dangerous.

"You've let a few things slide, haven't you, then?" Trentwood said, lifting a book cover with distaste.

Mary wasn't certain how to respond, or what to respond to first. He was right; in the face of his illness she had lost track of the everyday matters. Rather than responding to that nitpicky topic, however, she realized she had never actually seen Trentwood move anything since his death. His previous talents had only included appearing out of thin air and walking through solid objects.

Not that either talent, if one could call such abnormalities talents, had been very easy to adjust to, only... he had show-cased them from the start.

No, this was too much to absorb. Better stick to safer topics. Mary pulled a handkerchief from her pocket and began dusting the pile of books nearest her. "Things were a bit hectic, if you remember."

Trentwood shrugged and took a seat nearest the fireplace, though no fire burned and wouldn't warm him anyway.

"I don't suppose you could help me? Maybe you could float to the top shelving and dust?" Mary smiled at his affronted expression. She had never dared speak to him in such a fashion when he was alive, and she didn't know what inspired her to take such a tone with him now. But oh, how delicious it felt to speak her mind without fear of censure.

"Just who do you think I am?" Trentwood demanded, leaping to his feet.

All right, so there was still some residual censure. Her mouth seemed to have a mind of its own as she retorted, "To be honest, I've thought you a nuisance. So I'm very glad to have found a task for you to do."

Trentwood's mouth dropped open. "What did you say?"

"If you're going to haunt me, make yourself useful, if you please. I've enough to worry about without your meddling." Mary slapped her handkerchief at the pages of the book in her hand and coughed at the cloud of dust she dislodged. "What do you know about Hartwell, for instance? You're a ghost, can't you spy on him? Confirm he is who he claims to be?"

"You would have your own father spy on a guest in his house?" Trentwood fumed, a blue vein popping in his fore-head.

Mary rubbed her forehead in empathy. Talking back to the ghost was almost more trouble than ignoring him. "No, I wouldn't. I'd have my father's ghost spy on a guest in my house. Or did you not leave the house to me?"

Trentwood's mouth thinned to a furious line, but he couldn't refute her, and she knew it. "I refuse to do anything so underhanded. Now what do you think about that?"

Mary lifted the pile of books and replaced them on a sagging shelf. She made a mental note to have Pomeroy look at stabilizing it. "Suit yourself. If you won't help me dust and you refuse to be underhanded, you can take your questions elsewhere."

"Really, we must stop meeting like this," Hartwell said from the doorway.

Mary dropped the book she was inspecting.

"Ah yes, the youth from the tomb," Trentwood said, sidling over to Hartwell. "What do you think happened to him?"

Mary opened her mouth to snap at Trentwood, but the words fell away upon seeing Hartwell's face. He kept his hair long and brushed to the side to hide his pinched skin. Mary moved closer. His eyes were very dark—almost black. So dark, she couldn't read any expression in them. The left eye had a collection of little scars that cut through the brow, down over his eyelid, and onto his cheek. The scars pulled on his eyelids, dragging the upper to meet the lower before it ought, and pulling the lower to reveal the inside of his eye socket. In total, the scar had the odd effect of making his eye look lazy when it was not.

When Hartwell shifted his weight, Mary realized she was staring. She cleared her throat.

"I have decided," Hartwell announced firmly, "you are doing it on purpose."

Mary paused. "I'm sorry, doing what on purpose?"

"Being contrary."

"Contrary?" Mary exclaimed.

Trentwood chuckled. "Whoever this chap is, let's keep him a while, shall we?"

Mary scowled.

"Oh, yes," Hartwell said, warming to the topic. "Talking to yourself, telling me to play your footman when I've inspected your house and know quite well that you haven't any footmen, admitting you knew I was listening to you and your aunt—"

"Ah!" Mary pointed an accusatory finger at Hartwell. "I knew you were listening!"

Hartwell grinned. "This is all an act, Miss Contrary Mary, and heaven help me, I'm curious."

"Careful, Mary," Trentwood cautioned, "do you know what you're dealing with?"

Mary shifted her eyes from Hartwell to Trentwood and back. She couldn't help it—she stole a glance at Hartwell's scars again and flushed in response to his embarrassed flinch. She stepped back to retrieve the book she had dropped. Startled when Hartwell swooped in to pick up the book for her, she swallowed a gasp.

"Mary Wollstonecraft?" Hartwell said, turning over the book in his hand. "Your father let you read such texts?"

Mary snatched it from him, but it was too late, Trentwood had found her out.

"I told you to throw that trash away!" Trentwood snapped.

"My father didn't come into this room; this was my library," Mary said, hugging the book to her chest.

Hartwell chuckled. "You are, without a doubt, the most contrary person I've ever met, myself excluded."

Trentwood snorted.

Mary backed away from them. What could one say, after having been found out to have read—and absolutely loved—A Vindication of the Rights of Women? Nothing, really. She inhaled slowly and waited for the tirade she was certain to receive.

She waited to be labeled a menace, a suffragist, a pain. That was what Trentwood called such groups of women, and while Mary had no inclination to wrestle the vote from British men, she had liked Wollstonecraft's words. She liked the idea of having her sense of reason acknowledged.

Trentwood paced the room deep in thought, though he glanced at Mary now and again as if trying to decide just what punishment he would most enjoy meting out.

"Curiouser and curiouser," was all Hartwell said. He rubbed his chin as he pondered Mary.

"You are a highly irregular man," was all she thought to say.

Hartwell laughed, really laughed this time, and it sent a pleasant chill down Mary's spine. "This coming from the woman who talks to herself. I respectfully claim the term 'irregular' is relative."

Mary scowled. "In any case, I don't understand why you insist on speaking to me in such a familiar manner. Calling me Contrary Mary, of all things!"

Hartwell nodded with heartfelt understanding, smoothing his hair back from his face and behind his ear. "My mother complains the same. She never could cure me of it. Does my familiarity bother you? I can try to stop, but you'd only laugh at my attempt."

Mary gave him an odd look. "It's not really in my nature to laugh," she admitted.

"That is the saddest thing I think I've ever heard, Mary Trentwood."

At this, Trentwood disappeared, his voice whispering in Mary's ear, "I like him, don't you?"

Mary twitched away. "No."

"No? What? No what?" Hartwell said.

Mary faltered. "No... I suppose you are right. My mother used to laugh a great deal."

EIGHT

IN WHICH POMEROY SNEEKS

THERE WERE FEW TASKS Pomeroy would not do for the Trentwoods, and many he did without their knowledge. Snooping through Hartwell's satchel, for instance, was in no way a part of his duties in normal or extenuating circumstances. Pomeroy's mother, God rest her soul, had always said, "What's done is done," and had taken great pains to ensure this was his philosophy.

So when the house had settled for the night, and Pomeroy took a letter from his breast pocket, the well-worn one he had found in Hartwell's satchel, he felt all the proper emotions as his mother had taught. His hands were sweating, his head ached, and he suspected he was developing an ulcer. Guilt was felt deeply in the Pomeroy family, being the closet Catholics they were, and the butler Pomeroy at the manor house of Compton Beauchamp was no exception.

Pomeroy had locked himself in the silver room, which was sadly barren of the family silver. It was more of a closet than a room, with drawers and shelves made of wood darkened from years of sweating hands sliding the silver in and out of place. Pomeroy shook his head every time he had the misfortune to enter; it just wasn't right, to leave one's only child, one's only daughter, with a pile of debt and naught else.

But that was neither here nor there.

Pomeroy flipped the letter over, having settled his candelabra on a shoulder-height shelf. Puzzling how the letter lacked an address. Perhaps Hartwell had never sent it? Unfortunately, Pomeroy had only enough time to snatch one letter from the satchel, and this one was the easiest to access without disturbing anything else. What a wasted opportunity, he thought dourly, until he began to read its contents.

The handwriting was erratic, scrawled across the page by the writer in a violent emotion. The writer never named the recipient, nor did the writer sign his—or her—name.

Not that Pomeroy blamed the writer, as the letter reeked of blackmail. It was dated four months ago, which was around the time Mrs. Durham had moved to the manor house as Trentwood's days drew to an end.

"You have been naughty," the blackmailer accused. "I know it. Would that your husband knew the depths of your betrayal. Rest assured, one day his name will be cleared of your cuckolding."

Pomeroy folded the letter, following the careworn creases. He tapped the letter against his temple. Mrs. Durham had been very quick to eject Hartwell from the house that morning. And Hartwell had been more than pleased when Mrs. Durham didn't arrive for dinner, having begged off with the insufficient claim that she suffered a monstrous headache.

Now, one could find reasons, of course. One had to be blind not to see the interest in Hartwell's eye and expression when speaking with Mary. Therefore, Hartwell could have been glad Mrs. Durham hadn't joined them for dinner because he wanted to talk to Mary more. It was certainly plausible.

And Hartwell's initial concern that Mrs. Durham was the mistress of the manor house? A logical reaction to having the door slammed in his face.

Neither of these points excused the final one, however, the fact being that no one seemed to know who he was, or why he was at the manor house but for Mrs. Durham.

Pomeroy sighed and rolled his shoulders free of the kink in his neck. As if there wasn't enough to concern him and Mary already when it came to all things with Mrs. Durham. He checked the time on his pocket watch, glowering at the hands as they ticked past midnight.

Blackmail at the manor house. What was the world coming to?

Pomeroy ruffled his white hair with a low grumble. He blew out his candle and slipped from the empty silver room, tucking the letter into the breast pocket above his heart.

The matter could rest until morning, surely. He would let Mary sleep. Her day had been far from normal, and that was considering abnormal had become the norm over the last month. Yes, Mary should sleep. When she woke feeling rested, she would see sense in his suggestion that they call the authorities before Hartwell became any wiser.

Pomeroy yawned behind his hand. In the morning, Mary would be her logical self and follow his suggestion and the manor house could go back to its quiet mourning. Really, it was an excellent plan.

"Hartwell? Blackmail?" Mary's smile stretched across her face and her lips quivered in the traitorous moves of laughter. She sat on the floor in the library, sewing together the ripped open seam of one of the chair armrests. Her curved needle glinted in the daylight, which shone brightly through the newly scrubbed windows. "Pomeroy, really."

That had not been the reaction he had expected. Pomeroy drew to his full height. He looked down his long nose and said in his stiffest tones, "I have evidence, Miss, which supports me."

Mouth still trembling, Mary held out her hand. "I think you've been indoors too long; you ought to take a walk now and again," she said, accepting the letter.

Pomeroy shifted his weight as Mary read the short missive, noting with smug—if silent—satisfaction how her brows furrowed together, her mouth down-turned, and her shoulders hunched in embarrassment.

"He didn't write this," Mary said, flinging the letter at Pomeroy.

"How can you know, Miss?"

"I can't," Mary admitted, accepting Pomeroy's help as she stood. She brushed her hands down the front of her working apron and threaded the needle through the apron's hem. "I've only known him a day, but I doubt the laughing man I ate dinner with last night is a blackmailer. The handwriting seems… feminine, somehow. And Alex is a barrister, his occupation is to uphold the law, not circumvent it!"

Pomeroy's smile was far too kind, making it drip with pity and condescension. "Be that as it may, Miss Mary, he wouldn't have to be a good sort of barrister, now would he?"

Mary wrinkled her nose and crossed her arms over her chest. "What is your suggestion, then?"

"Call for the authorities at once, of course."

She nodded slowly. "And what then? Have the gossip-mongers on my lands, harassing my tenants, wanting to know all about how the hermit Miss Mary Trentwood was harboring a blackmailer? Thank you, no."

Pomeroy's jaw set as he mimicked Mary, crossing his arms over his chest. "What is your suggestion then?"

Mary paused a moment, her attention caught by something at the window, or through the window, Pomeroy couldn't tell. She frowned at whatever it was that had caught her attention. Pomeroy cleared his throat. He raised his brows when Mary lifted her hand in the ever familiar motion that asked for silence. "Really, Miss…"

Sighing, a slow smile spread across Mary's face. "We won't call the authorities, not until we have more information. I'll write to my father's solicitor for word of Hartwell and any disreputable dealings attached to him. In the meantime, wouldn't it be safer if we kept him here where we could prevent his mischief?"

Pomeroy's mouth sagged open and his hands fell to his sides.

"I see we are in agreement. Excellent." Mary clapped her hands and smiled. "Now then, shall we have breakfast and welcome our potentially-blackmailing-guest to Compton Beauchamp?"

Unbelievable.

Oh, this was rich. Stupendous. Excellently timed. Mary couldn't keep the smile from her face as she led Pomeroy from the library. She didn't care if Hartwell was a blackmailer or not; the fact was she had a bit of information on him that he didn't know she had.

Well, that wasn't entirely true. Mary didn't want Hartwell to be a blackmailer. She rather liked his warm smile and delighted in the way his laugh, when triggered, sent a chill up her spine. Though she would never admit it, dinner with Hartwell the night before had been, easily, the highlight of the past year.

Mary had woken that morning smiling, for heaven's sake, for no reason at all. It hadn't been the weather, as the day was dull and threatened rain. Again. It hadn't been her industriousness, as she had broken two needles while repairing the chair arms in the library and poked herself often enough that her thumbs were numb.

No, Mary suspected the reason she rose from bed with an amused smile had everything to do with Hartwell taking Mrs. Durham's position as her dining companion.

That, and the loveliness of having an evening with someone her age, or if not her age, around her age, interested in talking about books and culture and music—interested in talking with her.

If Trentwood had haunted her last night, Mary never noticed.

That was enough to make Mary smile for days.

Mary entered the dining room alone. Pomeroy had left her without calling attention to himself, though she probably wouldn't have heard him, what with all of her thoughts bouncing around her mind screaming for her notice. Hartwell and Mrs. Durham had yet to emerge from their bedrooms, leaving the modest buffet free for Mary's less-than-thrilled perusal.

Roasted tomatoes, again, with burned toast, jam and clotted cream, fish leftover from dinner, and coffee. It was enough to send anyone's appetite away, shrieking bloody murder.

Mary knew better than to complain. Mrs. Beeton was doing the best she could with the supplies at hand. Mrs. Beeton was, in fact, doing exactly what Mary asked, which was use everything in the stores until it was absolutely necessary to send out for more. That Mrs. Beeton was sticking to this order, even when Mary wanted to renege with a passion, was one of the many reasons why she had been kept on, while other servants had been let go.

Mary's thoughts continued to wander. Hartwell came to the forefront quickly. Blackmail? She tried to imagine him in a dark, dank room smelling of grease and polluted with the sounds of children's screams, penning that awful letter with a vicious smirk plastered across his face. Even with his scar, it didn't seem to fit.

But if Hartwell had written the letter, Mary knew that Pomeroy's plan was the most prudent. She shuddered. The gossip would be fierce, to say the least. But if Hartwell hadn't written the letter, then who did and why did he have it?

"Woolgathering again?"

Mary flinched, missing her cup as she poured her coffee.

Trentwood sat at the head of the table, his customary spot. He didn't look quite as pale as she was used to seeing him—funny, that, to realize one was used to seeing one's dead parent in the first place. His improved color was, perhaps, owed in part to his sitting in shadow. "Woolgathering about your Mr. Hartwell?" Trentwood prodded when Mary remained silent.

Mary sat at Trentwood's right, her customary spot. "I would hardly call him *my* Mr. Hartwell, Father."

"Especially not if he's blackmailing your aunt?"

Mary speared a bit of tomato with her fork. "Precisely so."

"Even if she deserves it?"

Mary stopped cold, her fork halfway into her mouth. "What do you know?" she asked, setting her fork on her plate.

Trentwood shook his head, the motion telling Mary he didn't know anything, he was just provoking her, as was his way. "I don't think he's blackmailing anyone, do you?"

She rubbed her thumb along the side of her mouth as she thought, wiping away an errant bit of tomato pulp. "The letter could be evidence. For a case he's working on."

Trentwood nodded his approval. "Certainly would explain the careworn edges, if he had to reference it often."

Oh yes, Mary liked this theory. She bit into her tomato, enjoying the way it squirted sweet juice. "I'll have to send my compliments to Mrs. Beeton," she said between bites, "this may be a modest breakfast, but it's delicious." As she chewed, she caught the way Trentwood watched her and realized how broadly she was smiling.

"Do you like the blackmailer?" he asked, leaning forward.

"We don't know he's a blackmailer. Why are you calling him a blackmailer all of a sudden?" Mary protested. Blast the man, he always knew how to get under her skin. "Even so," she said, trying to dig herself out, "it's comforting to know something about him that he hasn't told me himself."

"Oh?"

"Father, he had the definite advantage over me yesterday. He knows a great deal about us and we nothing of him. Pomeroy's snooping, while unpardonable, gave me a—a trump card, of sorts."

"And that pleases you?" Trentwood said.

"Very much indeed." In fact, Mary knew much of her surliness yesterday stemmed from being caught unawares by Hartwell—twice. Both times it had looked as though she was talking to an empty room.

The idea of Hartwell knowing Mary spoke to herself, or rather, spoke to someone no one else could see, was mortifying.

Knowing a potential secret of Hartwell's? Yes, that pleased Mary greatly.

"Even if we discover it is something completely unrelated," she said, finishing her unspoken thought before sipping her coffee.

"Unrelated to what?" Hartwell said, entering the room. He had foregone wearing his entire suit, instead opting for a shirt loosely tucked and a waistcoat to maintain some decency. He looked at home and glad to see Mary. She found herself wondering if Steele would have joined the house so painlessly.

Not that Hartwell's arrival was painless, lest she forget everything that happened at Wayland's Smithy.

"Your lovely eyes are making me blush," Hartwell said after Mary had stared at him for a minute or more.

Mary blinked and coughed, spluttering into the coffee she still held at her mouth.

"You really ought to get that checked out," Hartwell said as he turned his attention to the sidebar, taking no pains to hide his grin.

"What?" Mary said between coughs she struggled to suppress.

"That whole talking to an empty room. What must your servants think?"

"Ha. What servants have I left to frighten? Pomeroy has been with the family since before I can remember, as has Mrs. Beeton, and the house staff are the children of my father's—I mean my—tenants." Mary realized she was babbling, but the momentum was too strong to slow down. "There have been odder things, I'm sure."

Hartwell joined Mary at the table, sitting at Trentwood's left and across from Mary.

How odd; Mary had often imagined Steele sitting in that seat. Seeing Hartwell there, both the night before and now, made Mary want to miss Steele. It was familiar to miss Steele, and startling that she didn't. When had that happened?

Certainly not when Hartwell arrived, she was not so shallow. When was the last time she had pined for Steele? Mary glanced at Trentwood. His eyes, his terrible eyes, pierced her as if he could read her thoughts, and worse, approved of them.

Hartwell cleared his throat, snatching Mary's attention from Trentwood. "You are completely correct, there have been odder things. I once had a client who wanted to sue his neighbor's dog for… ahem… pressing his amorous attentions on my client's wife."

Mary's mouth dropped open even as her lips curved into an incredulous smile. "You didn't take the case, I hope!"

"I didn't have to," Hartwell said, spreading jam over his toast, "the defendant had his dog sent to his mother in the country before the trial, which suited everyone fine."

Mary looked at Hartwell askance. "You're making fun of me."

"Upon my honor, I'm not," Hartwell said, lifting his hand in solemn truth. "That dog was a menace anyway, and the owner was lucky my client didn't shoot the thing. No, sending the dog away was the best solution all around."

"What *are* you talking about at this ungodly hour?"

Hartwell and Mary both jumped in their seats. They turned to find a horrified Mrs. Durham standing in the doorway, clutching close to her chest her lapdog, inappropriately named Petit-Ange, or "Little Angel." The dog yipped, and Mary's lip curled.

"Mr. Hartwell, my aunt, Mrs. Durham, and her dog, Petit-Ange." Mary turned to him and murmured, "The dear little angel is not, as you so elegantly put it, fixed. I've more than half a mind to do it myself while my aunt sleeps, though. I've lost more pillows and shoes to that menace than the little beast is worth."

Hartwell snorted and tried to cover it with a rasping cough.

Mrs. Durham was neither fooled nor amused. She marched to the sidebar, Petit-Ange tucked beneath her arm.

Mary hid a smile as she watched Mrs. Durham realize she couldn't hold Petit-Ange and pile food onto her plate at the same time. This had been Mary's sole morning entertainment before Hartwell's arrival.

Now, Hartwell sat across from her and seemed to have noticed her amusement. He turned in his seat so he could watch Mrs.

Durham also as she shifted Petit-Ange around, scolding him for trying to eat her food, yet purring at him for being so cute.

Mary rolled her eyes, as was her wont, only this time Hartwell happened to see her do it. He grinned at her, and she found herself grinning in return.

"Making friends with the enemy? Is this your strategy?" Trentwood said, reminding Mary that yes, he haunted her still and yes, he sat at her left and yes, he just so happened to believe Pomeroy that Hartwell was a blackmailer.

Odd, though, that comment about Mrs. Durham deserving blackmail. Mary had no idea what Trentwood meant by that, and as her thoughts converged on that little mystery, her grin faded.

She ruminated on the topic, not noticing that Mrs. Durham was walking toward the head of the table until it was almost too late. Just when Mrs. Durham was about to sit on Trentwood's lap, Mary pointed her finger and shrieked, "No, not there."

Mrs. Durham gasped, dropping Petit-Ange to the floor and her plate to the table.

"What did you do that for?" Trentwood said, peeved, as he stood to get out of Mrs. Durham's way. "I was going to move, or did you think I'd like to have that thing on top of me?"

Mary swallowed. *Good Lord, now I've done it.* Hartwell and Mrs. Durham stared at her as if she had lost her mind, and really, Mary was fairly certain she had. "There was a spider," she said weakly.

Hartwell shoved his toast in his mouth to muffle his guffaw, Mary could only assume. She slouched in her seat while Mrs. Durham inspected the chair, finding nothing wrong.

Mary's eyes darting around the room trying to find Trentwood's new hiding place. Not that when Trentwood hid, anyone else could see him anyway. He did, however, at moments such as this, attempt to be a little less obtrusive. At least, that's what

Mary liked to think Trentwood was doing when he disappeared like that. *Blink, my father's haunting me. Blink, the ghost is gone. Blink, I'm definitely mad.*

And worse yet, Hartwell and Mrs. Durham ate their food silently, studiously, letting her take whatever time she needed to collect herself. They weren't trying to have a conversation and pretend like Mary hadn't just screamed at the top of her lungs, no, that would have been a kindness on Mrs. Durham's part, and she had a limited supply of kindnesses, of that Mary was certain.

"I'm so glad your headache subsided, Aunt," Mary said, finally.

"Whatever do you mean?" Mrs. Durham said. "Even if my headache had subsided, it's back with a vengeance now."

A light whimper escaped Mary's lips, one she was certain Mrs. Durham did not hear. Hartwell, on the other hand… Mary was beginning to realize that nothing got past him. He managed to notice her when she wasn't worth noticing; indeed, it was when she wasn't the center of attention that his attention was on her. Perverse man.

"Did you sleep well, Mr. Hartwell?" Mrs. Durham asked, chewing on the leftover fish from dinner. "That guest bed is quite stiff, I ought to know, I slept there for three months before Mr. Trentwood died, and let me tell you, I still haven't worked out all my back pain."

Hartwell smiled at Mrs. Durham, much to her—and Mary's—surprise. "I slept as if angels had put me there." He turned to Mary. "Your butler, Pomeroy, is very attentive. Does he always lay out your guests' papers on that little table for them?"

Mary clasped her hands together in her lap where Hartwell and Mrs. Durham couldn't see that she was digging her nails into her palms. "I'm not certain I understand your meaning."

Mrs. Durham ate her food calmly, as if she hadn't heard the warning that rumbled in the undertones of Hartwell's question.

"I wasn't sure if it was a country custom, or perhaps something particular to Compton Beauchamp. As I understand it, personal possessions are exactly that—personal." Hartwell continued his disarming smile, even as his tone grew colder with each passing word until he finally spat out the last.

Oh, I could kill him, Mary thought, closing her eyes. What did it matter if Pomeroy had been with the family for thirty years? To have stolen a piece of correspondence from a barrister was bad enough, but to leave the papers out in a blatant disregard for secrecy of the robbery! Did no one have any logical sense anymore?

At the very least, Pomeroy was going to get a stern talking to.

"There must be a misunderstanding," Mary stuttered, her mind racing ahead to lay down a plausible storyline. "Pomeroy was in the library with me this morning. We were going over some papers before the solicitor comes."

Hartwell leaned forward, resting his elbows on the table. "So the solicitor is coming today, then?"

"Yes," Mrs. Durham said.

"No," Mary said simultaneously.

"What are you two playing at?" Hartwell said, frowning.

I could ask the same of you, Mary thought. "I received word that he would be arriving tomorrow, and I wanted to speak with Pomeroy about where we could lodge him. You see, you and my aunt are in the only guest bedrooms."

That, at least, was the truth. Pomeroy had approached her in the library first to say that he had received notice of the solicitor's arrival. It was only after that had been settled had he the nerve to pull out that stupid letter.

"Why did you think the solicitor was arriving today, Mrs. Durham?" Hartwell asked, his eyes narrowing.

The effect was rather terrifying, and Mary had to commend her aunt for not staring at that left eye, which had become nothing more than a patch of scarred flesh. Whether or not Hartwell was blackmailing Mrs. Durham, there was certainly something going on there. When he spoke to Mary, he was all smiles; with Mrs. Durham, he was as Mary imagined he would be in court. Terse. Suspicious. Indignant.

"Well, that had been his original plan. I'm sure I don't know what's taking him so long."

Mary stared at Mrs. Durham. Why did she lie? They hadn't known at all when the solicitor was coming, hence the reason Mary thought Hartwell had been the solicitor only the day before. Mary watched Mrs. Durham finish her meal, the thought that she didn't really know much about her aunt, other than the fact that she was her mother's younger twin, scaring her a little.

Just what had Trentwood meant, Mrs. Durham deserved to be blackmailed?

What good was it to have a ghost for a father if he wouldn't divulge the secrets he knew? Really, the situation was impossible.

"I thought perhaps since I've stayed the night, that I could do you a service in return, Miss Trentwood, and sit with you when your solicitor comes," Hartwell said, his voice carefully even.

Mary's eyes lit with obvious relief, then dulled with a shifty wariness. "I don't really know you, Mr. Hartwell. Why should I trust my family finances to you?"

He shook his head. "Not to me, with me. I have no intention of representing you, only sitting beside you in case your solicitor decides to play any tricks on a grieving daughter. It has happened before, you know."

Mary stiffened.

"I'm not implying that you've lost any of your senses in your time of mourning," Hartwell rushed to add, "only that it might help to have someone sitting beside you, silently sitting beside you, who is familiar with all the terminology."

He was right, Mary was a trifle terrified about having to deal with the solicitor. This was a city man, coming to talk to her about Trentwood's debts and investments, which she had only begun to wrap her mind around over the past year as her father's health declined. When Trentwood was alive, he hadn't the energy to guide her. But now that he was dead, and haunting her...

"All right," Mary said. "I will take you up on your offer."

Now it was Mrs. Durham's turn to shriek. "Are you out of your mind?"

"What?" Mary said, "isn't he your friend's brother? Is he not trustworthy?"

"He's extremely trustworthy, he's a barrister, and a good one at that," Mrs. Durham fumed.

"Then why are you upset?" Hartwell asked, his voice low, calm, soothing. To Mary, at least, it was soothing; to Mrs. Durham it seemed to incite her further.

"I'll not accept charity from your sister, that's why. I want nothing to do with her."

"Have you had a falling out?" Mary asked.

"Yes," Mrs. Durham spat. "And she's sent her brother to rub it in."

Hartwell laughed then, and Mrs. Durham became purple in the face. "What nonsense. I didn't hear of any falling out. If I had, you ought to know I wouldn't be here. I quell disagreements, I don't start them."

Mrs. Durham tried to come up with a retort, her mouth flapping, wordless. She looked like a fish grasping for crumbs. Mary allowed a small smile at the thought, a very small smile so no one would notice.

"Aunt," Mary said, "you aren't accepting his charity at all. I am. These are my finances now, and I need to understand them. I need all the help I can get."

With Trentwood standing beside Mary, he could make certain Hartwell advised her properly. With Hartwell sitting beside her, Pomeroy could try to find other blackmail letters in Hartwell's satchel, or anything to provide further context. Provided, of course, that he put everything back in place. "Thank you, Mr. Hartwell, for being so kind to offer."

"If I'm to help you, I insist you call me Alex. I only give my services freely to my friends, and my friends call me Alex."

So very forward, this man, so determined to be on friendly terms. Why? "Well, if I'm to call you Alex, I suppose you ought to call me Mary."

Hartwell grinned. "Excellent. Mary it is."

Unbidden came Trentwood's voice asking her, "Are you sure you know what you're doing?"

Truthfully, Mary didn't. But then, she wasn't really in the habit.

Nine

In which rules are established

"WELL, MRS. DURHAM WAS vexed at breakfast, wasn't she?" Trentwood said as Mary shut the bedroom door behind her.

She had spent the remainder of the morning calming Mrs. Durham and feeding Petit-Ange dog treats while Hartwell had escaped to his bedroom. Coward. At this point, the last person—thing—Mary wanted to see was Trentwood's ghost, so of course he would appear right when she was about to throw herself to bed to sleep away her pounding headache.

Mary rubbed her temples. "What do you want?"

"Why do you think I want something?"

Mary leveled a look at him that translated, roughly, to "Are you really going to play that game?"

"And just what do you hope to accomplish by looking at me like that, young miss?"

Her chuckle was without mirth. "Father, you know I haven't been considered young for years." She brushed past him, noting when she did so the hairs of her arms stood on end and a chill ran down her back. Shivering, she sat on the edge of her bed. "I would like to propose a few rules, if you please."

Trentwood pulled his watch and chain from his waistcoat pocket. He spun the chain so the watch circled outward, rotating around his hand. It was his thinking motion and signaled to Mary she would need all her wits at the ready, for he would be determined to thwart her. How that was different from any other conversation lately, Mary wasn't all that certain. Still, it didn't hurt to be prepared.

"Rules?" Trentwood prodded.

Mary cleared her throat and kicked her feet out from her skirts. Right then. "I've got to keep appearances, Father. You don't want me sent to the asylum, do you?"

He stood impassive.

Mary scoffed. "I see. So you would rest in peace knowing your only child and heir was wasting away in filth?"

"Seeing as how I'm not resting in peace now, I'm uncertain what your point is."

"Father!"

"How do I know you aren't mad?" he countered. "I'm not the one speaking to ghosts, am I?"

Mary threw up her hands in exasperation. "All right then, be that way. Send me to the madhouse. I'm practically living in one anyway since I'm not allowed to ignore you, you keep startling me right when someone comes in the room, and everyone seems to have secrets that I can't make sense of."

"Send you to the madhouse? Don't see why I'd do any such thing. Do you think I've grown heartless since my death?"

"I was fairly convinced of it when you were alive," Mary muttered, glaring at the floor.

Trentwood disappeared.

Mary jumped, startled by the sudden lack of a conversation partner. She swallowed. She waited. He was doing this to scare her, that's what he was doing. He was trying to teach her a lesson. He was forever trying to teach her lessons.

"Father?" she whispered, her eyes focusing and refocusing on every little movement in the room.

Her bedroom window was open a crack, letting in a sliver of cool air that made the brocade curtains shift slightly. A beetle scuttled along the hardwood flooring. Mary squeaked and lifted her feet.

Really, she ought to have known better than to say such a thing to him. Her shoulders slumped.

Trentwood reappeared close to Mary, so close that his nose hovered inches from hers. "Care to try that again?"

Mary held her breath. Her entire body shuddered in response to the cold Trentwood emanated. She forced herself to concentrate on the peppermint scent that almost masked the lingering stench of dirt and decomposition.

So he was trying to punish her. Her temper flared as it never had while he was alive, and she found herself snapping, "You never did explain why Steele wasn't good enough for you." Her voice was low.

"I said he wasn't good enough for you, remember?"

"Obviously not," Mary said, sidling away from Trentwood. "And just what would have made him good enough for me, Father? What would have proven his worth to you that he was good enough for me?"

Trentwood's smile was tight, a little cruel, and a little sad. "Let me ask you: did he ever once try to see you again after that party?"

No, he never did, both she and Trentwood knew that very well. She backed away from him, shaking her head.

"Did he ever write?"

Not that Mary knew of, but then Trentwood could have confiscated the letters before Mary saw them. Not that he would have, he could hardly move without her or Pomeroy helping him after that awful fever had taken hold. In fact, she had read his correspondence to him, and written his letters for him, as he had difficulty holding a pen.

"Have a friend ask after you or pass some word your way?"

Mary swallowed. Her lip began to tremble. Stop it, she wanted to shriek. Stop it. Why are you doing this?

"What has that dandy done over the last year—year, mind you!—that has you so convinced he intended to offer for you?"

By the time he finished speaking, Trentwood was shouting at Mary from across the room. His eyes, once pale and washed out, had adopted a frightening green hue. A vein at his temple bulged… as if blood still flowed there. His watch was hanging, forgotten, from his waistcoat pocket.

Mary pressed her lips together. She was not going to cry. She had cried about Steele, but only when alone in her bedroom when her loneliness had crept into her bed with the night shadows. Or when she had taken her solitary walks in the afternoons when her father had napped. But she had never cried before Trentwood, and she certainly wasn't about to begin now.

And anyway… "How do I know you didn't have Pomeroy hide his letters from me, or prevent him from seeing me? Pomeroy would walk through hellfire for you."

Trentwood shook his head and sighed. His eyes lost their greenish hue and he seemed a bit more natural, or as natural as he could be, given the situation. "You don't understand me at all, do you?" He drew up his watch by its chain and tucked it into his waistcoat pocket, the motion giving him time to find the correct words. "Don't you think, if I had seen an inkling of spirit, of courage in the boy, enough for him to send one measly letter, that I would have respected him for it?"

Mary moved to the window, clenching the curtain between her white fingers. Trentwood was telling the truth. She didn't know how she knew, but she knew he was, and there was the rub. She felt her cheeks grow hot and a lump form in her throat.

"Did you think I enjoyed watching you, day-in, day-out, waiting for a sign of his affection?"

She had, indeed.

"Do you think I wanted to die, leaving you with Mrs. Durham as your sole companion?"

Mary hugged her arms tightly to her chest. "Why are you here?" she whispered.

Trentwood's sigh of relief was so loud it made Mary jump. That wasn't exactly what she had expected.

"Finally," he said, "you're beginning to ask the right questions."

Mary spun on her heel, her mouth sagging. What did he mean, asking the "right" questions? How could there be wrong questions? And was she imagining it, or did he manage to say something that didn't end as a question just then?

"You aren't ready for the answer yet, but at least you're asking the question. Can't believe it took you a month. Thought you were rather more clever than that."

Mary rubbed her temples fiercely. She couldn't make sense of what he was saying. What had they been talking about, anyway, before he had derailed the conversation with all his talk of Steele?

Rules, that's right, Mary had wanted to lay down some rules.

"Would it really be too much if you somehow gave notice of your... arrivals so I'm not quite so startled, at least?" Mary asked. "And could we try to keep your appearances to when I'm alone?"

"You could develop a thicker skin, you know."

"My apologies that it's taking me so very long to become accustomed to my father's ghost popping in and out of vision without warning."

He grunted.

"So then, will you warn me before appearing out of nowhere?" she pressed.

Trentwood nodded his acquiescence nobly, if a bit grudgingly.

"All right then." Mary cleared her throat. "Now, what do you really know about Aunt Ophelia and Mr. Hartwell—I mean, Alex?"

"That he's standing outside your door, for one."

"What?" Mary dashed across the room and threw open the door to find, yes, Hartwell standing there, cool as silk with his hand raised to knock. "What are you doing?" she said flatly.

"Hello Mary," Hartwell said, his hand hanging in the air.

"What is it? My aunt isn't harassing you again, I hope."

"Careful, Mary," Trentwood cautioned, moving to stand behind her. "He suspects something."

Suspects something? Mary eyed Hartwell warily. What did he suspect? That she suspected him of blackmailing her aunt? That she suspected her aunt of something so awful her father wouldn't tell her? That she was haunted by her father's ghost?

There were quite a number of mysteries needing to be solved, she realized suddenly.

"You really are one of the most frank women I've ever met," Hartwell muttered, his voice almost low enough that Mary couldn't hear him. Almost. "No, your aunt isn't harassing me. You sounded distressed. I don't know who you were talking to or what you were talking about, but I thought if you wanted to talk, the least I could do is offer to listen."

Trentwood chuckled. "He's lying."

Mary twitched.

"Look there."

Mary followed where Trentwood's finger pointed and caught sight of Pomeroy sneaking around the corner of the hallway.

"Poor Pomeroy," Trentwood said, still chuckling. "He thinks you've lost your mind."

Maybe I have, Mary thought, closing her eyes. Her fingers of one hand clawed into the doorjamb while the other gripped the door handle. "Is that so? You want to listen?" she said to Hartwell.

"Oh yes. I'm very curious to know who Steele is. Pomeroy wouldn't tell me."

Trentwood roared with laughter.

Mary pointed an accusatory finger at Hartwell. "Ah-ha! Pomeroy thinks I'm speaking to myself and he wants you to distract me, that's what you mean. How dare you speak about me with my butler behind my back? Who do you think you are?"

Hartwell threw his palms up in mock surrender. "The man cornered me in the guest room. I had nowhere else to turn!" He shoved a lock of hair out of his eyes. "Anyway, I am curious about this Steele chap. He sounds like a right bounder for leaving you."

"I don't believe this," Mary muttered.

Hartwell smiled and Mary was struck with the thought that he had been handsome once, intimidatingly so. Thank goodness for small miracles like facial scars to remove her usual fear of handsome men…

"I like this one," Trentwood announced. He wiped nonexistent tears from his dry cheeks, a residual habit from his previous life. "He has spirit."

Excellent. Wonderful. He had known the man for less than a day and already liked him more than Steele, whom he had known a month. Mary set her jaw, determined not to answer Trentwood with Hartwell right in front of her. But oh, how she wanted to.

"In all seriousness, Mary," Hartwell said, "I was wondering if you cared to walk about the property. The sun is fighting its way from the clouds, and I'm still a bit stiff from my jaunt with the Browns yesterday." His gaze flitted to a spot behind her shoulder. He frowned.

Mary held her breath and froze in place. Hartwell was staring right at Trentwood. Did he see him? Did he see the ghost? Was she really haunted and the ghost wasn't just her imagination?

No, she must have imagined it, for now Hartwell was frowning at her. Dimly she realized he was asking if she was all right.

"Show him the gardens, Mary, he'll like that," Trentwood said.

Mary sighed. She wasn't entirely sure which was worse: Trentwood asking questions or issuing directives.

"If you go with him right now, I promise I won't tag along," Trentwood offered.

"I'd love a walk," Mary blurted.

"Excellent," Hartwell said as she grabbed her heaviest shawl and a thick felt hat to protect against the March chill. She didn't notice the way he watched her. If she had, she would have noticed the cold glint in his eye, the grim line of his mouth.

Fortunately for Hartwell, Mary didn't see the betraying expression, and so had no idea what she was walking—no, practically jogging—into.

TEN

IN WHICH MRS. DURHAM PONDERS

MRS. DURHAM WATCHED FROM the library window as Mary ventured out on a walk with Hartwell. She had listened to them talk from her bedroom, and followed as they left the manor house.

It had been Hartwell's idea to take a walk, one that Mary hadn't seemed too thrilled about, which was odd considering Mary was always gallivanting to that tomb. Mrs. Durham knew it wasn't because Mary disliked Hartwell that made her hesitate to walk with him; she had seen the pretty blushes that stole across Mary's cheeks when Hartwell looked at her just so.

Therein lay Mrs. Durham's emerging problem. She knew she was a guest at the manor house, and at mercy of Mary's whim… if Mary realized and exercised her power. Trentwood had been quite clear on his deathbed when he had asked to speak to Mrs. Durham alone. He had left nothing for her, and why should he?

He was the husband of her twin and had no true allegiance to her other than that.

She knew Trentwood had never liked her, which had suited her, really, because she had never liked him. Yet to be told she could never touch a cent of her sister's money through lips cracked dry from fever, now that had been the deciding factor. What could Trentwood do about it? He was dead. Things had been progressing rather nicely, really, up until Hartwell's arrival.

Mrs. Durham dug her nails into the wooden window sash as Mary and Hartwell disappeared around the corner of the house. They were taking a turn around the grounds; Hartwell had made up some excuse about wanting to see the gardens that he had heard his sister speak of so fondly.

Yes, she would think of them fondly. That was where she had seduced herself a husband. An uncharitable thought, but that didn't make it any less true.

"What in the world am I to do?" Mrs. Durham muttered. Petit-Ange, at her feet, sneezed. "Bless you, dearest."

The fact of the matter was it simply wouldn't do to have Hartwell at the manor house any longer than absolutely necessary. Mrs. Durham's mouth felt sour at the thought of having to face him at dinner. He had his sister's eyes, and mouth, and smile, God help her. It made Mrs. Durham want to vomit, his sister's smile, the very one that charmed Mary so.

She wanted to claw out his sister's eyes and feed them to him.

No, no, that wasn't right. Surely she hadn't just thought such a grotesque act. Mary and Hartwell passed in front of the library window again, the wind pulling at their clothing. Mrs. Durham couldn't see their faces, but she could tell by the way they leaned toward one another that they had, over the course of their walk, found more topics of discussion to amuse them. Mary even burst into laughter. When was the last time she had done that?

Mrs. Durham frowned. This had to be stopped. There was absolutely no way she would allow Mary to entertain feelings for a Hartwell, of all people, even if he happened to be the only honorable one alive.

Yet what could she do about it? Mary had all but agreed to give Hartwell access to her finances, the little brat, and so Hartwell was certain to stay until the solicitor left.

If only there was someone else to confuse Mary's affections.

Mrs. Durham smiled. It was a cruel smile, a smile meant to wound even as it apologized.

"Come, Petit-Ange," she said, scooping the dog into her arms. "Mama has a letter to write."

She took one last glance out the window to confirm Mary and Hartwell had decided to take one more turn about the house.

Mrs. Durham chuckled, tucking Petit-Ange under one arm so she could lift her skirts to sashay from the library to her bedroom.

"She won't know what hit her, Petit-Ange, will she?" she crooned. "Your Auntie Mary is going to forget all about her precious Mr. Hartwell and that horrid man will leave and you and I will get our house back. Just you wait and see."

Petit-Ange barked and whined. Mrs. Durham looked down at her skirts, which had felt very warm at her hip, suddenly.

"For heaven's sake," she snapped, "couldn't you wait until I put you down? This is the only black dress I have, you naughty thing." She was going to write her letter smelling of urine.

Somehow, it felt so very typical.

ELEVEN

IN WHICH HARTWELL PONDERS

HARTWELL HAD BEEN IN the middle of writing a series of questions into his journal when Pomeroy had burst into the guest room with the suggestion which sounded like a demand that he invite Mary for a walk.

That annoying butler was lucky that inviting Mary for a walk had been on Hartwell's mind for most of the morning. Otherwise, he'd have suffered the boxing of his life for interrupting a rather important chain of thoughts.

No matter, Hartwell was outside now, and it was easier to think outside. Well, usually it was easier to think outside. Something about being in Mary's presence seemed to stunt his wits a little. Happily, she seemed comfortable with the silence between them, allowing Hartwell to run over his list of questions in his head:

1. Who is Steele?

No wait, that wasn't the first item on the list at all.

Focus, man, focus.

2. Why is Mary interested in a man who hasn't thought of contacting her in a year?

Really, this was getting embarrassing.

3. Why had Pomeroy insisted he take Mary for a walk? Why not distract her himself?

Ah, now that was a question worth asking, as it suggested Pomeroy knew something more than what he let on about the situation. Just what did Pomeroy know? And whom did he know it about? Hartwell glanced sidelong at Mary, who puffed a sigh into the cool air. It took him a moment to realize they walked at the same pace, kept the same sort of rhythm.

What an odd thing to notice, and what an odder thing to have in common. He had long legs for a man. He couldn't imagine how long her legs must be to keep in stride with him.

The last thing he needed to be thinking about was Mary Trentwood's legs when he had a blackmailer to catch. For all he knew, she was the blackmailer. Really, this wasn't what he had in mind when he left London yesterday.

Hartwell scowled. Absolutely ridiculous, this growing attraction to such a brusque woman who could very well be the person determined to ruin his sister with information that he hadn't even been able to wring out of her uncharacteristically closed mouth.

All Hartwell knew was that if anyone knew anything, his sister Lady Kirkham had said, it would be Mrs. Durham. And that was all Lady Kirkham would say, even after hours of interrogation.

How Lady Kirkham expected him to help her when she wouldn't confide the dastardly secret that her blackmailer held against her, Hartwell didn't know. But he would try, of course he would try, for he loved his elder sister. Even when he wanted to strangle her. Which was most of the time, to be honest.

So then. Back to the list of questions.

1. Who is blackmailing my sister?

2. Does Mrs. D know anything about it?

3. If Mrs. D does know something, how am I to get the information from her if she's determined to dislike me?

4. Does Mary know anything about it?

> 5. If Mary does know something about it, how am I to
> get the information from her if I'm beginning to like
> her?

Hartwell winced, not liking to admit the last point to himself. But if he was to be objective, he had to be honest. He liked Mary, inasmuch as a man could like a woman he'd known for a day. She was blunt, and he liked bluntness.

It suggested openness, honesty, a lack of guile. She had an honest face, the kind that splayed her innermost thoughts and feelings when she thought she had impassive control. All of which suggested she wasn't the blackmailer and he was free to explore whether these feelings were of friendship or something deeper.

"Are we quiet because we like it, or because we have nothing to say?" Mary asked.

Hartwell coughed, not expecting her to speak while he had been trying to decide if he had romantic feelings toward her. "I was rather enjoying the silence after this morning's breakfast discussion. And then I thought perhaps you might enjoy the silence after your… discussion in your bedroom," he said wryly.

Mary stiffened. "My aunt had no right to be so irritated."

He studied Mary, noting that every time Mrs. Durham had her attention, her face tightened, her hands fidgeted, and her eyes darted about as though calculating every escape route. Mary had no deep love for her aunt, of that Hartwell was certain.

"I'm surprised you accepted my invitation," Hartwell said, keeping his tone light. "I thought I was interrupting something."

"You were," Mary said, "but I welcomed the interruption."

"Ah." He followed along as Mary turned the corner of the house. The ground clung to their feet, and he wondered if Mary had put boots on to protect her feet from the cold. But then she was a walker, and most likely wore such boots out of habit rather than necessity. He shook his head slightly. Back on track!

"I was certain you'd deny me the pleasure of your company, as you didn't seem to enjoy my company at all yesterday."

Mary looked at him sharply. She relaxed at the sight of his smile and allowed a small one of her own to break through her troubled expression. "I could say the same of you, you know."

"Quite," Hartwell said. How to get Mary to speak of blackmail? He was rather appalled by his lack of interrogation skills when outside of the courtroom. But then, he'd never had to interrogate a woman, and certainly not a woman like Mary Trentwood. Dangerous thinking, for if she were a blackmailer and blackmailing his sister besides, he would have to see her in court and mount evidence against her.

Without evidence, he had no case.

What was it about this woman that made Hartwell think in circles? He ought to have stayed in London and learned more about the people living in the manor house. While stuck here, he had no resources, no way to access his solicitor quickly, no way to know if the blackmailer had sent another letter to his sister.

Blast and damn, sometimes I wish I thought things through a bit more before jumping on a train to the middle of nowhere.

Mary placed her hand on his arm. He looked at her with a start before realizing she was gesturing at a rise in the ground that would have made him stumble. She, on the other hand, was watching the house, the windows specifically, it seemed. She knew the grounds of her home so well that she didn't need to watch her step. She knew them well enough that she could stare at the house solemnly and warn Hartwell of his own misstep without hesitation.

Just how often does she do this? he wondered.

Mary was looking at the bay window belonging to the library, he realized. Hartwell caught his breath at the sight of a shadow lurking behind the murky panes of glass. Was that the mysterious father Pomeroy had warned him about?

No, for there was a dog in its arms. The very same dog that had used his leg as an itching post at breakfast. Very un-ghost-like. So Mrs. Durham watched from afar, did she? Best give her a show.

"So this is the family home, then?"

Mary nodded. "We've been here since Compton Beauchamp came into being, since the Tudors, I think." She sighed at the crumbling stone steps that led from the back of the manor house to the lackluster garden. "It's a bit worse for wear."

"It's charming," Hartwell lied. The place was a deathtrap if he ever saw one.

"It's falling apart," Mary retorted, shifting her shawl around her shoulders with a sniff. "But I'll not leave it, not while my—" She cut herself off.

"Not while your dear retiring aunt is in such dire need of your tender care," Hartwell finished for her, his tone the very definition of admiration and understanding, with the requisite undertones of sarcasm and amusement.

Mary choked on a giggle that turned into an amused snicker.

"Has she always lived with you?"

"No," Mary said quickly. She stopped walking.

"Well, that sounds like a story begging to be told," he said, rounding on her with a grin. He saw Mary glance at his expression and turn from it. He dropped his grin as if it burned his already scarred face, realizing she turned from him whenever he smiled.

Just like everyone else.

"A story for a story," Mary said, her hazel eyes bright and her cheeks a bit flushed as she turned to face him.

No, not just like everyone else, he thought, as the wind ruffled his hair. Others looked away in disgust, fear, ashamed curiosity; they never looked away with blushing embarrassment. Good heavens, not only was Mary Trentwood *not* afraid of him, was it possible she actually found him attractive? Poor girl, she obviously needed a quizzing glass. Or two. Or three.

"A story for a story?" Hartwell said slowly.

"Indeed." She smiled, warming to the subject. "I tell you a little about myself, and you tell me why you're really here."

His brows rose and his mouth took a mulish turn. "Meaning you don't think I'm here at my sister's bidding?"

Mary opened her mouth to reply, but he cut her off before the words left her mouth.

"It just so happens I'm not here at her bidding, so good for you for sensing it. But I am here because of her, if you'll acknowledge the difference." Hartwell clamped his mouth shut before it decided, quite of its own accord, to blurt anything else. Just what had gotten into him? He was supposed to be gleaning information about Mary and Mrs. Durham, not volunteering his own.

"I do see the difference," she mused, "and wonder at it."

He waved a finger at her. "I've told you something; now you must tell me something."

"No, my aunt hasn't always lived here," she offered.

After waiting a moment or two, Hartwell exclaimed, "But I already knew that bit, you can't count that. Tell me something new." Oh, how his peers in London would be roiling with laughter at the sight of him now, stumbling over the basest game of sharing information. And what was Mary doing? Was she—oh yes, she was!—she was laughing.

That laugh settled into every corner of his mind and warmed him. Hartwell didn't care if he had to volunteer everything he knew, as long as he could make her laugh again.

"Fine," Hartwell said, fascinated by the way Mary's eyes sparkled in the sunlight, and how strands of hair had blown free of her chignon to be held captive between her still trembling lips. He watched her inhale quickly, and he knew she knew he was staring boldly at her mouth. He dragged his eyes back to hers. "This is a very odd game, Mary Trentwood."

"My mother and I used to play one very like it," Mary said, resuming their walk to dissipate the charged awkwardness that had sprung between them. Or so Hartwell assumed. She clasped her hands behind her back as she walked, a very mannish thing to do, yet she somehow made it look very feminine, very natural, very her. "We would each volunteer a sentence to a story, and we came up with the most ridiculous tales."

"I assume a princess was involved."

"Oh, yes," Mary said. "Someone had to save the prince."

"I beg your pardon?"

"Well, it's just that in our stories, the prince was always marrying the wrong woman." She frowned, and he heard her toe tapping against a rock. "I can't remember why, for the life of me. But he was marrying the wrong woman and didn't know he was a prince, and the princess had to show him the errors of his ways."

Hartwell snorted. "Don't you think if the princess had to show the would-be prince the error of his ways, perhaps she ought to have waited for a prince who knew he was a prince and knew the princess was right for him?"

Mary's expression darkened and she continued walking, briskly this time. Hartwell dashed to catch up to her.

"How often have your friends married their match, Mr. Hartwell?" she snapped. "How often have they had the foresight to marry a woman who could give them a proper home, a proper marriage, a proper partnership?"

Hartwell licked his lips. His sister, he knew, had thought she had married her match. He didn't know what she thought now. And his peers in London? They made sport of their wives in a very unsportsmanlike manner, quelling the youth within Hartwell who had spent his childhood reading tales where the prince did save his princess and cherished her.

"None," he admitted gruffly.

"It's your turn. You must tell me why you're here."

He touched her arm and she stopped. She would not look at him, and he suspected there were tears under her cold tone. She wouldn't cry, heavens no, she was too proud for that. But that didn't prevent the emotion from being there anyway.

"I didn't mean to tease about your mother. I'm terribly sorry, that was awful of me."

"Yes, it was."

"My mother always said my mouth would get me into trouble."

"It has."

Hartwell scowled. "I'm trying to apologize, Mary, will you kindly let me?"

She tried to suppress a smile but failed. "Very well."

Thank heavens for that. He was certain he had insulted her deeply, but there was a smile lurking. For all that Mary said she wasn't one to laugh or joke, she was certainly in fine form at the moment. Best take advantage of it while he could.

Really, all Hartwell had to do was wait until the solicitor came with the Trentwood papers. He would know, then, if she had been accepting funds from his sister. He could even ask the solicitor, on the sly, about Mrs. Durham's finances. Hartwell was well known in London for his fairness and diligence. The solicitor would trust him, surely.

Hartwell swooped to kiss Mary on the cheek. "My sincerest apologies. My mother would be absolutely mortified by my behavior." He grinned at the sight of a pretty pink hue washing over her face. "And I'm here because my sister tells me your aunt, of anyone she knows, would know who is blackmailing her."

And there was pale, scared Mary again, staring at him, stricken. Hartwell could have kicked himself.

"What?" Mary breathed.

"My sister. Someone is blackmailing her, and she swears your aunt knows who would do such a thing." Hartwell shrugged. He turned, noticing a carriage ambling up the gravel lane to the house. "I don't know if I can believe her. My sister often goes into flights of fancy, shall we say. But it's all I've got, and I'll not let my sister be threatened if I can do anything about it. Say, were you expecting the solicitor so soon?"

But Mary didn't reply, not verbally, at least. She took a step forward, stopped, took another step forward, and frowned.

"Mary?" Hartwell said.

A man stepped from the carriage, slapped his hat against his legs to dislodge the dust from travel, and looked up. He was a tawny sort, well built and quite assured of himself. He was unforgivably attractive, even Hartwell could see that. And he was staring at them just as they stared at him.

"Steele," Mary breathed.

TWELVE

IN WHICH MARY REMINISCES

IT HAD BEEN A year since the candle-lit chandeliers had bounced overhead the strenuous motions of the dancers. The ballroom had smelled of perfume and body odor, and the air was littered with conversation, music, and laughter. Mary had stumbled from the dance floor laughing, her hand resting on the arm of her dance partner. He had taken her to her father, who had watched sternly as they approached.

"Father, I'd like you to meet Mr. Steele," she had said, motioning to the towheaded man bowing beside her. She had been panting a little from the dance, which explained the flush in her cheeks and brightness in her eyes.

"A pleasure, sir," Steele had said, his voice faltering a little, betraying his nerves. He had watched Trentwood as they had approached, and somehow knew he had been found lacking. He shared a small, tight smile with Mary.

It had been the way Trentwood's lip had quirked to the side ever so slightly that had worried Mary.

She had looked at Steele, trying to see what she suspected Trentwood saw: a young dandy determined to engage his daughter in nefarious acts.

Steele had taken great care with his appearance. His shoes had shone in the gaslight, his pants hadn't a wrinkle, and though he had been far too young, not even thirty, he had tucked a quizzing glass surreptitiously in his waistcoat pocket. Still, there had been much in him to like, such as his carriage: broad-shouldered and standing tall. He had not been afraid of Trentwood like the other gentlemen she had brought her father's way, merely respectful.

"You've danced with my daughter twice now," Trentwood had said. He had crossed his arms over his broad chest. "There will not be a third."

Mary had pressed her lips together, praying to her dearly deceased mother for patience. "Come now, Father, give him some credit. He wouldn't dare, not without your permission."

Steele had shaken his head vigorously. "Indeed, sir, I have brought her to you with the hopes I might call upon you at a favorable time tomorrow." He had squeezed Mary's hand resting on his arm.

"You may not," Trentwood had replied. "Mary, get your things, we're leaving."

Mary had sent an anguished look Steele's way, but had taken her father's arm. She had followed his lead to the door and had accepted her wrap without a word. She had waited for the proper moment to say something, anything, which would have changed her father's mind.

It wasn't until they had been alone in the carriage, bumping along the road in tense silence, that she had gathered the courage to say, "I don't understand."

"What?" Trentwood had snapped.

"I don't understand why you didn't like him."

Rather than responding, Trentwood had yanked the window sash so the cool winter air had access to charge into the little carriage. With the window open, Mary had heard hoof beats charging down the dirt road, taking her farther away from Steele. She had felt pressure rising up through her chest and into her throat. Her eyes had begun to burn.

"I liked him."

"No, you didn't," Trentwood had said, eyes not meeting her begging expression. "He turned your head with pretty words and fancy footwork. If I allowed him to pay a call you'd be sorely disappointed." He had looked at her then, his expression somber. "You'll thank me, one day."

A brisk wind had whistled through the crack in the window sash on the opposite side of the carriage. Mary had shuddered, hugging herself. "We'll catch our death of cold."

The next morning, Mary had entered the dining room with sunken cheeks and bags beneath her eyes, hinting at how the remainder of her night had fared. She had pulled a couple of rashers, a roasted tomato, and a slice of toast onto her plate from the breakfast buffet to accompany her strong tea. She had sat at the table and ate because it was habit, not because she was hungry.

I am in love with him, Mary had thought with dull surprise. I am in love with Mr. Steele.

Mary had not been able to understand just what Trentwood disliked about Steele. Steele had been eligible, able to provide for her, and he had been interested. What more did a father want for his daughter? Furthermore, Steele had been her last chance; she had been certain of that.

One simply did not receive many interested suitors by the time one turned twenty-six, that was the way of the world. Mary had been resigned to a future of tending her father's house, until Steele came along with his smiles.

A rattling cough had startled Mary from her reverie. She had looked up to find a haggard Trentwood shuffling into the dining room, his eyes bloodshot. He had, it seemed, refused aid from his valet for his hair hadn't been combed, and he still wore his evening finery beneath his dressing robe.

"Did you sleep at all?" Mary had ventured to ask, watching him shovel food on his plate.

"Damned cough," he had rasped, "kept me up all night." He had dropped his plate to the table, accepted a strong cup of coffee from the silent servant, and rested his forehead in his hands.

Alarm spread, chasing away the dull surprise of Mary's feelings for Steele and the memory of her own haggard night. Trentwood had taken a chill last night, just as she had feared, and was ill, far more ill than he was letting on. She had shoved away from the table and waved the servant away impatiently. She had circled the table to stand beside Trentwood. After a moment's hesitation, she had pulled his hand from his forehead and replaced it with her own. She had gasped, snatching her hand from his burning skin.

"Send for a doctor," she had snapped at the servant. "My father has a severe fever."

"Utter nonsense," Trentwood had muttered.

"Father, I'm taking you to your room. You need rest."

"Not until I've had my bacon."

Mary had slapped the fork out of Trentwood's hand. "Bacon! You can hardly lift the fork to your mouth and you're worried about your bacon?" She had tugged at his arm, shocked by how heavy it felt. "Come, you are going back to bed."

Trentwood had tilted his head when he looked at her, his expression slack but his eyes bright with fever. "Gertrude?"

Tears had sprung to Mary's eyes. "No, I'm Mary. Your daughter." She had stooped so she could drag his arm around her shoulders to help him from the table. She had managed to get him to the doorway before she had to stop, hardly able to breathe due to her rising panic.

Thankfully, Pomeroy, her father's valet, had appeared at her elbow and taken Trentwood from her. "The apothecary is on his way, Miss."

Mary had sighed. When her mother was alive, they had been able to afford a surgeon. What a disgrace to be relegated to the local apothecary.

The apothecary had arrived to bleed Trentwood and alternate bathing him in wet cloths while piling blankets high atop him to break the fever. Trentwood had recovered after a week, but never quite fully. He had never managed to regain that solid dependability Mary had assumed was inherent to her father. He had come to rely on her for most everything from the moment he woke fever-free.

Mary had not recognized this man, this man with the body of her father. Most nights, she had cried herself to sleep, unsure whom she mourned more, the loss of Steele or Trentwood.

She had shouldered the burden of being master and mistress of the manor to distract herself. She had balanced the ledgers, addressed the farmers' complaints, and continued managing the servants and general household management that had been her original duties.

Trentwood, meanwhile, had refused to eat unless she fed him. He had refused to sleep unless she read to him.

Yet even with all these distractions, it had never been quite enough to fill the ever-widening hole in her heart.

A year later, Trentwood had died in his sleep, holding the miniature of Mary's mother, Gertrude. Mary had relied on her aunt Mrs. Durham for the funerary details, knowing she would be unable to face her father's burial, and resurrection, alone.

87

Thirteen

In which Steele arrives

Mary rubbed her eyes. After a year of imagining his fine carriage rolling up the gravel drive to her front door, stepping down and slapping his hat against his legs, she was certain she had finally, most definitely, lost her mind.

"Is there a man, a blond man, standing at the front door beside a carriage?" she murmured. When Hartwell didn't respond, she looked at him to find a puzzled, almost hurt, expression before it was masked by a pathetic attempt at calm indifference. "Humor me, Alex, I am often questioning what I see these days."

There, that ought to spark a response from him; she knew Pomeroy must have told Hartwell about her supposed ghost—not supposed but real. And indeed, Hartwell worked his jaw a bit as he pondered a reply.

"There is a man, yes. What did you call him?"

Mary stepped away from Hartwell. "Mr Steele." She hugged her shawl tight around her as she moved toward this stranger, this so very welcome stranger, who watched as if she was a ghost.

"Miss Trentwood," Steele said as soon as she was within hearing, and he rushed forward to clasp her hands in his. "Miss Trentwood I'd no idea about your father. I'm terribly sorry."

Mary smiled. She smiled and smiled and looked down at her hands and up at Steele and smiled. *You came back for me.*

Of course, the phrasing was a bit off, as Steele had never actually been to the manor house, but that was a triviality. He had come back to her. That was the important thing. He had come back, and he was holding her hands, and though she was being an absolute ninny about such a small act of friendship, of compassion, of tender feeling, she delighted in it.

"I'd no idea when Mr Fredricks sent me out here that I would be tending to your business, of all persons," Steele said. "He gave me strict instructions not to touch anything or look at any of the papers until within the sight of the departed's family."

Mary's smile began to waver. What?

"But how very glad I am it is you that I'm to help!" Steele squeezed her hands.

A jolt of fever blasted from her hands, up her arms, nestled in her breast, and set her cheeks aflame. *Really, Mary Ryan Trentwood, you're almost twenty-eight years old. There is no call for such dramatics.*

"I'd ask how you've been this past year, but I can see it hasn't been easy for you," Steele continued.

He was everything Mary had remembered him to be. Tall, broad-shouldered, easy manners and all smiles beneath that tawny mustache of his. He held her hands sweetly, confidently, eagerly. He leaned toward her when he spoke, as if he couldn't get close enough but knew he had no right to come closer.

Mary stepped closer to him. Steele had come to her, it was the least she could do. She willed him to see how she had waited for him. She waited for him to acknowledge the plea in her eyes. She wished him the courage to kiss her as she had dreamed it.

Steele's smile grew to the point of splitting his face in two, and Mary had never seen anything lovelier. He smelled of the city, or what she assumed was the city, as Hartwell had similar lingering scents upon his arrival: coal, sweat, exhaustion.

"You must come inside," she said.

Steele nodded, and then caught sight of Hartwell behind her. He raised his brows. "Who is your friend, Miss Trentwood?"

Hartwell came to Mary's side, his brows also raised. "Indeed, Mary, who is your friend?"

Mary looked from one to the other, not liking how Hartwell had mimicked Steele's tone, or how Steele had bristled at the sound of Hartwell using her given name. Steele dropped her hands and looked Hartwell over. And heaven help her, Hartwell was looking Steele over. Really, they were being quite silly.

"Jasper," Mary said, "this is Alexander Hartwell, brother to my aunt's friend. And Alex, this is Jasper Steele, my…"

Oh dear. What could she say? *This is my long-lost love come back to me.* No, that spoke of dramatics she could never sustain. What about, *this is my Jasper?* No, the words had never been spoken between them.

"I'm her solicitor," Steele offered, prioritizing his right to be at the manor house over Hartwell's.

"You are?" Hartwell said, sounding at the same time delighted and disheartened.

"You are?" Mary said, all former feelings of warmth deflating in the face of such stark truth.

Steele hadn't come for her.

The sun broke through the clouds just then and shone in full force on Hartwell, Mary, and Steele. Hartwell had his hat in his hands, as did Steele, and they continued to measure one another in the increasingly awkward silence. Hartwell remained cool, disinterested.

It was a mask Mary was beginning to recognize. As she looked at Steele and saw his revulsion at the sight of Hartwell's face, and saw Hartwell's responding apathy, she knew one expression didn't exist without the other.

Or rather, she was beginning to suspect, perhaps, that Hartwell's lighthearted manner around her could very well be because she did not mind his scar so very much. In fact, she hardly even thought about it, except when seeing someone else react to it.

Why, Steele even looked green at the sight of Hartwell! How could he begrudge a man his ugliness, when it was so very obvious Hartwell didn't begrudge him his beauty?

Mary felt her arms go limp to the sides of her body, feeling the weight of her chilled hands and the loss of Steele's warmth.

He isn't here to see me, she reminded herself. *He's here because he's paid to be here.*

She missed her initial exhilaration already. It was a cold place to be without her resurfaced hopes, and she shivered. Mary looked at Hartwell and shared a grim expression with him. She wasn't sure why he looked grim; surely he faced strangers every day who reacted to his warped eye, but she appreciated the company.

"It's a bit biting out here," Steele said, shifting his weight. His mustache danced as he chewed his lip.

"Yes," Mary said, flailing her arm at the front door. "You must come inside and warm yourself after your journey." She wanted to sound warm, caring, excited that Steele had come to see her, but she knew her voice sounded flat, perhaps even a bit peevish.

Well, she had a right to sound peevish, didn't she, after waiting an entire year and then some, losing her father, being forced to tolerate her aunt moving in, and only after all that did he decide to show his face?

With these thoughts in mind, Mary had no intention of taking Steele's arm and walking him into the manor house. She had no intention of anything at the moment for she was indulging her feelings of hurt and anger and frustration and disappointment, and had no energy or inclination to think past those emotions.

When she saw Steele raising his arm to lead her into the house, her eyes widened in horror. *Good lord*, she thought, *he can't be serious.*

Hartwell, the absolute gentleman that he was, slipped past Steele's arm as if he hadn't seen it. Steele was a little to Hartwell's left, after all, and Mary could only assume that Hartwell had somewhat of a hard time seeing on that side. Not, of course, that she had seen any evidence to that effect, but really, why linger over such minuscule details?

Mary accepted Hartwell's arm gladly. She took comfort in his solid, silent strength as she instructed the carriage driver to warm himself in the kitchen with Mrs. Beeton's hot brandy.

Pomeroy exited the manor house just then, gloved and dressed in layers. He cast an admonishing eye at Mary, who wore only a heavy shawl and hat against the cold, before saying to Steele, "Might I carry your things for you, sir?"

"Thank you, Pomeroy," Mary said, "Please place Mr. Steele in the… Oh dear." She looked at Hartwell, whose bland smile grew a bit. Where to put Steele, if Hartwell was in the guest room? She didn't dare put them together. She wouldn't want both of them sleeping in the room beside hers.

No, there was only one thing to do.

"Pomeroy, ask Aunt Ophelia if she would mind moving to mother's bedroom. We shall have to put Mr. Steele in her bedroom."

Steele blinked at Mary. "You only have two guest bedrooms?"

Her mouth sagged open at the blatant dismay darkening his tone. He knew she wasn't rich, and he had told her he had liked her anyway. But then, that was a year ago.

"Beggars can't be choosers," she snapped. She inhaled. She dug her fingers into Hartwell's arm. She became aware she was hurting him only when he placed his hand atop hers to disguise the fact that he was prying off her claw-like grip.

She opened her mouth to apologize but was cut off by Hartwell saying, quite smoothly, "I fear there's been something of a mix-up in Mary's plans, Steele, as she wasn't expecting me at all, and had only one guest bedroom prepared. In fact, Mary is only out here in the cold because she was humoring my need to stretch my legs after the train ride from the city. This isn't the easiest place to get to, as I'm sure you know."

Steele nodded, a bit dumbly, Mary thought.

"In any case, I'm fairly certain Mrs. Durham already dislikes me. I'd hate to have her dislike two persons who are disrupting her peace and quiet because we want to help her niece." Hartwell paused. "That is why you're here, isn't it?"

"Of course," Steele said, bristling.

Oh yes, of course he is here to help me, Mary thought. Funny, that, as he hadn't even known whose house his employer had dispatched him to.

"I thought so, you seem quite an upstanding man, Steele, and I'm glad of your company. So glad of it, that I'm willing to move out of the guest bedroom and into Mrs. Durham's and face her wrath. For I'm certain she shall be quite livid?" Here Hartwell looked at Mary for confirmation.

Mary frowned at Hartwell. What was he trying to do? A thread of their conversation before Steele's arrival meandered to the forefront of her attention, what was it?

Drat it, that's right, blackmail. And Hartwell claimed he wasn't the blackmailer, but that her aunt knew the blackmailer, or knew someone who might know the blackmailer, or… to be honest, Mary hadn't quite understood what Hartwell had been saying when Steele had pulled up to the manor house, for she'd quite lost interest upon seeing Steele alight from the carriage.

She narrowed her eyes at Hartwell. His smile was in every way benign and harmless. Which meant he had to be up to something.

"My aunt won't like having to move," Mary said slowly, tasting each word before she spoke it. "But unless you want to go back to Swindon tonight you'll have to stay here."

Steele motioned at the two large-ish bags at his feet. "I certainly didn't intend on this being a day trip, Miss Trentwood." He put heavy emphasis on his formal address, giving Hartwell a snide look in the meantime.

"It's settled then, I'll take Mrs. Durham's room, Mrs. Durham will take your mother's room, and Steele will take my room." Hartwell turned to Steele, his grin cheeky. "You know, it's beside Mary's room, and the walls are paper thin."

"Alex," Mary gasped.

"That was highly unnecessary information, sir," Steele said, drawing up to his full height and yet still managing to fall short of matching Hartwell. "One hardly speaks of a lady's bedroom and of her walls being paper thin in front of her!"

Mary squinted in the sunlight, trying to discern Hartwell's intent as he schooled his expression into impassivity. It was rather alarming how she was already able to pick up some of the finer subtleties of his expressions; even though he looked cool and apathetic, she could feel his pulse racing beneath her fingertips. He enjoyed teasing Steele almost as much as he enjoyed teasing her.

No, that wasn't right; Hartwell enjoyed teasing Steele more than her, because Steele had all the posturing of a gentleman, without the actions to back it up.

Good heavens, Mary thought, feeling a bit nauseated, *Father was right. How annoying.*

"I take it you mean that one would rather speak of a lady's bedroom and of her walls being paper thin behind her back?" Hartwell tsked at Steele, looking a brotherly sort of disappointed. "For shame, Steele. And in front of a lady, too."

"Let's have a cup of tea," Mary blurted, seeing how red Steele's face was becoming. Really, Hartwell needed to hold his tongue. "Pomeroy, you'll take care of Jasper's things, I trust?"

"Of course," Pomeroy said. He grabbed Steele's bags with one hand and waved at the driver of the carriage to follow him round the back of the house. "Mrs. Beeton already has a pot ready to go for you, Miss, and Mrs. Durham has been waiting for you in the library all this time."

Mary had been walking toward the house, flanked by Hartwell and Steele, but stopped when hearing that last bit. "She's been waiting for us?"

"Yes'm, she was writing a letter, but stopped when she heard the commotion." Pomeroy scratched his white hair. "Oddest thing, Miss, she actually threw away the letter when she saw the young man step from the carriage. Said Providence had provided for her."

"Why, whatever can she mean by that?" Mary said.

Pomeroy shook his head. "I'm not certain, Miss, but she beat you to the arrangements. She's already put Mr. Steele in her bedroom, and moved her belongings to the late Missus's bedroom."

Mary frowned.

First Hartwell appeared out of nowhere with a letter that stank of blackmail. Then Pomeroy insisted on sending Hartwell after her. Mrs. Durham had a conniption over Hartwell staying in the house, yet without warning volunteered her bedroom for Steele, who hadn't given an indication of his arrival anymore than Hartwell had. And then there was still the business with her father…

Oh Lord. My father.

Somehow in the middle of everything else that was going on, Mary had managed to forget that little detail about her father haunting her. He was already rather displeased with her. The sight of Steele in his house was sure to drive him mad.

"You go inside without me," Mary said brightly. "I've some business to tend to with Pomeroy."

"And leave us to your aunt?" Hartwell said with an incredulous laugh. "I think not, Miss Mary Contrary. No, you're coming into the house with us, or we're all staying out here in the cold."

"I think I'd rather be inside—" Steele began, frowning at Hartwell's presumption at knowing what he wished.

"No," Hartwell said, interrupting Steele, "you wouldn't. Trust me on this one, old man."

Steele's jaw jutted out. "Pray excuse me, Miss Trentwood," he said, slapping his hat onto his head. He spun on his heel and entered the house.

Mary closed her eyes. She counted to five. She concentrated on the pit of her stomach. Maybe her father wouldn't notice. And maybe he would decide to stop haunting her, magically.

"What in the hell is this damned fool doing in my house?" Trentwood's disembodied voice roared.

Mary almost retched. Apparently wishful thinking didn't work when ghosts were involved.

Fourteen

In which Trentwood reacts

Trentwood stood just inside the front door, flexing his stiff fingers. Everything felt stiff these days. An effect of being dead, he supposed, the thought of which only fueled the churning feeling in his gut. He glared at Steele, who stood before him, his eyes searching rather frantically from left-to-right.

Steele had burst into the house with a great lack of aplomb, his face red from being in the wind, Trentwood assumed, and perhaps also from seeing Hartwell with Mary.

Trentwood certainly hoped it was the sight of Hartwell and Mary together that had so nonplussed the London fool.

Steele hadn't continued into the house to meet Mrs. Durham, however, which surprised Trentwood. In fact, Steele had stopped a mere foot short from him. Almost as if he had seen him and didn't want to run into him.

To be sure, the thought had frightened Trentwood more than he cared to admit to himself. He had grown used to popping in and out of places with impunity. He liked it. Trentwood had realized that other than Mary, only animals seemed to know he existed. There was something satisfying about scaring Mrs. Durham's dog just when she had managed to get it quiet. And he liked the idea of watching over Mary to make up for the time when she had watched over him.

So when Steele had stopped before him with a great shudder, Trentwood had stepped back, muttering an oath. He had assumed he would never see that ridiculous mustache, that flop of blond hair, or that weak chin again. And he certainly had never thought he would see all three after his death.

Steele released his breath, which Trentwood hadn't realized he had been holding. "Buck up, chap," Steele said, shaking his head clear of whatever he had been thinking. "You're just cold from having stood outside for so long." Steele glanced over his shoulder with a sneer. "What kind of girl is she to walk about in this frigid air with only a shawl? And to expect me to stay out there with her?"

Trentwood flexed his fingers before closing them into his palm to make a fist.

"And with that monstrosity of a man! Really, Miss Trentwood," Steele continued, calming as he ranted quietly to the supposedly empty hallway. "You have surely been put-down upon by your father's death if you willingly consort with such characters."

Trentwood tasted bile at the sound of the pity Steele ladled into his tones.

But then, Trentwood usually had a slight taste of bile on his tongue. Steele made the taste stronger, far more distasteful. He gritted his teeth as Steele shook his head at the sight of the threadbare rugs spread across the hallway floor. His nostrils flared when Steele clucked his tongue at the tarnished silver tray empty of mail, incoming or outgoing. Gertrude had bought that tray.

When Steele walked further into the hallway, not bothering to wipe the mud and sleet from the soles of his boots, it was more than enough to justify roaring, "What in the hell is this damned fool doing in my house?"

That brought a rather green-looking Mary rushing inside, with Hartwell not far behind.

"What is it, what's wrong?" he was asking her.

Mary barreled into Steele, and they both almost toppled over. Mary certainly would have fallen, as Steele wasn't nearly quick enough to turn and catch her, if Trentwood hadn't grabbed her arm and jerked her upright.

The action caused both of them to freeze.

Her arm had felt his hand and the strength behind it.

They stared at one another, forgetting Hartwell and Steele. Trentwood didn't dare speak, and neither, it seemed, did Mary. Her eyes were eloquent enough; they seemed to scream, "What are you?"

Mary gagged. Her eyes widened. Her hand flew to her stomach, and she jerked away from Trentwood in the direction of the empty silver tray where she emptied her stomach with the most awful retching noise.

Trentwood stared at his hand.

Steele threw a perfumed handkerchief over his nose and frowned at Mary.

Hartwell was at Mary's side, an arm around her shoulders as she dry heaved, tears streaming from her eyes. He glared at Steele. "Good God, man, the woman is obviously ill. How can you stand there doing nothing? Fetch her aunt, fetch a servant, fetch some water, or get out of here!"

Steele stepped back. "I'm here as her solicitor, not her errand boy. And I'll certainly not fetch anything for a woman who has obviously chosen her... associates... poorly."

There was no mistaking what Steele implied.

Trentwood had heard quite enough, as had Hartwell. Almost as one, they turned from Mary with their fists and gave Steele a hit that sent him sailing.

"I ought to kill you for your lack of respect," Trentwood and Hartwell shouted.

Trentwood shook his head in disgust at the same time Hartwell did. Trentwood noticed, dimly, that his fist flexed in time with Hartwell's fist. And he seemed to blink when Hartwell blinked.

They returned to Mary's side, drawing their arms around her shoulders that heaved now not from stomach convulsions, but from quiet tears. "There now, you'll be feeling quite all right once the tears dry."

It had been something her mother always used to say when she was little. Trentwood didn't understand why Mary was looking at him with growing horror.

"Get out," she rasped. "Get out of him right now."

"What?" Trentwood said. He cleared his throat, for his voice sounded a bit off. "What did you say to me?" Funny, he was sounding a bit like Hartwell. He looked in the mirror that hung above the silver tray now full of Mary's half-digested breakfast. He saw Hartwell's reflection, though it was almost as if in the shadows of Hartwell's face, he saw himself.

"Well, that's different," Trentwood mumbled.

Mary's eyes rolled into the back of her head. Hartwell dropped to his knees to catch her while Trentwood remained standing, staring into the mirror.

"What on earth is going on here?" Mrs. Durham shrieked, standing in the library doorway.

What on earth indeed, Trentwood thought, fading away in a beam of sunlight.

FIFTEEN

IN WHICH STEELE AWAKES

STEELE SHIFTED HIS HEAD. His cheek rubbed against a smooth fabric he recognized. Silk, he thought it was. He kept his eyes closed, enjoying the way his head was cushioned by layers of the filmy fabric. It seemed Miss Trentwood had come to her senses and left that Hartwell, now to be known as Quasimodo, as she well should have done.

The cushion supporting his head was warm and soft. It was almost too warm, and it shifted beneath him as he jerked with the sudden realization that his head rested in a lady's lap.

"Are you coming to, Mr Steele?"

Steele's eyes flew open. Mrs. Durham's face was inches from his, and he could see every pore, every crease, every disappointment there. He swallowed. He extracted himself from her lap, pulling away from her soft arms. He ought to have known better. Women were fickle, of that he was certain, but he doubted the particular woman known as Miss Mary Trentwood was quite that fickle.

Whatever Quasimodo had done to win Mary's loyalty, it had been enough to ensure she was administering to his wounds, whatever they were, and not Steele's, which seemed very perverse.

"Have some tea," Mrs. Durham said, handing him a cup.

They were sitting on an old sofa, the kind that ought to have been thrown away years ago but was kept for its sentimental and worn-in value. In fact, Steele realized, as he studied the room in which he sat with Mrs. Durham, all the furniture was old. All of it was worn. All of it looked well loved.

It was rather distasteful, really. Very bourgeois, as if Mary couldn't afford any better. Or worse yet, that she could afford better, but chose not to.

Terrifying.

Steele accepted the teacup with one practiced hand while he prodded his aching jaw with the other. He sipped the tea and winced. Mrs. Durham looked at him, her expression expectant. If nothing else, she had to be related to Mary, for Steele had just realized he had no idea who she was, why she had been cradling his head, and how she managed to drag him into what he assumed was the library.

He sneezed. Yes, he was most definitely in a library. Books always gave him the worst conniptions of the nose. It was something to do with the dust, he assumed.

It was the woman's eyes, Steele realized as he sipped his tea, that made the familial connection to Mary so obvious. These were sharp, dark eyes, which noticed his every move and guessed at his every thought. He felt trapped beneath their inquisitive stare. "And you are?"

"Mrs. Durham, Mary's aunt on her mother's side."

Steele nodded, and winced at the increase in throbbing. "Thank you for the tea."

"Certainly," Mrs. Durham said. "Do allow me to apologize for my niece. She has been without a mother a good many years and does not know where her attentions ought to be focused."

Steele coughed, unsure how to respond.

"You must understand," Mrs. Durham said, her tone forlorn as she wiped the palms of her hands across the black silk of her dress. "My niece is quite mad with grief. She has latched herself onto this stranger in the desperate hope that he will bring her out of her low spirits, and for a time, I suspect he has." Tears began to gather at the corners of her eyes.

Steele scooted closer to her. He placed a consoling hand atop her trembling one.

"I fear he is determined to ruin her, Mr. Steele. I'm so very glad you have come."

Steele's hand tightened its grip on her hand. "Rest assured, Mrs.—Durham, was it?—I have come with Miss Trentwood's best interests at heart." All right, so that wasn't a complete truth, but he was hired to be her solicitor and walk her through her father's finances. Though, why his employer insisted he explain such things to a woman, and a woman such as Mary Trentwood who already had rather odd notions of independence, was beyond Steele.

Still, Mary was very pretty. She had a lovely smile and a rather seductive voice. Unbidden came thoughts of her voice speaking to him late at night, carrying a smile in its undertones, as she ran his fingers through her hair. He shivered.

Surely if Mary can learn to like Quasimodo—Steele really was warming to that name for Hartwell—then she could learn to like Steele again. For he knew she had liked him, she had liked him very much. And he had liked her too, at the time.

Mrs. Durham clutched Steele's hand. "Thank you, Mr. Steele. I knew I could depend upon you. You understand, of course, that you must be very cunning. Mr. Hartwell is the definition of the word and will go to great lengths to disarm you."

Steele recoiled a little at the name. It hadn't sounded familiar before, not until it was paired with '"cunning" as a descriptor. "How long has he been here?"

"No more than a day."

"And he hails from…?"

"London," Mrs. Durham said, her lips stiff with an emotion Steele couldn't name.

No matter, Steele had his own emotions to handle. He pulled his hand from Mrs. Durham's as a wave of nausea almost bowled him over.

"Mr. Steele?" Mrs. Durham said, alarm making her squeak.

"Mr. Hartwell of London, you say," Steele managed, "he wouldn't happen to be a barrister?" He could be someone else. He could be any number of Hartwells in London. Couldn't he?

Mrs. Durham waved her hands dismissively. "I suppose so, yes, I think Mary said something to that effect, perhaps."

Steele groaned. "I wish you had not given me the charge of protecting your niece from him." He sneezed and dragged a handkerchief from his pocket. This was supposed to be a simple assignment. Go to the back of beyond. Read the details of a recently found will to a grieving daughter. Go back to civilization and the plump arms of his pretty doxy.

"Why ever not?"

Steele wiped a bead of sweat from his temple. "The only cases Hartwell has ever lost are the ones he intended to lose. Depend upon it, Mrs. Durham, if your niece is his goal, there will be little I can do to stop him."

Mrs. Durham stood, jerking her skirts away from him as if his presence carried a foul stench. "Then my brother-in-law was right, and you never deserved my niece."

Steele, mouth agape, watched her sweep from the room in as grand a manner as any opera singer he had seen. Just what was that supposed to mean? Steele sneezed again. Damn her if she thought he was going to give up that easily. Hartwell only lost cases he intended to lose, yes, but Steele had nothing to lose in this instance.

And that, he thought smugly, *makes me a rather dangerous man.*

SIXTEEN

IN WHICH HARTWELL CONFERS WITH POMEROY

HARTWELL RESTED HIS ACHING forehead in the palms of his hands, his elbows digging into his knees. He kept his eyes squeezed shut. Every time he opened them, they watered. His mouth was dry, his throat scratchy, his tongue leaden. The veins hidden by his scar pulsed sluggishly. His stomach flipped one moment, and flopped the other.

"Might I offer you a cup of tea, sir?" Pomeroy said.

Hartwell grunted, taking care not to move a muscle. He felt drunk. No, not drunk. He felt hung over. No, not hung over. He felt like death.

Which didn't make much sense; one moment, he was concerned about Mary—what in the world had made her ill, he had eaten every bit as much as she had at breakfast—then he was carrying Mary up to her bedroom, Pomeroy applying a cold compress on her forehead. Nothing in that round of events should have made him feel so wretched.

"Might I ask what happened before I returned to the foyer, sir?" Pomeroy said.

Hartwell sat on a chair just outside Mary's bedroom. It was the chair from the writing desk in the guest bedroom; the thought of being in Mary's room longer than necessary, even to drag a chair to sit, had seemed ill-bred. Pomeroy stood just before him, still dressed in layers to protect against the cold. He had arrived moments after Mrs. Durham had happened upon the commotion.

Cool-headed as Pomeroy was, he hadn't bothered asking hysterical questions like Mrs. Durham. He had disappeared in the direction of the kitchen, Hartwell assumed, and returned with a bit of wet, folded cloth. Pomeroy had administered the cloth to Mary's forehead, and asked Hartwell if he would be so kind as to escort Mary to her bedroom, as she was obviously incapacitated.

"Escort," was the term Pomeroy had used, and it had made Hartwell smile at the slight formality. The hallway had begun to smell with the stench of Mary's half-digested breakfast. Yet Pomeroy had helped Hartwell lift Mary and had prepared her bed so Hartwell could deposit her in it. The man deserved an explanation after all that.

"I haven't the slightest idea," Hartwell said.

Pomeroy raised his brows. "Is that so?"

Hartwell cleared his throat. He peeked through one eyelid, saw green spots, and clenched his eyes shut again. "You won't believe me, I'm certain, but you'll have to, Pomeroy old boy. Mary became violently ill, Steele said something unseemly, and you appeared soon thereafter."

"That sounds you know a great deal more than not having the 'slightest idea.'"

Hartwell scowled, and groaned at how that small movement made it feel as though someone was stabbing pins into the crown of his head.

"Besides which, I figured as much, sir. I knew from the moment I saw you that you've been trained a little in the ways of a good fist fight."

Hartwell decided not to respond to that.

"But I can't see how Mr. Steele could have inflicted any damage upon you, sir, and that is where my confusion lies. What on earth is wrong with you?"

"I haven't the foggiest," Hartwell moaned. "I wish I knew. I feel as though I've been beaten soundly, left for dead, and then trampled upon. Get me a brandy, will you, Pomeroy?"

Pomeroy patted Hartwell on the shoulder. "Sorry, sir, but we haven't any. You drank the last of it at dinner last night."

Hartwell was fairly certain he was going to cry. "How is Mary?"

Pomeroy peeked into the bedroom. "She's sleeping." He shifted his weight, and Hartwell could sense a sort of embarrassment in the action. "Thank you for carrying her," Pomeroy said, "I couldn't have managed myself. Bad back."

"I hardly noticed her weight," Hartwell admitted, leaning back, resting his head against the hallway wall. "In fact, I didn't even feel it when I punched Steele. I've never felt so strong in my life. It was almost supernatural." He squinted at Pomeroy. If he squinted, it didn't hurt so badly. "I felt as if nothing could hurt me. As if I had nothing to lose. Isn't that odd?"

Pomeroy shrugged. "I had felt the same, back in my fighting days. I was a prize one, once upon a time." He paused and smiled wistfully. "When Miss Mary found out, oh, how she laughed!"

Hartwell opened his eyes fully and took measure of Pomeroy. "She said she isn't one to laugh."

Pomeroy nodded. "She isn't now, but once…"

Hartwell pushed away from the wall. He took a moment to steady himself before attempting Mary's bedroom door.

Mary slept fitfully, a vicious frown furrowing her brow. Beads of sweat gathered at her temples and on the bridge of her nose. She was tangled in the bed sheets and seemed to be fighting her way out without much success.

"You help her," Hartwell said, "I'd frighten her if I did it."

With gentle hands, Pomeroy unwound Mary from her cocoon. "Why are you here, Mr. Hartwell?" he murmured.

Hartwell joined him at Mary's bedside and they watched as she drifted into a deeper slumber, one marginally more peaceful.

"I'm not entirely certain anymore. I came to stop a crime. I suspect that's still my reason. The crime, I think, has changed."

This time, Pomeroy grunted. After a moment, he brought the chair from the hallway into the bedroom. "I would stay, but there are chores to be done. I trust you will keep the door open?"

Hartwell sank into the chair and nodded, hearing the quiet plea in Pomeroy's helpless tones.

"If she wakes screaming," Pomeroy stuttered, "she'll calm down if you take her hand."

Hartwell didn't say anything as Pomeroy left him with Mary. He inhaled deeply. Unconsciously, his breathing slowed to match hers. Every time he thought he had her figured out, or her history, some new bit of information was thrown in his lap.

He leaned closer so he could brush a strand of hair from Mary's face. "What happened to you?"

SEVENTEEN

IN WHICH MARY DREAMS

MARY DREAMED SHE WAS sitting in her bedroom, reading at her window. She was playing with a lock of her hair, pulled back from her face with a ribbon, as her eyes sped across the page. Only the page was blank, yet she was riveted. Somehow, knowing in the way one knows the truth in dreams, Mary knew she was fifteen, though she looked her true age of twenty-seven.

She was fifteen, she was reading a book in her bedroom, and her parents were still alive.

Mary was reading Persuasion, her favorite book, though she was fairly certain she didn't quite understand all the nuances Miss Austen had carefully inscribed. She did think it horribly romantic, though, that Anne had waited all those years for Wentworth, and that, at the last, Wentworth had not forgotten her.

A part of Mary realized, dimly, that this was an odd thing to dream about.

As dream-Mary turned the page, she heard a commotion that must have come from the front door. Doors were slammed, heavy footfalls rushed about, and her father was shouting for help.

Mary dropped her book. She grabbed her skirts. She bolted from her bedroom, down the stairs, skidded to a stop at the sight of her broken, bleeding mother cradled in the arms of her father.

Trentwood glanced at Mary, not seeing her. "Laudanum!"

Mary stared at her mother, who stared at Trentwood.

"Don't be an idiot," he shouted, "get her some laudanum!"

Mary spun on her heel and stumbled up the staircase. She crashed into her mother's bedroom. The door slammed against the wall. Blinded by the white haze before her eyes, she felt across her mother's vanity for the little bottle saved for the worst migraines. She tripped over her skirts. She almost dropped the precious bottle. She clutched it to her panting breast and returned to her parents.

Her mother was still staring at her father's pale face. Her father had buried his face in her shoulder, sobbing softly.

Mary held out the laudanum for Trentwood to take from her.

Her mother didn't blink.

Mary dropped the laudanum. She didn't flinch when the glass bottle smashed into pieces, when the liquid seeped into her cloth house shoes, when she stepped on the glass shards to close her mother's unseeing eyes.

"Don't touch her." Trentwood pulled the body away from Mary's caress. "She had a migraine. She'll be all right in a moment."

Mary bit her lip.

Trentwood saw Mary standing on the shards and spilled laudanum. He inhaled. "You've broken it. You've broken her laudanum. She needs that! You idiot, she needs that!"

Something in Mary snapped, and she was no longer fifteen. She drew up to her true height. "She's dead, Papa, she's dead."

Trentwood swayed, hugging the body close.

Mary grabbed him by the shoulders. "Papa," she screamed, "she's gone. She's dead."

This was a typical dream for Mary, when she did happen to dream. It was an exhausting dream, one where she seemed to scream in real life. Or so Pomeroy would tell her when she woke. This time, however, someone took her by the shoulders, wrenching her away from her inconsolable dream-father.

"This is what you dream when you wake screaming?"

Mary stared at Trentwood, not the dream one hugging her dead mother, but the one who had possessed Hartwell and punched Steele. Only this ghostly Trentwood was as real as she, and he didn't reek of decay and peppermint, and his eyes were that same dull—once lively—brown, rather than an unnatural pale.

"Marianne Ryan Trentwood, answer me."

"What are you doing?" she shrieked, shoving him away.

"I wanted to know why you woke screaming," Trentwood said. "You're frightening poor Hartwell out of his mind, and there's no one around to help him, Pomeroy's in the kitchen helping Mrs. Beeton, and Mrs. Durham is tending Steele, or she was last I saw."

Mary shook her head. She looked behind her at dream-Trentwood, who smoothed her mother's hair from her face.

It had been an awful migraine that did it. Mrs. Trentwood had been taking her daily constitutional around the house, when a migraine hit her so badly that she tripped and fell down the stone stairs into the mouth of the garden. Later, it was estimated she had lain there for an hour before anyone found her.

"You're not real," Mary said to the ghostly Trentwood. "You're not real, you're not in my dream."

"Would it be better if I left now?"

"Yes."

"And wait for when you wake?"

Mary shuddered. "Thank you, no."

"Well then." Trentwood pulled out his pocket watch and swung it from its chain. "What say you to having a little chat about all this, hmm?"

Mary turned her back to him. "I would rather wake up."

Mary started awake with a shuddering gasp. Someone was shaking her, she realized, or had been shaking her, for her head and neck ached, and she wasn't settled against her pillow but rather half-lifted from the bed by a pair of strong hands. She looked up into Hartwell's mangled face, shadowed by his long hair. She sighed. "You've no idea how glad I am to see you."

Hartwell's chuckle was more than a bit strained. "Pomeroy said if you started screaming I should take your hand, but you wouldn't stop and I didn't know what to do." His grip on her arms tightened. "I'm sorry. I didn't know what to do."

Mary nodded. She reached up, laid her hand on one of his. "Thank you." She peeled his fingers off her arm and inched away. "Thank you for waking me. I'm terribly sorry Pomeroy put you in such an awkward position. He ought to have known better."

Hartwell's shrug was rough, embarrassed. "There was no one else to do it, it seems." He brushed his hair out of his eyes. "Your resources have become very reduced, haven't they, since your father's death?"

Mary pulled her coverlet around her shoulders so it made a thick, impromptu shawl. The warmth seemed to ward away the chill she was suffering, but slightly.

Hartwell, seeming as though he needed to be doing something, began to tuck the other coverlet around Mary's legs. It was a simple gesture, wordless and intimate. He looked at her, and she caught her breath. She could tell him everything, she knew, and rid herself of years of needless burden. She knew she wasn't to blame for her mother's death, but that initial response from her father…

"Even before his death, we operated on a limited income," Mary said.

Hartwell reclaimed his seat.

"When I was young, I knew we weren't rich, but we were comfortable." She swallowed. "I know there were funds put aside for me, but I haven't been able to determine their location, or the terms of retrieving the funds. So I've had to let the servants go. All but Pomeroy and Mrs. Beeton, who insist on staying though I can't pay them."

Hartwell nodded. "Sometimes a roof over one's head and a bed of one's own is enough. And the appreciation of a child you've watched grow into a loyal young woman."

Mary grunted, which made a smile peek from the corner of Hartwell's mouth.

"So this solicitor, then," Hartwell said, "he's to tell you where your funds are?"

Mary nodded. "I'm afraid my father's been a bit clever and made arrangements that I'm not to see the funds unless I follow his instructions."

"Would he have done such a thing?"

"Don't all fathers?" Mary turned from Hartwell and stared into the opposite corner of the room, where Trentwood stood with his arms crossed. "Don't they?"

Eighteen

A Series of Escalating Letters

A letter postmarked for London, March 1887
MY DEAREST LADY KIRKHAM,

It has been far too long since my last letter; I do apologize for the tardiness.

Though I suppose you know the reason for my tardiness? Of course you do, I've been very amused by the thought of you petitioning your honorable brother to come to your unchaste rescue.

Did you think I would not catch wind of his journeying from London in search of me? Did you think I would allow any of your family to move anywhere without my knowledge of it?

Really, my lady, you ought to be ashamed. Sending your baby brother to clean up your mess. For this is your mess. You have made your bed. Revel in it.

How is your darling son? He would be almost a year old, is that not correct? Does he have startling blue eyes and blond hair? Does the skin around his eyes crinkle just before he's about to laugh?

What have you named the boy? What does your husband think of the boy? Or is that far too personal a question? Good day, my lady. My fingers tire and my soul aches with the burden of knowing your indiscretion.

Another letter, sent moments after the previous

MY DEAREST LADY KIRKHAM,

Keep a close eye on the boy. It shall not be my fault if you were to lose him in the rough streets of London.

A tear-spattered letter sent from London to Compton Beauchamp
ALEX,

Please find enclosed two of the most awful pieces of paper I've ever had to set eyes upon. This brigand, this criminal, is threatening my child, my heir! I am frantic. Mama's of no help. You must return to London immediately. I am at my wit's end. I've ordered all but our most loyal servants out of the house. I'm not attending any of the parties that I ought to deign by matter of course. Mama swears she knows the identity of the letter writer, but when pressed she says she doesn't know at all, and the "spirits" are teasing her and won't tell her a thing.

Alex, I fear Mama is losing her mind. She tells me she can speak to ghosts. She's as much as admitted that when she suggested to me that you go to Compton Beauchamp to ask after Mrs. Durham, that the "spirits" told her to do so.

Alex, come home. You are on a fool's errand. You must return and protect me. Protect us. Baby Henry is inconsolable without his uncle. I've a fair mind to run about the house screaming. It wouldn't be out of place. The house is so empty!

Please return to us. We are all in pieces without you to anchor us.

Ever devoted,

Your sister, Florence, Lady Kirkham

NINETEEN

IN WHICH HARTWELL SEES

HARTWELL SAT IN THE chair at Mary's bedside. He shifted, thinking maybe that would grab her attention, but no.
He continued to wait for her to emerge from behind the
emotional fortress she had erected upon regaining some
semblance of lucidity.

Mary's bedroom matched the remainder of the house in
terms of once-subtle wealth turned shabby from age. There
were pillows propped on two chairs and piled on the window
seat. Throws made of lace were draped across the vanity,
which she had made functional by propping a portable writing desk against the mirror. Indeed, it seemed the vanity was
her writing desk more often than not, if the piles of paper
on either side meant anything.

It was, on the whole, a comfortable escape of a room from
the rest of the manor house. The colors were muted but not
dreary. There were books piled on the bedside table, and each
had a ribbon in it to mark where Mary had left it.

Hartwell decided he liked that. He wasn't one to be
satisfied reading just one item at a time either. And while
his reading habits were, perhaps, a bit more pedestrian than
Mary's, for he would never consider Greek a bedside read, he
took comfort in knowing he was not the only bluestocking
left in all of England, as his sister was so often fond of
whining.

Hartwell shivered. Though the window was closed, the room felt frigid. He envied Mary her two coverlets. She seemed unaware of their warming existence though; she shivered as violently as he did. He had half a mind to rub his hands down the length of her arms, both for the exercise and to help her regain some heat.

Mary stared into the far corner of her bedroom, which was, Hartwell suddenly realized, where it seemed the frigidity came from. Odd.

Hartwell followed Mary's line of sight, making note of the fact that she pouted as though being lectured. He had affected the very same expression once upon a time when his own dear father had been alive to lecture him. He stared into the corner. What was she looking at?

Hartwell squinted. He frowned. He rubbed his aching forehead. He turned away to face Mary, and in doing so, saw from the corner of his eye the eerie shape of a shadow where none had been a moment before.

Hartwell swiveled in his chair. There was nothing in that corner. The room seemed to drop a degree in temperature. He rotated, slowly, so when he looked at the corner of the room from the very edge of his periphery, he could see the shadow of a man quite clearly.

Hartwell jumped from his seat. The chair toppled to the floor behind him.

"Have you seen something, Alex?" Mary said. Her voice was flat, and her pupils dilated. She turned to him almost mechanically.

Hartwell hesitated. He looked in the corner. Nothing was there. He couldn't see anything. Yet, when he relied on his peripheral, there stood a man in the corner. He was certain of it. He was as certain of seeing a man in the corner as he was certain he stood on two feet.

His stomach rumbled unpleasantly. He met Mary's apathetic gaze. "You know, I think perhaps your cook has poisoned us."

That shook Mary out of her trance, or whatever it was that had her in thrall. "What?"

"Why, you were violently ill not an hour ago, and now I'm seeing things. We must have eaten something rotten."

Mary's expression cleared, then brightened. "Yes, that must be it." She nodded. "We must have eaten something rotten."

"Either that, or you're trying to poison me so I don't accuse you of blackmail. Believe me, poison is a worse offense."

Mary's mouth dropped open. "What did you just say to me?"

"I'm certain I can't speak plainer, but I'm game to try. If you're blackmailing my sister and think by poisoning me you're going to scare me away, you're out of your mind."

"I must be out of my mind." Mary swallowed. "You're accusing me of poisoning you! I became ill before you. Why would I poison myself?"

"I've seen your life, it isn't the happiest. I've seen people in better situations take their lives, however unnecessarily."

Mary squeaked her outrage.

"For all I know, you ate the poisoned food to escape this labyrinth you're in the middle of, and decided to take me with you to keep you company."

Mary's mouth flapped as she fought to find the words she wanted to fling at him. Unable to, she kicked the coverlet from her legs and jumped to the floor. "That's the most idiotic thing I've ever heard," she fumed. "I'm not the happiest of ladies, but I've met far unhappier, as have you, or have you—very conveniently, I might add!—forgotten about my aunt? She has lost her parents, her sister, her husband, her brother-in-law, all in the last fifteen years! If you must point your misdirected and heartless pity somewhere, point it at her."

Hartwell hissed on the inhale. Mary wasn't done.

"If you're so convinced I'm blackmailing your sister, we will have Jasper pull out my papers right now. He will be able to show you not only do I not have the funds that your blackmailer has most likely been extorting from your sister, he can also tell you I haven't the funds for new pen and paper to write the letters!"

Hartwell pointed at the stacks of paper at her vanity.

Mary stormed over to the vanity, lifted her arm high in the air, and swept both piles to the floor. "Bills," she screamed, "debts, liens. Reminders my father fell ill and died before he meant to."

Hartwell was afraid she might empty her stomach again. Though he doubted she had anything left to vomit after that impressive, if disgusting, display downstairs.

Mary began to advance on him.

Hartwell backed away from the livid glint in her eye. He flinched when she grabbed his hand, but didn't fight when she towed him down the stairs. Her grip was strong, not painful.

"You're so certain I've something against you, or your sister, when I've never heard of either of you. So let's see this precious paperwork of my father's so I may sleep exonerated tonight."

Hartwell figured he should have been more afraid of Mary at that point. Instead, there was the oddest sensation of admiration and respect welling inside him, which felt ironic and perverse, to say the least. And satisfying, to know he had broken her shell. She had spirit. He couldn't fault her that, especially when she applied it so unlike his sister.

"All right," he said.

Mary stopped. She rounded on him, skirts swirling around her ankles, mouth open to spew another litany at him. "What?"

"I agreed to look over your paperwork, so I shall. I'll admit I wanted to do so originally because I wanted to confirm you were or were not the blackmailer." He smiled. "At least now I don't have to pretend otherwise."

Mary's hands bunched into fists.

Hartwell wondered if Pomeroy, being the "prize one" that he was, had taught her a thing or two.

When her fist connected with his jaw, he had his answer.

TWENTY

IN WHICH MARY INSISTS

"MISS MARY, YOU'RE AWAKE. Good," Pomeroy said as he entered the foyer with a tray of tea. "I was just about to check on you and Mr. …pardon me, what have you done?"

"She's just decked me, is what she's done," Hartwell said, rubbing his jaw.

Pomeroy smiled. "I was addressing you, sir. I was asking you, what have you done?"

Hartwell grunted.

"Did you know he never cared to make certain my solicitor wouldn't cheat me, he wanted to look at my papers all this time just to confirm or deny that I'm the blackmailer," Mary seethed. Her hands were gathering into fists again.

Hartwell backed away. "Temper, temper."

"It's rather lucky you never met Mr. Trentwood, sir," Pomeroy said. "His temper was far worse than Miss Mary's."

Mary nodded. "Say one wrong word and he laid you flat to the floor."

A searing pain shot across Hartwell's forehead and he realized all of a sudden that his hand ached. It ached as if he had just punched someone, rather than Mary having just punched him. He didn't remember doing any such thing, but then, where was Steele?

A bell rang from the parlor. Everyone turned at the sound.

"Pomeroy," Mary said slowly, "who is in the parlor?"

He shifted his weight uneasily. "Mrs. Durham and Mr. Steele."

"No one is allowed in the parlor, Pomeroy."

"I know, Miss, but Mrs. Durham insisted."

"No one."

Hartwell watched this exchange, working his jaw a bit to get rid of the ache. He had wondered why he had been sent to wait in the library. It had been a rather odd thing at the time. But then, a number of odd things had happened since leaving London, and in the relative scheme of things, he had forgotten about it.

"Yes, Miss," Pomeroy said, "but you weren't there to stop her, and I was sent for tea and a compress for Mr. Steele. There's little I could do."

Hartwell's brows rose. Even he couldn't mistake the frosty tone Pomeroy used. He looked at Mary. She stuck her chin out and blinked rapidly. She was going to cry if she wasn't careful.

"That is my mother's parlor, Pomeroy, and Mrs. Durham has no right to it."

Hartwell frowned. But wasn't Mrs. Durham the sister of Mary's mother? The dullness in Mary's eyes prevented him from voicing the question. Best to wait until he knew her better, he supposed. Though why he assumed he would have the opportunity to get to know her better, after she had soundly displaced his jaw for a moment or more, was beyond him.

The bell rang more insistently.

Mary met Hartwell's gaze and they shared an odd, intimate look. He was unsure what she meant by her look. It was vulnerable, yet resilient. Soft, yet angry. It was an expression that needed comfort, and he hoped he sent some her way.

"Pomeroy," Mrs. Durham screeched.

"For the love of all that is mighty," Hartwell snapped, "give me that." He grabbed the tea tray from Pomeroy. "The woman needs to calm down. There are other people who need tending to." He stomped down the hallway to the door that had heretofore been closed: locked, he had assumed. Had Mrs. Durham stolen the key, or were there things about her household Mary didn't know?

"What are you doing here?" Steele said when Hartwell entered the room.

"I'm giving the woman her damn tea." Hartwell almost dropped the tray on the marble top table before Steele and Mrs. Durham, but the look of panicked alarm that flew to Mary's face made him set it down gently.

For all he knew, this was her mother's tea set. And damned if he was the one to break it just to spite the likes of Mrs. Durham.

"Rude, awful creature," Mrs. Durham sniffed.

Hartwell barked a laugh. "Rude? Awful? Takes one to know one, my dear Mrs. Durham, or did it not occur to you to inquire after your niece when she was so obviously ill not an hour ago?"

Mrs. Durham's eyes narrowed. "What are you talking about?"

"Did Steele not tell you that Mary had emptied her stomach and collapsed?"

"Let's not dwell on that," Mary rushed to say. "We've other matters to concern ourselves with."

Steele turned an awful shade. "Yes, such as why your guest would attack me!"

"Yes, such as why your solicitor would be so bold as to insinuate that you are not the lady of *quality* you are," Hartwell growled, crossing his arms over his chest.

"What?" Mary spun on her heel. "You said what about me?"

Steele threw up his hands in a sort of mock plea. "I didn't know you when I said those things!"

Mary gulped her air. "Know me! I've been unconscious for… I don't even know how long! How can you possibly know me better now, if what Alex says is true?" Her hand flew to her mouth. "I can't believe I'm saying it, but my father was right about you."

"What *are* you all going on about?" Mrs. Durham said.

Hartwell opened his mouth to explain, but Mary held up her hand to silence him.

"We've other matters, Aunt. I'm sorry, but Jasper will have to nurse his jaw—that looks rather painful, nicely done, Alex—over his papers. I'm determined to prove something to Alex, and I want it done now."

Hartwell flinched. He had hoped, futilely it seemed, that Mary would have forgotten about his accusation in the midst of all this hysterical confusion. She really was one of the most annoyingly common-sensical woman he had ever met. Even more annoying was how greatly he enjoyed seeing her at work.

"Yes, indeed," Hartwell said, "Mary and I have a score to settle, and we need to see the papers right now, Steele."

Steele stood from the sofa he shared with Mrs. Durham. He was quiet for a moment, studying Mary and Hartwell, looking confused and displeased. "I'm only authorized to go over the papers with Miss Trentwood and her associates."

Mary and Hartwell exchanged a look.

"I appoint Alex as my associate," Mary said.

"I accept said appointment," Hartwell said.

"I think you're being ridiculous," Mrs. Durham said.

"No one asked you, dearest," Mary replied.

"Bravo," Hartwell couldn't help but say.

Steele's jaw clenched. He nodded, and bent to retrieve his satchel at his feet. He flipped it open, stuck his hand inside, and looked at Mrs. Durham. "Terribly sorry, Mrs. Durham, but I'm under strict orders to ask you to give the bereaved and her chosen associates some—" He swallowed, looking a bit green. "—privacy."

Mrs. Durham was quite gracious about it, actually, which surprised Hartwell. She rose from the sofa, nodded stiffly, and left the room with nary a word, which was just how Hartwell liked her. Silent. Gone.

TWENTY-ONE

IN WHICH THE WILL IS READ

"MUST ADMIT, MARY, YOU'RE more like yourself than I've seen you in years," Trentwood said, standing just behind her.

Mary jumped. She looked at Hartwell and Steele quickly, but they were busy pushing aside her mother's knickknacks on the coffee table so there was room for the papers. She scowled at Trentwood. She wondered if he could hear her thoughts, now that it seemed he could jump into her dreams at will.

She shuddered. What an awful thought.

"I'd watch it if I were you," Trentwood said, pointing his finger at her. "We're going to have that talk, and we can do it with our mouths or minds. I don't care either way."

Mary pressed her lips together in a stern pout. So he could read her mind. Fine then.

What are you doing here? I told you I didn't want to speak to you.

Trentwood smiled. *No, what you said was you would rather be awake than talk to me about your mother. Well, now you're awake. Good for you.*

Mary inhaled. Her nostrils flared.

Waving his hand in a dismissive fashion, Trentwood moved to stand behind the sofa where Steele and Hartwell sat. They were laying the papers on the marble top table, murmuring to one another. *I'm here to make certain neither of these fools do you wrong, that's why I'm here. For the moment.*

Mary's nod was terse.

"We may begin as soon as you are ready, Miss Trentwood," Steele said, looking up at Mary with that little frown of his.

It didn't suit him, frowning. It made his face seem pinched.

"By all means," Mary said. She turned around, unsure which chair she should sit in. One had been her father's, the other, her mother's. Her father's chair was leather, with masculine lines. Though the parlor was her mother's domain, she had allowed the chair because she had liked her husband to sit with her before the fire on a long winter's night.

It had been a compromise Mrs. Trentwood had been happy to make, Mary remembered. She remembered laughter when the chair had been plopped in the room. Her mother's was a deep, rose-colored velvet. Its arms and legs mimicked the curves of a woman's body, seductive in their gentle slope.

Before Mary knew it, Trentwood sat in his chair. He motioned at the chair beside him.

Mary sat in her mother's chair. Her back was stiff, and she gripped the arms until her knuckles turned white.

"Calm down," Trentwood cautioned, "or you will make them wonder what is wrong."

A valid point. Mary exhaled, having not realized she had been holding her breath. She closed her eyes. "Go ahead, Jasper."

"Well," Steele began slowly, "it seems you may be a rather rich woman, Miss Trentwood."

Mary opened her eyes. "May?"

Hartwell cleared his throat. "According to these papers, your father had a trust set aside for you. There is no one left in your family, no male heirs anyway, and so the house has been left to you. He took advantage of that new law and put it in your name should he die."

Mary swallowed.

"Yes," Steele said, cutting Hartwell off from saying any more. "Mr. Trentwood set aside a trust for you, it's true. But there are provisions to your access to the trust."

"Of *course* there are," Mary said.

"Watch your tone," Trentwood said.

"You watch your tone," Mary snapped.

"I beg your pardon?" Steele said.

Mary colored. "I—what are the provisions to the trust?"

Hartwell leaned back from the papers. It was as though he had lost interest in them. It seemed they told him everything he needed to know: Mary was poor for the time being, but as soon as she knew what she needed to do to access her trust, she would be provided for. There was no reason for her to blackmail his sister.

And if Hartwell were as smart as he seemed to think he was, he might have figured that out sooner rather than later. In the meantime, his attention was focused on Mary. The way his eyes settled on her face made her squirm in her chair.

"Stop that," Trentwood said. "You're not a school girl."

Ready to retort, Mary caught sight of Hartwell's brows rising. She snapped her mouth shut.

Steele shifted in his seat. He looked more than a bit discomfited. "The provisions are that you will have access to all the monies, as long as you have the key."

Mary sighed. Of course. Wait, what had he said? "What key?"

TWENTY-TWO

IN WHICH A KEY MUST BE FOUND

MARY PRESSED THE HEEL of her hand against her throbbing temple. "What key?" she repeated through gritted teeth.

"I'm not certain," Steele said.

Mary looked at Trentwood from the corner of her eye. "What key?" she demanded.

Steele sputtered a bit. "Miss Trentwood, I assure you, neither I nor my barrister know of any key, or why, it seems, you haven't its possession."

"Don't think she was talking to you, chap," Hartwell muttered.

Trentwood lounged in his chair, his whitish eyes meeting Mary's flashing ones calmly. "The key to your mother's lock box."

"The key to my mother's lock box?" Mary said, incredulous. She put the heels of both her hands to her temples.

"So you knew of the key listed here?" Steele said, leaning forward with obvious relief.

"Of course not," Mary snapped. "I only just realized I needed a key. How could I possibly have known?"

Her jaw working as she watched Steele and Hartwell exchange glances, Mary managed to bite her tongue. Her father was right, she wasn't a school girl anymore. She couldn't go around boxing the ears of everyone who annoyed her, though she had so very little patience left for this farce.

"So then, your mother's lock box?" Steele said.

"Well, apparently it's the key I want." Mary spoke slowly, as though he was hard of hearing.

Hartwell leaned forward then. "Who told you that?"

Her mouth opened, but the words wouldn't come out. *My father did, you idiot.* She felt her mouth make the motions, but her voice failed to make a sound. She looked at Trentwood. Her eyes widened.

Still don't know enough about these Londoners, she heard Trentwood's voice echo in her mind. *No need to let them think you've gone mad.*

"Perhaps I have gone mad," Mary whispered.

"I'm sorry?" Steele said. He had been gathering the papers with a furious frown, muttering about not understanding why his employer had sent him out to this back of beyond village for something he could have written in a letter.

"She thinks she's gone mad," Hartwell offered.

"I didn't ask you, Quasimodo."

Mary's mouth dropped open. Hartwell burst into laughter.

"Quasimodo? Really? Is that really the best you can do?" he said, wiping tears from his eyes. "No wonder you're only a solicitor."

Steele shoved the papers into his satchel and stood. "Beg your pardon, Miss Trentwood, but my duty has been fulfilled."

Also standing, Mary said, "You must stay the night; the roads will be dangerous with the rains."

Steele looked as though he wanted to tell her she was as mad as she feared, but Hartwell stood just then and seemed to scare off the words. "Of course, thank you, that is most kind."

"Too kind," Trentwood said. "You ought to let the idiot freeze in the snow after what he said about you. You owe him nothing."

Not wanting to respond, Mary was glad that Pomeroy chose to enter just then with the mail.

"Two for you, sir," Pomeroy said, handing two poorly-addressed letters to a shocked Hartwell.

"They're both from my sister," he said in monotone.

"Nothing bad, I hope," Mary said quickly, watching Hartwell scan the little pieces of paper.

His expression was grim. "More blackmail. And now a kidnapping threat."

"Oh," she said, her voice weak.

"Blackmail?" Steele exclaimed.

Mary sank into her mother's chair. "The information about my finances... Alex thought perhaps I was blackmailing his sister. But I would never threaten a baby." She waited until Hartwell tore his tormented eyes from the paper clenched in his shaking hand. "I would never threaten a baby."

Hartwell blinked away tears of a different sort. He nodded and cleared his throat. "I believe you," he said, his voice rough.

"Would someone tell me what is going on here?" Steele snapped, looking from one to the other. He jumped when Hartwell grabbed his shoulders. "Unhand me," he said, sounding calmer than he looked.

"You've stumbled into quite the story," Hartwell said, his voice sounding a bit crazed. "I came here determined to find out who was blackmailing my sister, and now I've no evidence, no information. But you're a solicitor. It's your occupation to find information. I'll enlist your services and you'll stay here until you find evidence that the blackmailer has something to do with this house."

"Wait a minute," Mary said, "I just proved I'm not the blackmailer!" She shivered beneath the glare Hartwell aimed at her.

"Which leaves everyone else."

TWENTY-THREE

IN WHICH MRS. DURHAM PACES

MRS. TRENTWOOD'S BEDROOM HADN'T been opened since her death. With the unexpected guests, there had been no other choice but to place Mrs. Durham there for as long as the Londoners saw fit to stay in Compton Beauchamp. Mrs. Durham knew that couldn't have been an easy decision for Mary. Why, the girl practically worshipped the memory of her mother, however mistaken she was in believing her mother deserved such piety. The way Mary clung to that silly pendant from her mother made Mrs. Durham want to rip it from Mary's thin neck.

No, no, that's not what Mrs. Durham wanted to do. She wanted to understand why her sister was so loved, when she was so alone.

No, no, that wasn't true either; it made her sound too pitiful, and Mrs. Durham refused to be considered pitiful by any means.

She was a survivor. She had survived her husband falling out of love with her. She had survived losing what riches she had. She had survived living on her brother-in-law's begrudging generosity.

It was only natural, therefore, that Mrs. Durham assumed she could survive her niece's temper tantrums about opening a room or two. Or three. And if not her niece's temper tantrums, then her tantrums by proxy, also known as Mary's new lap dog, also known as that upstart Hartwell.

It was as if Hartwell didn't realize Mrs. Durham had seen him in his swaddling clothes, once upon a time. She had known him before his face had been mangled, such was her history with his sister Lady Kirkham.

Mrs. Durham stopped her pacing. If she wasn't careful, she would wear a path through the already fragile rug that covered the majority of Mrs. Trentwood's bedroom. She shuddered.

The room still smelled of her sister. Rose water and laudanum. Thankfully, her sister hadn't been brought up here after her death for the funerary preparations. Mrs. Durham knew she wouldn't have been able to stay the night, if that were the case.

Everything was as Mrs. Trentwood had left it on her morning constitutional around the garden. Her hairbrush with golden hairs still caught within its bristles laid carelessly at the edge of the vanity. A discarded newspaper crumpled at the foot of her bed. The curtain pulled open an inch, allowing a ribbon of sunlight into the room. Her afternoon tea dress pressed and waiting, coated with a layer of dust.

Had there been servants available to strip the room down to nothing but a skeleton of furniture, Mrs. Durham would have ordered it done in an instant.

It was one of many things Mrs. Durham would have liked to have done.

"This is all your fault, Henry," she muttered to her reflection in the vanity mirror. She sat at the vanity and began to brush a lock of her graying hair with her sister's hairbrush. She wondered how her husband would have responded.

"This is as much my fault as it is yours," he probably would have said, smoothing his mustache. He was always smoothing his mustache, even though he had enough wax in it to keep it in place for years at a time, Mrs. Durham had always thought.

Once upon a time, when he had been in love with her, that implacable mustache had been one of his many charms.

"My fault!" she would have replied. "Was it my fault you fell out of love with me?"

He would have sighed and shaken his head, and given her a look of affectionate annoyance. "Why you insist I've fallen out of love with you, I'll never know. You have everything you could need. I don't know what more you could want."

"And what do I need?"

"A home to care for, a husband."

"A child?"

He would have frowned at her then. He probably would have turned his back to her. He would have picked up his hat and cane. He would have announced he was going for a walk. He would have left even as she begged him to stay, even as she clung to his arm, apologizing hysterically.

"I couldn't help it," Mrs. Durham would have told him.

"Yes, you could have," he would have said, shutting the door in her face as he left for his club.

Mrs. Durham kept brushing the lock of hair. She continued brushing even as she ripped hairs from her head. She felt no pain. Her hand moved mechanically. She stared into the mirror. She was lost in the reflection of her eyes. Her husband had once called her eyes bewitching. She wondered if it was true, if she could bewitch with her eyes. Or was it just another one of Henry's lies?

Mrs. Durham was fairly certain she would never know.

TWENTY-FOUR

IN WHICH HARTWELL SPEAKS HIS MIND

HARTWELL TOWERED OVER STEELE, his fingers digging into Steele's thin arms. It never occurred to Mary that Steele was a thin man. Not lanky, just… delicate. That is, he looked delicate compared to Hartwell, who, while not brawny, had more to his frame.

Hartwell seemed grounded even while in an obvious panic. His hands didn't shake, his voice was even. The only indication of his distress was his hair falling before his eyes, and the way he clutched Steele. Mary envied Hartwell's ability to maintain control.

"You could maintain control if you learned to breathe once in a while."

From the corner of her eye, Mary saw Trentwood inch just out of view. There were matters to be dealt with. "I'm going for a walk," she announced. "I'm going for a walk, and you two shall have to do without me."

"What?" Hartwell snapped. He dropped Steele to the sofa as if he were nothing more than a child's toy.

"I'm going for a walk," Mary said, rising. She still had her thick shawl draped around her shoulders, and her walking boots—good heavens did they put her in bed with her boots still on?—and if she moved quickly she could grab one of her father's old jackets she kept tucked away in a back corner of the library.

Hartwell blocked her path.

Mary refused to look him eye-to-mangled-eye. She stared at his muddied boots and fitted breeches that flattered his muscular calves. For a barrister, he was surprisingly fit.

"You may not be the blackmailer, Miss Trentwood, but someone is," Hartwell growled.

She arched her brows. "Might I remind you, Mr. Hartwell, that you are a guest in my home? I didn't take to hearing your accusations that I am a blackmailer lightly, and I certainly don't take to hearing accusations of anyone in my household, either!"

"Be that as it may," Hartwell said, "someone in this house is blackmailing my sister and I'm determined to find the cause of it."

"Why are you so convinced of this? Why can't you just pay this blackmailer and leave me and my family be?" Mary said.

Hartwell's mouth dropped as he staggered back a step.

Steele took this moment to join the conversation. "If what he says is true, my dear Miss Trentwood, then he couldn't simply pay off the blackmailer. Such characters are never satisfied. They will come again, ever stronger."

Mary resisted the urge to shrug. How that was her problem, she didn't know. She wasn't the one being blackmailed.

"Forgetting all that, how can you feel safe living in a house with a mind bent to criminal activity?" Hartwell stepped closer. "How would your father have liked it?"

"He'd have disliked it, and you know it," Trentwood said in Mary's ear, making her flinch. "Listen to him, he speaks sense."

Which one? Mary asked. *Which one am I to believe? The one you possessed, or the one you dislike?*

Distracted by her conversation with Trentwood, Mary didn't notice Hartwell's hand coming toward her cheek until it was too late. She froze as the very tips of his fingers brushed against her skin. She caught her breath as her flesh flared with a bold heat that betrayed her embarrassment and… was it possible? Her eyes flickered in Steele's direction.

"Honestly," Hartwell said softly, though his tone carried every morsel of his annoyance, "do you think any honorable man would allow you to be victim to such a person, if he knew it was in his power to protect you?"

Hartwell's fingertips moved from her cheek to smooth an errant hair behind her ear. Mary swallowed. A chill ran down her back. Such reactions were for schoolgirls, not mistresses of the manor. She pressed her lips together and blinked rapidly in a vain attempt to break her gaze from Hartwell's dark eyes.

Really, when one got used to his face and felt the effect of his smile, there were only his eyes of which to truly take note. Dark though they were, Hartwell's eyes spoke promises that made Mary feel hot and cold in turn.

"I haven't asked for protection from anyone," Mary said with a falter. "I don't need protection."

Part of Mary wanted Hartwell to take her in his arms so she could outright bawl. Part of her wanted to run away so she could sort through her jumbled thoughts and emotions alone. Still a third part wanted to lean so her cheek rested in Hartwell's hand.

"I shall stay to ensure whatever harm could come your way will not come from Mr. Hartwell," Steele said, jumping to his feet to slap Hartwell's hand away from Mary.

"Finally," Trentwood said, "the boy shows some gumption."

Mary's nod was terse at Steele, glad he had been strong enough to do what she could not. The way her stomach had fallen to her feet, no, not to her feet, but to the basement below, made her quite certain that if Steele hadn't been in the room, Hartwell might very well have kissed her. She wasn't entirely certain she would have pulled away. What would her father have said at such behavior?

"Agreed," Hartwell said, his tone crisp and business-like. He smiled, brightening her mood as daybreak brightens the night. "Do forgive me, Mary, if I've overstepped my bounds. I'm certain you've seen I think you're a funny little thing." He shrugged. "It's been what, a day? Not that time matters when it comes to such odd circumstances as these. The fact is I don't want to see you get hurt. I'm not certain how much more you could take."

"I'm not some delicate piece of china, Alex."

Hartwell nodded. "Of course you aren't. China doesn't have feelings, Miss Contrary. Or stomachs."

"You're impossible," Mary said.

"Indeed," he said, grinning.

After a very unladylike grunt, Mary muttered, "I'm going for a walk. Tell Pomeroy to not wait for me if I don't come back in time for dinner."

"Why Miss Trentwood," Steele exclaimed, "you can't be thinking of walking alone."

Hartwell shook his head with a little laugh. "You're going to lose this battle, friend."

"Jasper," Mary said, her voice deceptively sweet, "stick your nose back in your papers." She turned on her heel to face Trentwood, who looked far too pleased for a man who had been dead for a month and more. *You are coming with me.*

Trentwood snorted. *As if I'd have it any other way.*

By the time they reached Wayland's Smithy, it had begun to rain. It was the kind of loud rain that spoke of the end of winter and the coming of spring. Mary had been forced to jog that last one hundred yards to the black opening of the Saxon tomb. She had slid on the slick rock floor covered with decaying leaves, and Trentwood's tight grasp on her arm righted her. She jerked away from his unnatural touch.

Mary huddled beneath the sheltering rocks of the sarsen stones that made the ceiling, her arms wrapped tightly around her waist. *I haven't anything left from breakfast to feel so ill to my stomach.* "Tell me what happened back there."

Trentwood stood in the shadows beside her. She could feel his white eyes watching her and fought the wave of nausea that shuddered through her body. Those white eyes had, for a brief moment, looked at her through Hartwell's eyes. Certainly she hadn't imagined that. That Trentwood had, for a time, stepped into Hartwell's body so he could land a devastating punch to Steele's jaw? One couldn't imagine that. Just as one couldn't imagine one's father becoming a ghost.

I'm not mad. Please, tell me I'm not mad.

Outside, the rain plummeted to the ground more furiously than Mary had ever seen. It was as if the sky vomited on her behalf. She closed her eyes and leaned her forehead into the moss that clung to the vertical stone walls. She sighed as the cool rock soothed the pounding at her temples.

"What would you like to know?"

She wasn't sure where to begin. "How did you do it?"

Trentwood shrugged. "One minute I was watching you thrash about in bed, and I heard you scream that terrifying scream of yours, and the next minute I was in your dream. I haven't the slightest clue how it happened."

Mary's tongue felt heavy in her mouth. "I was talking about when you possessed Alex."

Again, Trentwood shrugged. "I'm as new to this being dead folderol as you are in watching it."

Wiping beads of sweat from her brow, Mary whispered, "You will limit such… jaunts… in the future, I hope?"

"Indeed," he said with a short laugh. "It pains me to do it as much as it seems to pain you to watch it. Do you know how difficult it is to be dead, hopping around from one mind or body to the next, not knowing how you got there, or how you'll get out?" He stepped closer, and she could smell his death-stench.

"No, I don't. I never thought it was a skill I would need to learn," she said.

"Inherited your mother's morbid sense of humor, I see."

"Given the circumstances, I think I'm glad of it."

Trentwood stepped closer. "Mary, we must talk about your dream. We must talk about your mother's death."

Mary's smile was grim at best. She spread her palms flat against the stone behind her waist and leaned against the cold stone wall. An odd sort of fuzziness encroached her vision. She tried to shake her head free of it, without success, so instead she fought to focus on Trentwood. "Very well."

"What's wrong?" he asked flatly.

"No—nothing," she gasped.

The world became very dark. A dark cloud, probably, passing overhead. Though that hardly made sense, as they were properly sheltered by the stone ceiling of the tomb. Perhaps a tree had fallen? Mary hadn't heard the shrieks of splintering wood, or the crack of a thunderbolt.

No, a tree hadn't fallen, she had. There was no other explanation for why her cheek was nestled among the decaying leaves, or why Trentwood's boots were so close to her nose.

It was actually rather comfortable. Mary closed her eyes. Perhaps it would be best if she slept a bit. Yes, sleep was exactly what she needed.

Twenty-Five

In Which Trentwood Panics

TRENTWOOD JUMPED AWAY FROM Mary when she fell at his feet. Breathing heavily, he squeezed his eyes shut, waiting for her screams and the terrible rushing sensation he had felt the last time he had appeared in her dream.

A minute passed, though it seemed an hour. He opened an eyelid and then the other when he realized he was still in the godforsaken tomb with Mary at his feet. "Mary?" He crouched beside her, a hand held before her mouth and nose to feel for warm puffs of air.

She was breathing, faintly. Rather than warming him, her weak breaths left his skin feeling clammy, which again reminded him of how unnatural he was. He felt as if his skin was ready to molt from his body… though he wasn't entirely certain he had a body beneath this skin, however solid he felt when he touched Mary.

Trentwood stood. Mary had fainted, if he could interpret anything from the clumsy way she had fallen, as if she had forgotten what it meant to stand upright. It was no wonder, really, given the last day, no, month—if he were being brutally honest, year—that she had tolerated.

But how to move her? Trentwood shuddered at the thought of touching her, now that he knew he could jump into her dreams. What other nightmares did she suffer, with him as the misinterpreted villain?

More importantly, how to get her back home? For she would, in her weak condition, catch influenza or pneumonia if she continued lying in those wet leaves. Hmm. Trentwood pulled out his pocket watch and swung it by its chain. Perhaps he could startle a farmer into running into the clearing? Or better yet, could he get Pomeroy to come?

The next thing Trentwood knew, he stood where he had never stood while alive: the servants' room off the kitchen. Pomeroy sat at a roughly-hewn wooden table with a canvas apron covering his chest and lap. He was polishing the silver tray, now empty of Mary's vomit, whistling as he did so.

That man was always far too cheerful for Trentwood's taste, but then, his cheerfulness always suited Mrs. Trentwood, and Mary, too. Trentwood had to admit that when left to his own devices, Pomeroy was incredibly resourceful; he could think of no other man who juggled the responsibilities of butler, valet, and footman with a smile.

Trentwood shivered and somehow seemed to know it wasn't he who shivered, but Mary, lying on the floor of the tomb. "Mary is in trouble. You must go to her," he said to Pomeroy.

Pomeroy lay down the tray and lifted a tarnished spoon.

"Did you hear me, man? You must help Mary!"

Nothing. Not a blink, flinch, or gasp. Pomeroy, it seemed, was a lost cause.

To the parlor, then, where Hartwell and Steele drew up plans to investigate everyone still residing at the manor house.

"I doubt Pomeroy is blackmailing my sister, he's far too frank," Hartwell was saying when Trentwood walked through the wall into the parlor. "If the man wanted to ruin me, he would do it with his fists, not with his words." He paused. "Though he's got a wicked way with those, too."

"What could he do to you that nature hasn't already done?" Steele said.

Hartwell leveled a look at him. "And this is why you'll never be more than a solicitor. You're supposed to solicit the information from me, not throw judgment calls at my face, about my face! There is a subtlety to being a barrister which you simply lack!"

Steele scowled, but didn't say anything, giving Trentwood the opportunity to whisper in Hartwell's ear, "Mary needs you."

Crying out, Hartwell pressed the heel of his palm to the side of his head.

"What?" said Steele, "what is it?"

"Mary! It's Mary! You must go to her!" Trentwood insisted.

Hartwell stumbled to his feet. With his hands before him as though blinded by the pain, he felt along the overstuffed chairs littering the parlor on his way to the window hidden behind heavy brocade curtains. "How long has it been raining like that?"

"I don't know, an hour?" Steele replied, also rising to his feet.

"Where is Mary?" Hartwell looked at Steele. "We've been talking for an hour and she's trapped in the rain?"

"I warned her it was dangerous to walk alone," Steele offered, weakly. "She was too ill!"

"We're wasting time," Trentwood snapped.

Hartwell rolled his neck as though he had a kink in a muscle and suffered a full-body shudder. "G-get your coat, we're going after her."

"You can't be serious," Steele protested, following Hartwell from the parlor. "I haven't the clothes to go rushing out into a country storm! And neither, I think, have you! Send her servant, that Pomeroy man."

Hartwell turned his back to Steele as he shoved his arms into his jacket and wrapped a woolen scarf around his neck. "If you were a man, I'd lay you flat."

Trentwood hooted his laughter. "Well said, son, well said."

"I hardly think that was necessary," Steele said under his breath as Hartwell slammed the door behind him.

Steele watched Hartwell run from the house, splashing through puddles and paying no heed to his surely ruined clothing. He watched Hartwell, feeling a knot gathering in his stomach. The man moved like a man in love.

Which was impossible, of course, for Mrs. Durham had admitted that Hartwell had been a guest at the manor house for all of a day and then some. Sensible men like Hartwell didn't fall in love easily or quickly. Steele knew this because he was not the most sensible man in the world, he knew it and accepted it, and he happened to fall in love easily and quickly.

Such as a year ago, when a laughing, dancing Mary had admitted she found him the most interesting man in the room. It had been such a forward thing to say, so very un-English of her. He had fallen in love instantly, thinking that she must have loved him greatly to be so brash, so... American.

But then her father had fallen ill, and Mary had dropped off the face of the earth, and Steele had fallen in love with another young woman, a true American with no name worth remembering, but enough wealth to catch any man's attention, sensible or not.

Yet here Steele was with Mary back in his life. Surely it meant something. And with Hartwell off on his madcap rescue, it seemed only right that Steele perform his own great deed.

"Pomeroy," he shouted, "Pomeroy, prepare the parlor."

Pomeroy came sprinting at Steele's shout, for it sounded more like a scream of agony. "What is it, what's happened?"

"Miss Trentwood—something's happened to Miss Trentwood and we must find blankets and... and I don't know what else, but she will be cold, surely, and must be warmed. What shall we do? What shall I do? I've never met a pair of such ninny-hammers, running out in weather like this!" Steele returned to the front door, throwing it open to stare at the lane devoid of Hartwell and Mary.

Pomeroy, to his credit, seemed to understand Steele's frantic rambling. "If you would be so kind, sir," he said, his tone firm, "do enlist Mrs. Durham for any extra blankets she might find. I will warm some chocolate and get the fire in the parlor to a healthy blaze again."

Steele nodded. "Yes, yes, good man for thinking of it." He sprinted upstairs, his head swiveling. "Mrs. Durham?"

For a maddening minute, there was no answer. Then came Mrs. Durham's head poking from her doorway, a cautious, yet oddly blank, expression on her face.

"Mrs. Durham, you must pardon my rudeness, but it seems something has happened to Miss Trentwood, and Mr. Hartwell has gone to fetch her but we are in need of blankets," Steele rattled off, brushing past her so he could whisk the blankets from her bed. He coughed at the cloud of dust that he disrupted. "Good lord," he wheezed, "is there no one to do the housework?"

"No, no one," Mrs. Durham said dully.

Steele moved to the window to pick up a knitted throw and to the vanity to grab a heavy shawl. All were covered with dust. His lip curled. "When Miss Trentwood is returned and feeling well, we shall have to press upon her the risks of such living, Mrs. Durham!"

"Yes, of course," she replied.

"Thank you for your kind understanding, Mrs. Durham, you must understand this is a special circumstance, for I would never in my right mind burst into a gentlewoman's bedroom and steal her bedclothes from under her! No indeed, I should have asked you to do it yourself, but you see, I've no idea when or if Hartwell will return with Miss Trentwood, and so we must be at the ready. Surely you understand, Mrs. Durham."

"Oh yes, quite clearly."

Had Steele been less frantic, he might have noticed how Mrs. Durham moved as though she struggled against the tide. He might have noticed that her hair was half-undone, her hairbrush bloodied, and her fingertips raw. He might have noticed that he had lifted not only every available bit of linen in the room, but also a pile of unaddressed letters that had been tucked in a fold of the blanket by the window.

No, it was not until Steele was in the parlor, laying the extra linens around the fire to warm them for Hartwell and Mary's arrival—no, not Hartwell and Mary, for the thought of them together, even in a simple address, made his heart feel sour. To be more accurate, it was not until Steele was in the parlor, laying the extra linens around the fire to warm them for Mary's arrival that he found the letters.

By that point, he was far calmer. Pomeroy had forced a cup of hot chocolate into his hand, and he had half-drunk the cup by the time the letters had fallen to the floor.

Steele lifted one, his brows rising as he recognized the handwriting. It wasn't that he knew the writer, per se, but that he had seen the writing before, and recently. Leaving his cup of hot chocolate by the fire screen, he lifted the letter he had been studying with Hartwell, before Hartwell's freak announcement that Mary needed help.

Of course they would be the same handwriting. Of course it would be Steele who would have to tell Mary the truth about her aunt. Of course. Dammit.

TWENTY-SIX

IN WHICH HARTWELL BERSERKS

IN MARY'S DREAM, SHE was lifted by a handsome beast with arms as thick as a steam engine. The beast shot out from the tomb much like a runaway train, roaring through the trees and farmer's fields back to the manor house. He kept repeating her name, but she couldn't answer. She wanted to, but her mouth wouldn't open, and neither would her eyes.

"Mary, wake up!" she heard her mother cry.

Mary woke with a gasping shiver. It took her a moment to realize she was no longer sprawled across the floor of the tomb, but in someone's arms. They raced along the slippery lane to the manor house at superhuman speed.

"Put me down," she rasped, thinking it was Trentwood who carried her, for who else could move so quickly while carrying her? She wasn't the smallest of women.

"Can't," Hartwell said, panting. "Too cold. Besides, don't think I could stop if I wanted. Tried already. Lost control. Of my legs."

Mary clung to his neck as the fields surrounding her house whizzed past them. "Seems as though you've got firm control… Could you slow down a bit, if you won't stop?"

"Tried that, too."

Mary bit her lip. Hartwell looked panicked, and not simply for having found her fainted away on the floor of a tomb. He looked terrified, frightened out of his wits for his wellbeing. His eyes were dilated, his nostrils flaring. The wind and rain had torn his hat from his head and his hair was plastered to his face.

With everything else that had happened, Mary believed Hartwell wanted to stop, most dearly, but couldn't, for purely supernatural reasons. *Do I dare?* She winced when Hartwell looked at her from the corner of his eye. Yes, she did dare, she must.

"Father," Mary said, "Papa, I'm feeling much better now."

Hartwell looked at her sharply.

"Papa, please."

Hartwell shuddered to a standstill. He stopped so quickly Mary would have flown from his arms had he not tightened his grip. He panted so heavily that she worried his lungs would burst from his chest. Suspecting her legs were still too weak to carry her weight, she remained in his arms, feeling sheepish as she clung to his neck.

"I'm sorry about all this," she said after a moment or two.

Without a word, Hartwell moved one foot forward with a quizzing expression on his face. He took another step, and another, until satisfied he controlled his movements. "I don't suppose you would mind telling me what all this is about," he said, not looking at Mary.

Mary tightened her hold around his neck as he stepped over a large puddle in the road. "You wouldn't believe me."

"If this is about ghosts, I'll have you know my mother thinks she's been speaking to them for years, and let me just say that none of them have had the same effect yours seems to have on me."

There was a low whooshing sound Mary had come to recognize as Trentwood appearing from nothing. She glanced over Hartwell's shoulder to find Trentwood following a pace behind them.

"He's a quick one, isn't he?" Trentwood said.

"He's here, isn't he?" Hartwell said. "Your father?"

"How can you tell?" Mary whispered.

"My head feels like it's about to split open," he replied through gritted teeth. "I think it's his proximity. He's very close, isn't he?"

Trentwood, with a great frown, stopped walking so the distance between them grew until he was three yards away. With a low sigh, Hartwell's expression cleared.

"Much better, thank you, sir," he said.

"I don't understand," Mary said. "You know my father is haunting me? And you don't think I'm mad?"

Hartwell's laugh was short and without mirth. "No more mad than I. I've suspected for a while, or wondered at least, if you believed you were being haunted. But today, the oddest things have been happening…"

"Such as not being able to control your legs?" Mary offered.

"Or knowing you needed help," Hartwell replied. "We were in the parlor, Steele and I, and all of a sudden I had an awful headache, and I knew, somehow, that you were at the tomb. And then… I lost time earlier. I thought little of it, but now… you and Steele are under the impression I punched him, and my hand does hurt, so perhaps I did."

Mary leaned her chin on Hartwell's shoulder, watching Trentwood follow at a respectful distance. *How can I tell him?*

Tell him what you must, Trentwood said, his voice echoing softly in her ear.

Clearing her throat, Mary said, "My father began haunting me the day of his funeral. I don't know why, or how this came to be. He doesn't seem to know his strength."

"You don't know why he is here?"

Mary shook her head. A lump gathered in her throat and tears in the corners of her eyes. She swallowed the lump and buried her face in Hartwell's shoulder. She felt Hartwell stop walking and hold her closer to him in a semi-embrace. She pulled her arms ever tighter around his neck, sniffling.

"You haven't had the easiest year, have you?" Hartwell said, his warm breath tickling the hairs on her neck.

She rolled her forehead against his shoulder in a silent, "No."

"And here I come, bringing accusations of blackmail to your door." Hartwell pressed his face against her neck and against her ear, trying to nose her away from his shoulder so she would face him. She pulled away, ashamed that tears streamed down her face, no doubt making her nose red and her eyes bloodshot. She was not a pretty crier, but she faced Hartwell, her lip trembling.

"For what it's worth," he said, "I am very sorry."

Mary licked her lip, tasting the sharp bitterness of iron. Apparently she had cracked her lip open during her fall. No wonder her father and Hartwell seemed so frantic. How awful did she look?

She couldn't look so very awful, not when Hartwell managed to look at her in such a way that made her chest tighten and her stomach flip.

They had reached the manor house by that point, and Mary was almost sorry for it. Her lips parted, wanting to say something, anything, to postpone Hartwell from announcing their arrival. Hartwell, at the same time, leaned a fraction closer. He had such nice eyes, such clear and gentle eyes.

The door opened to reveal Steele, ushering them inside as he tucked a warmed, woolen blanket around Mary nestled in Hartwell's arms, and another around Hartwell's shoulders. He guided them to the parlor, where a stoked fire raged and a pot of hot chocolate waited. The warm, soothing aroma hit Mary, and she sighed softly, already anticipating the velvety liquid touching her parched throat.

The sofa, angled to face the fire, was covered with all the extra blankets in the house, so when Hartwell placed Mary on it she didn't fear of water-staining her mother's furniture. She shivered violently as both men worked at peeling away her soaked shawl and waterlogged boots. Hartwell rubbed her hands between his own, and Steele dabbed at her wet feet.

Slowly but surely, Mary began to feel an uncomfortable tingling in her limbs. She hadn't realized they had gone numb in the cold. As the fire warmed her, and she sipped some of the warmed chocolate Hartwell pushed against her lips, her eyes began to droop.

"She knows I would never do anything to hurt her, doesn't she? She knows that I meant no harm when I spoke earlier, out of jealousy?" Mary heard Steele whisper.

Hartwell wiped the rivulets of water that continued to stream from her hair.

"Mary," she heard Trentwood's voice say, "you know I meant no harm when I spoke out of fear the day of your mother's death?"

"I know you didn't," she mumbled, falling into a deep, and thankfully dreamless, sleep.

TWENTY-SEVEN

IN WHICH A PARTNERSHIP FORMS

WHILE MARY SLEPT, STEELE showed Hartwell the letters.

"Dammit," Hartwell hissed.

Steele nodded. "That's what I said."

They watched Mary sleep. She burrowed under the blankets so they could only see her nose, closed eyes, and her damp hair. Hartwell dabbed away water that ran from her hair down the length of her nose. Steele tucked the blankets firmly around her bare feet. Together, they moved to the coldest corner of the parlor, as far away from the fire and Mary as possible without leaving the room.

"That was quick thinking, preparing the room for our return," Hartwell muttered.

Steele scuffed his shoe against the threadbare rug. "How could I have acted otherwise; you shamed me into doing it."

Hartwell said, "Well, I'm glad I said whatever I did then." He lifted the letters in his hand. "What are we to do about this?"

"I was hoping you would know. You came here knowing a blackmailer was in the house. Did you truly not know it was Mrs. Durham?" Steele whispered. He glanced over his shoulder at Mary to make certain she was asleep and couldn't hear them. She shifted, disappearing even further into her blankets with a little sigh.

Hartwell tilted his head from side-to-side in a physical show he had his suspicions. "The woman seems… erratic. I don't know her story, but she hasn't been good to Mary. Not understanding at all, given the circumstances. Which reminds me, you've been a sore point in this house, or didn't you know that?"

"Are you being serious?" Steele recoiled from Hartwell's implications. A sore point? Hartwell could only mean in terms of his relationship, or lack thereof, with Mary.

"Of course I am," Hartwell snapped. "Or didn't you know Mary's been pining after you since she last saw you? Did you not see how she looked at you when you arrived? For the love of all that's holy, man, you're the dumbest person I know."

Steele's lip curled. "Well, you're the ugliest person I know."

"Excellent." Hartwell grinned. "Now that we've gotten that out of the way, what are we to do about Mrs. Durham? She's obviously a bit batty, threatening my sister with me under her roof!" He tapped the letters against his lip. "Probably shouldn't accuse her outright."

"That would hardly be gentlemanly."

"No," Hartwell agreed, "it wouldn't. But it would be a lot of fun." He caught Steele staring at him. "What? What is it?"

"Sincerely, you are the ugliest man I've ever met," Steele said in wonder.

"Now that's what I call ungentlemanly. Who calls a man ugly to his face, I wonder?"

"What happened to you? This," Steele said, waving at Hartwell's disfigurement, "is not from birth, I assume."

Hartwell shook his head. "An accident." He clapped his hand on Steele's shoulder. "We'll go over it some other time, when we haven't a blackmailer in our midst. She's threatened to kidnap my nephew. I can't allow that."

Leaning against the wall, Steele rested his forehead on his raised forearm. "I could approach Mrs. Durham," he murmured, "she seems to have a fondness for me. Or rather, she's fonder of me than she is of you, and perhaps I could get a confession out of her."

Steele noticed the way Hartwell's brows rose and fell quickly. "I can do it," he insisted.

"She could be dangerous," Hartwell cautioned.

"No woman so attached to an annoying dog could be the slightest bit dangerous."

"I disagree. It's an unhealthy obsession. Makes me wonder what other sort of manias she might have." When Steele pouted, Hartwell rolled his eyes. "What now?"

"How have I been a sore point? Just how can you know such a thing?"

"It turns out, Steele, that if you're friendly to a lonely woman, you can learn about her, and this is the most shocking point, you can learn to care for her. Pomeroy filled in the details, but it was fairly easy to see she'd been jilted and wasn't taking it lightly, especially with her father's illness and death." Hartwell looked across the room at Mary, his expression softening. "She's a right foot soldier, that one, and puts up with much nonsense. It's a wonder she hasn't broken."

Steele scoffed, and Hartwell's attention swiveled to him. "And I'm to believe you, a man who's obviously jealous of my history with Miss Trentwood?"

Hartwell shrugged. "Think what you like. You can ask her yourself, if you're brave enough."

"Stop insinuating that I'm a coward!"

"Didn't think I was insinuating. I'm being quite plain."

Mary coughed weakly as she began to emerge from the blankets. "What are you two arguing about?" she rasped.

Steele and Hartwell were at her side instantly to push her beneath the blankets again.

"You shouldn't move; you're unwell," Steele said.

"You need the rest," Hartwell added.

"I don't know how I'm supposed to rest with you two bickering in the corner the way my aunt and mother used to do," Mary muttered, her eyes already closing again. "I can only assume it's either about me or this supposed blackmailer." Her voice began to drift off. "You're adults, I'm certain you can handle it."

Hartwell and Steele shared a look that said, "I hope so."

Twenty-Eight

In which Mary remembers

MARY DREAMED SHE WAS dancing with Steele. She wore a low-cut, cream-colored bodice decorated with pearls, and had a dragonfly barrette in her high-piled hair. Her dancing heels pinched her toes, and her elbow-length gloves were slipping.

She was aware, acutely aware, of the way his fingers tightened their grasp at her waist, and the way he led her so surely across the floor. He was in his dress blacks, and he positively shone golden beneath the candlelight.

She was just as aware of her father watching them from across the room, his arms crossed over his chest. Her throat constricted. Would Trentwood ever approve of a gentleman who showed interest in her? She would be on the shelf before long, if Trentwood kept up this inane protectiveness. Her brows knit together as Steele led her through a particularly tight spin.

If Mary was being completely honest with herself, then she, her dream self anyway, knew she was already on the shelf, and this entire dance was a farce. Steele wasn't interested in her anymore than he was interested in any of the other older women.

When the dance ended, she followed Steele to the refreshments table, smiling at a joke of his.

"Would you care to dance?" a low voice said from behind Mary as she accepted a cup of champagne from Steele.

She turned to find Hartwell. At least Mary thought it was Hartwell. He had the same dark hair as Hartwell and dark eyes. A smile burst across his face when she looked at him. Her breath caught in her throat. He was in his dress blacks as well, and looked almost dangerous in comparison to Steele's golden sheen.

He had no scar.

Mary stepped forward, her champagne forgotten though she carried it with her.

"Miss Trentwood?" Steele asked. "Miss Trentwood, we have another dance."

"Do we?" Mary said. She studied Hartwell's face. Without the scar, he was quite handsome, in an unconventional way. He had a large forehead and so he wore his hair long to minimize the breadth of it. His eyes twinkled at her in the candlelight.

"Is something amiss?" Hartwell said, brushing his fingers across his cheek. "Is there something on my face?"

Mary laughed. "No, indeed, there is a lack of something."

"Does it displease you?" Hartwell said, his voice low.

Mary tilted her head, thinking a moment. True, Hartwell was quite handsome… but he seemed to know it. He smiled as he always did, but his carriage was not easy and comfortable; it was stiff and self-conscious. He knew his beauty and was uncomfortable with it. Why?

Mary could only imagine what she might have done had she been as handsome. Married young… become the toast of London, be all the things her mother had been to Society.

And here Hartwell was, standing before her, as handsome as any man she had ever seen, and he disliked the attention. Even more confusing, he sought her out. She, average Mary, out of a sea of lovely ladies whose gazes stuck her with needles in a million and one places for pulling Hartwell from them.

No, the lack of the scar did not displease her, per se. It was the lack of what the history of the scar in Hartwell's past seemed to do to him.

The scar, Mary realized, had freed him of Society's expectations somehow. Had it chased away the marriage-mad mothers with their sniffling daughters in tow? Had it made him fearsome in the courts where before he had simply been a handsome, promising, young man? Had it given him the confidence to be who he wanted to be, rather than whom everyone else wanted?

"Miss Trentwood," Steele said, taking the still-full cup of champagne from her, "it is our dance."

Mary snapped out of her reverie. She looked up to find Hartwell watching her, bemused. "Perhaps the next one, Alex?"

Hartwell started. "You know my name?"

"Of course," she admonished, "we are friends, are we not?"

Hartwell opened his mouth, ready to say something, perhaps ready to argue, but Steele swept Mary away into a waltz, the sort that left her dizzy and laughing. The candle-lit chandeliers bounced over the dancers. The ballroom smelled of perfume and body odor. The air was littered with conversation, music, laughter, tension.

Mary stumbled from the dance floor, laughing, her hand resting on Steele's arm, Hartwell long forgotten. "Father, I'd like you to meet Mr. Steele," she said.

The air crackled, and the hairs on her arm stood on end. Her father was not her father.

"Mary," ghostly Trentwood sighed, rubbing his forehead, "why must you torture yourself like this? What good does it do you to remember times as you wish, rather than as they were?"

"I don't understand you," Mary said with difficulty, her tongue feeling heavy and thick in her mouth. She looked at Steele to find him frozen in place. "What have you done to him?" The more she talked, the lighter her tongue felt. "I swear, Father, you really must stop possessing the bodies of the men who take an interest in me. Surely you must understand how off-putting that is."

"I haven't done a thing. This is your dream."

"Dream?" Mary blinked. Oh yes, that's right. She touched her forehead as a sharp pain jabbed at her temple. The tomb. Hartwell carrying her home. Steele ready with chocolate and blankets. She was asleep in the parlor.

"Better?" Trentwood said, having watched her muddle through her thoughts.

She nodded.

"Are you going to wake up again to avoid talking with me?"

She shook her head, sheepishly.

"You," Trentwood announced, "are too preoccupied with the past. And not even an accurate past, but a past that tortures you."

"So then what am I to do? My past is who I am."

"No," Trentwood said, pointing a finger at her nose the way he used to when she was a child, "the past is what got you to where you are today. It is not who you are. You are not the cause of your mother's death anymore than you are the cause of mine. You are not deformed or average-looking, Steele is just a shallow idiot—exactly what I've been telling you the past year. And Hartwell…"

Mary glanced from the corner of her eye. Hartwell stood frozen as Steele in the shadows of the dance hall, watching the dancers spin and twirl and laugh and gossip. That is, his body faced the dancers. But his eyes were on her. They were on her, and Steele, and Trentwood.

Trentwood sighed. "Hartwell you have met before, and dismissed. And it's a wonder that neither of you remember it."

Mouth dropping open, Mary released her panicked hold of Steele's arm. "You're making fun of me, that's what you're doing, because maybe I'm starting to see that you were right about Jasper. How cruel of you! How awful!"

Trentwood's palm made contact with her cheek before she could think to duck away from the soft slap. "Do you really think I've come back from the dead to laugh at you?"

"Then why are you here?" she whispered.

Leaning close, smelling only of peppermint and pipe smoke, his eyes their original amber, Trentwood whispered, "Because you need me."

"Why do I need you? What for?"

"There are dark days coming, Mary."

Ready to ask what he meant, Mary jumped when Steele sprang back to life, saying, "A pleasure, sir."

"You've danced with my daughter twice, now," Trentwood replied, crossing his arms over his sallow chest. "There will not be a third."

Mary watched Hartwell from across the room. It was a dream, she knew she dreamed, but this felt too real. *Had* she met Hartwell before? Had he been interested and she too blind to see it?

"Come now, Father, give Mr. Steele some credit. He wouldn't dare, not without your permission." Mary spoke the words but did not feel the annoyance she had felt the first time around. Instead, she saw how Hartwell shifted his feet, unsure whether he wanted to approach or retreat. At the last, he retreated, sneaking out a side door, with three mothers trailing behind him, squawking their daughters' virtues at him.

"Indeed, sir," Steele said, squeezing Mary's hand, "I have brought her to you with the hopes I might call upon you at a favorable time tomorrow?"

Mary looked down at her hand as it rested on Steele's arm. He was squeezing it, but the caress she felt did not match the action. Someone was stroking their fingers along with her own.

Her actual fingers, not her dream fingers. That someone wove their fingers between hers. It was surreal, to watch this dream Steele do one thing, knowing fully well that someone, someone not in her dream, was touching her.

The realization made Mary jolt awake. She cracked her forehead into Steele's and fell back with a cry.

"Good God," Steele cried, "what on earth made you do that?"

"Why are you so close?" Mary replied, rubbing her forehead. "Let go of my hand at once."

Looking down at their intertwined hands, Steele turned an ugly shade of red and sprang away. "A thousand apologies, Miss Trentwood. I didn't realize you were awake."

"I wasn't, but that doesn't give you the liberty to take my hand without asking!"

"How was he to ask you, if you were asleep?" Hartwell said, entering the parlor with a new tray of hot chocolate. "Though I must say, the lady has a point, Jasper."

Mary pushed herself up from the sofa with one hand, still rubbing her forehead with the other. "How long have I slept?"

"It's about time for dinner," Hartwell said, his tone conversational though he gave Steele a dark look, "if you're feeling well enough for it."

Right at that moment, Mary's stomach decided to groan. "It seems I am." She accepted a cup of hot chocolate from Hartwell, staring at his face.

Rather than wincing, as he typically seemed to do, he met her curious gaze with a calm expression. "Is there anything amiss?" He paused, and grinned. "Is there something on my face?"

Mary smiled. Whatever had happened to him, she was grateful. There was openness in his smile that hadn't been there in her dream, a relief in his expressions that belied his knowledge he could do as he pleased. "No, nothing at all."

Steele looked on with a sneer. It was positively revolting, the way Mary looked at Hartwell. It wasn't that she looked upon that monstrous face with licentious thoughts. Mary was far too sweet for that sort of thing. But she definitely looked upon Hartwell-cum-Quasimodo favorably, which was, in fact, how she had once looked upon Steele.

And that, Steele thought, glancing at the mantle mirror to study his reflection, was an indication of madness if he ever saw one. Better to help Mary rid herself of such temptations, such as they were, than to watch her succumb to them.

"Miss Trentwood," Steele said.

"Yes?" Mary said, not noticing he had dropped to his knee before her because she was still smiling at Hartwell. Steele cleared his throat and waited.

"Yes, what is it, Jasper? Oh." Mary's expression fell when she directed her attention at him.

That wasn't entirely the reaction Steele had in mind, but at least she gave him a reaction, which was better than Hartwell's bored curiosity.

"What the devil are you doing on the floor?" Hartwell asked.

"I'd thank you to stay out of this," Steele said, his voice tight. "This is between Miss Trentwood and me."

"Well," Hartwell said, backing away with his hands in the air and a mocking smile tucked into the corner of his mouth, "who am I to get in the way of such things?" He stopped and tapped his finger against his chin. "But then, you certainly picked an odd time to have a private moment with Mary, what with me standing right here."

Mary's head swiveled from one to the other. "What are you two going on about now?"

"I believe," Hartwell said, "I am getting in the way of this man's proposal to you."

Steele reddened.

"Proposal to do what?" she said.

Steele's stomach dropped. He grabbed her hand, the one he had released not five minutes earlier, and brought it to his lips. "Dear Miss Trentwood," he said in impassioned tones, "your friend is quite right."

"Friend?" Hartwell interjected.

"Right about what?" Mary said. "I believe I must have hit my head very hard at Wayland's for I can't make out what either of you is talking about. Do be gentlemen and make sense!"

"I am asking you to marry me," Steele ground out.

At the door of the parlor, Mrs. Durham squealed and threw up her hands in jubilation, knocking a tray of snacks from Pomeroy's hands as he appeared at her side. "Why Marianne, it's what you've always wanted!" She stormed into the room, barreling past Steele to take Mary into her arms. "I'm so very happy for you. Of course I give my permission in lieu of your dearly departed father, and oh, do not mind the gossips for thinking you so very callous at marrying so soon after his death for who am I to step in the way of true love?"

Mary gasped in Mrs. Durham's arms, fighting her way out. "Pardon me, madam, but I've not replied!"

"Indeed, she hasn't," Hartwell said.

"I'll thank you to stay out of my family's affairs," Mrs. Durham said, waving her hand at Hartwell.

Steele, still on his knees, inched forward to be closer to Mary. "Dearest Miss Trentwood," he began.

"For heaven's sake, Jasper, you just proposed to me, oughtn't you call me by my Christian name? Really, sometimes you are so old-fashioned," Mary said, rubbing her temples. She kept glancing over at an open-mouthed Pomeroy, silent and leaning against the parlor doorjamb.

"Why Miss Trent—Mary," Steele said, amending himself mid-sentence beneath her suppressive glare. "I can't imagine what, or who, would make you say such things to me. Am I not allowed to afford you the respectful niceties I think you deserve?"

Snorting, Hartwell backed to the corner of the room farthest from the doorway, also rubbing his temples. The man looked like a beast, and so it was only fitting that he sounded like one.

"What's the matter—disappointed I had the wherewithal to ask her first?" Steele said, rounding on Hartwell.

"You would be far more threatening, my good man, if you weren't still on your knees, which you are. I keep telling you, it's all about the performance." Hartwell shook his head in a pitying fashion that Steele tried, and failed, to ignore.

His jaw jutting out, Steele said, "I'll not rise to my feet until I've an answer from Miss Trentwood."

All four of them—Steele, Hartwell, Mrs. Durham, and Pomeroy—looked to Mary. She shrank back from their silence.

"Miss Trentwood?" Steele said. He strove to make his voice soft, sweet, cajoling. "My dearest Mary, is it too late for me? Am I no longer the happy recipient of your affection?"

Mary started. "My affection?"

Nodding, Steele inched closer. His knees were beginning to ache, and he was fairly certain he was ruining his pants. Would linen hold up against rubbing one's entire body weight against the floor? He wasn't certain; he'd never been in such a position before.

Amazing how he had never truly thought to propose to a woman, yet here he was, waiting on baited breath for Mary's response. He was fairly certain he liked her. She was pretty and clever, and both were gainful for a solicitor's wife. She had kept a house together through her father's illness and death with dignity, though in reduced circumstances, which spoke to her domestic common sense.

And the happenings of earlier today? The unexpected dramatics and unfortunate connections to the very blackmailing woman sitting beside Mary, beaming at him with encouragement and glee? Well, that could be taken care of easily enough.

Or so Steele hoped.

"I have been told by a number of persons that you have waited for me, and I am appalled to know it. I never would have wished such torture upon anyone, the sort of waiting you must have done.

"To be alone, taking care of your father, hoping I would write. To suffer through his funeral, hoping I would call… however improper as you are in the very depths of mourning."

Steele inched closer when he caught sight of Mary swallowing against the tears gathering in her eyes. "I will do whatever you wish, my dear," he murmured, "I shall never make you wait again."

A tear ran down Mary's cheek, and she brushed it away impatiently. "I need to think."

Mary bolted from the room, chased by Mrs. Durham's shout that she ought to answer Steele.

Steele looked at Hartwell, who had leaned his head against the wall, wincing.

"Well played," Hartwell said. "You might be a barrister yet."

TWENTY-NINE

IN WHICH MARY MUST CHOOSE

MARY LOCKED HERSELF IN her bedroom. She leaned against
the door, her hands clasping the doorknob behind her as if
she was afraid it would turn of its own accord. *Unbelievable.*

"Well, that's one way to put it," Trentwood said. He
lounged against the vanity table, his legs crossed at the ankles
and his arms crossed over his chest.

Mary met his scrutinizing gaze. "What do you think?"

"About what?" he asked, incredulous. "Don't tell me you're
thinking of accepting the dolt, even after all that nonsense?"
When Mary shifted her weight, Trentwood scoffed. "You're
confused, Mary, that's what you are."

"Yes," she shot back, "I am. I thought that's why you're
here. To help me through my confusion."

"Oh, no," he said, "you'll not pin this on me, young miss. I
can't help it if you decide to choose one path over another."

Mary wrung her hands together. "How am I to know
which path is the correct one?"

"What's correct? How can one be correct about such
things?"

"I don't know! There ought to be some sort of correctness
somewhere, oughtn't there be?" Mary studied Trentwood
from the corner of her eye. "But then," she muttered, "there
is something so very incorrect about a father haunting his
daughter and possessing the men in her life."

A bark of laughter burst from Trentwood. "Don't make it sound so bad, Mary! I only possessed Hartwell, and he's none worse for the wear."

"None worse for the wear," Mary repeated in a heated tone, pointing at Trentwood, "except now he suffers migraines when you're near! Don't you see, Father, how you're affecting us?"

"Us?"

Mary flushed. She heard the suspicion beneath the simple word. So many implications by such a short syllable. Us. What did she mean by it? Certainly not that she thought of herself with Hartwell as a unit, as an "us." That would be silly. She had only just met him. No, "us" was the only noun that properly defined them, they who were both living, versus he, Trentwood, who was not.

"Yes, us. Those of us who happen to lack the ability to walk through walls and dreams and bodies."

With a scowl, Trentwood turned his back to her to stare out the window. "There's that damned morbid humor again."

"Forgive me, Father, if I attempt to make light," Mary said, her voice dripping with disdain. She ran her finger along her high-necked collar. Was it getting warmer? She swallowed and touched her temple to find it wet with sweat. She needed to get out of these clothes and into her dishabille at once if she didn't want to faint again. She stepped behind her changing screen.

"Forgive me, Father, if I make the best of a very unnatural situation. You must admit," she said, dropping her skirts and stepping out of the circle of fabric, "it was this morbid humor that kept you smiling during your last days. Or have you forgotten?"

He remained silent, staring out the window.

With deft movements, Mary unbuttoned her blouse and sighed in relief as the pressure in her neck abated. She hesitated a moment before unhooking the top half of her corset. It was a bit embarrassing to be undressing in the presence of her father.

A wonder, these new corsets that didn't require the help of a maid's nimble fingers. A shame that Mary now required such modern clothing in order to maintain propriety. She finished unhooking the remainder of her corset. A part of her cautioned against it; after all, she might have to face Hartwell or Steele again, and it simply wouldn't do to be without proper support.

Then her stomach lurched and she felt her forehead break out into a fresh sweat. Her hands began to shake, and Mary gave up the thought of dressing again. She had no need to return downstairs.

What she wanted, truly, was a deep sleep. Perhaps she would dream of Steele's proposition. Perhaps her dream self would know her feelings better than her awakened self. Or, at least, trust her feelings better.

Clad only in her chemise, stockings, and lovely lace dishabille that was loose and frilly and oh so very comfortable while still maintaining the absolute limit of decency, Mary stepped from behind her changing screen and met Trentwood at the window.

"What are you staring at?" she murmured.

He jerked his chin in the direction of the family plot. The dirt above his grave hadn't leveled out yet. The white cross made from the local limestone hadn't yet tarnished to a sickly yellow covered by green lichen the way the other grave markers had. The peaceful plot beside his that belonged to the late Mrs. Trentwood was flat, with hints of green poking through the dirt.

Mary's mouth went dry.

"I haven't been since the burial, you know," Trentwood mused.

Her brows arching, Mary said, "Really? Where do you go when you're not, that is, when I don't see you?"

Chuckling, Trentwood said, "Still afraid I'm just a figment of your imagination, eh?"

"Really, Father."

"I walk."

Mary frowned. There weren't many places Trentwood had walked when alive, and she couldn't imagine he would find new haunts—pardoning the pun, of course—when dead. "You aren't..."

"I keep thinking perhaps if I wait long enough, she'll appear."

Mary closed her eyes against the sudden pressure in her throat. No. He wasn't going to talk about her. Not like this. Not now.

"It was her favorite walk, you'll remember," Trentwood said. "And she did... well... we found her at the bottom of the steps and I keep thinking, maybe, just maybe, that she might be there. At dusk. When the setting sun hits the rose bushes just right."

Mary shook her head, backing away from him. This was much too much. She didn't want to be his grieving soundboard again. She had hardly been able to stand it when he was alive. Now that she had no idea when or if he would ever leave her in his current state, the thought of listening to him pine after her mother for the rest of her earthly-bound days made her lungs hurt.

Her lungs more than hurt. Mary doubled over. Her hand flailed. She made contact with the bedpost, which she used as a makeshift cane as she gasped for air. The world was closing in on her. Turning black. She blinked, her eyes dizzy. The floor was falling away. She fell to her knees, grasping for the solid wood beneath her. She couldn't breathe. She couldn't get enough air.

What is happening to me?

Breathe, Marianne, you must breathe. Her mother's voice.

This had happened before, once when Mary was younger, she remembered. What had she done? How had she battled the hysteria? Her mother had been with her.

Her mother had pulled her to the ground, demeaning though it was, commanding her to breathe.

Mary spread her palms flat on the floor, her knees scraping against the hard wood. Solid. Dependable. Steady. She sobbed air. Tears streamed down her face as her hair fell from its careful coif. She needed to breathe. In. And out. And again. And slower. And deeper. And she felt the rush of a cool breeze against her forehead and she sighed.

When she came to, Mary was curled up in a ball on the floor beside her bedpost. She shuddered as she righted herself.

"I'm not the best influence on you, am I?" Trentwood said, his tone awed and dismayed.

Her dishabille was probably ruined from the sweat pouring from her body, but Mary didn't care. She leaned against the bedpost, her legs sprawled in front of her. She looked up at Trentwood. "I daresay you're not."

"You were panicking. Hysterical. What did I say?"

It didn't really matter, Mary realized, what Trentwood did or said. The fact was he had a growing influence on her sanity. She was losing her mind. She knew it now, after so many attacks in one day. She had never heard her mother's voice before, in all the years since her death. She looked into Trentwood's terrified expression. She had to do it, to drive him away, to give herself a chance at normalcy, sanity.

"I think I'm going to marry Jasper, Father."

Eyes narrowed, he warned, "You do that and you will never see me again."

She nodded. "I know."

Thirty

In which Hartwell disarms

It wasn't until after dinner that Steele gathered the courage to say the words to Hartwell that had been burning his tongue at the table. Hartwell had never seen the man be so quiet, and though he hadn't known Steele more than a day at most, silent was not one of the adjectives that belonged to him.

"Why didn't you challenge me?"

They were walking from the dining room to the library, the room in which Mrs. Durham had announced she never set foot. It was the perfect room for their little chat for that very reason.

Hartwell couldn't help but smile, both at Steele's question, and at the fact that without speaking of it, both of them had moved toward the library immediately after the last plate was cleared from the table. Neither wanted to be cornered by Mrs. Durham, but Steele most especially, given his impending rela-tion-by-marriage to the woman. At least, that's how Hartwell would have felt.

"Challenge you? When would I have had the need to chal-lenge you?" Hartwell opened the library door, waving Steele inside with a large, disarming smile.

"You seem to forget I'm a man, Hartwell, and such charms don't work on me," Steele said between stiff lips.

"I suppose it depends on the effects one wishes to have on one's audience," Hartwell replied, his tone musing. He shut the door behind him and threw himself onto one of the stuffed chairs.

The library looked infinitely better since he had first laid eyes on it. Mary had spent more time than he thought in this room, tidying the books and darning the furniture. Handy little thing, she was.

"I don't catch your meaning."

"Sit man, you'll get uncomfortable leering over me like that."

"I prefer to stand. What sort of effects might one have on one's audience?"

Hartwell shrugged. "One can smile and hope it charms and disarms, of course, in the form of temporary stupidity due to a sort of immediate attraction. I can only assume that's what you mean by saying you're a man, and such charms won't work on you."

Steele nodded, but barely.

"And then there's the sort of disarming that comes from trying to get a man's back up on purpose. I call that my knowing smile." Hartwell demonstrated, smiling at Steele with his teeth, keeping a warning glint in his eye. "I know that by doing this, I'm bound to annoy you, set you on your guard, and thereby disarm you."

"What? You?" Steele scoffed, stopped, and turned red. "Dammit, Hartwell!"

"So what was it I'm meant to challenge you for?"

If Steele had his gloves in hand, he probably would have thrown them to the floor, he seemed so apoplectic in his anger. "For Miss Trentwood's hand!"

Hartwell felt his spine tighten and his eyes narrow. He inhaled slowly. He had to remain calm. It was cool, sound logic that would help him through this, not emotion, not whatever it was that fueled Steele's desperation. "Why would I do that?"

Eyes bulging, his careful moustache bristling free of its wax, Steele said, "Because you want her more than I do."

Now that made Hartwell stand up and advance on Steele so quickly that Steele actually tripped on an unseen ottoman and fell against a round table still covered with a few piles of books and a tasseled paisley throw. Hartwell glared into Steele's wide, terrified eyes. He felt his nostrils flare and heat rise at his temple. His mother had always said he looked rather ugly when he was angry, and Hartwell, in an errant thought, figured he must look worse now than as a child with his scarred face. It was a safe assumption, given the way Steele cowered.

"Say that again and I'll rip that idiotic hair piece right off your lip," Hartwell said. He kept his voice soft and silky, remembering how it had frightened his sister when they were children. It worked just as well on adults in the courtroom, and seemed to work even better on a fool such as Steele.

"If you're so upset by it, why haven't you offered for her hand?" Steele said, gulping.

"Because unlike you, I like to think things through before taking action. Do you think I'm about to propose to a woman knowing her aunt may very well be threatening the life of my nephew? Do you think any amount of affection would entice me to bring such a woman into my family? I would have to love Mary a great deal to want to bring Mrs. Durham along for the ride."

Steele almost looked impressed. "Why Hartwell, I didn't know you were so calculating."

With a great shove, Hartwell toppled Steele, the table, and the books to the floor. "It's not calculating, it's common sense. I came here for a purpose, and I'm not leaving until my family is safe. I can't be chasing after the skirts of a lovely woman just because you pose some sort of competition or threat."

"Aha!" Steele said before he caught the murderous look in Hartwell's eye. He scrambled across the floor in case Hartwell decided to kick him. "So you do think she's a lovely woman. You're a fool, Hartwell, not to have offered for her hand."

Steele was right, of course he was right, but Hartwell had no intention of showing he felt that way. Even though his chest felt a little tight at the idea of Mary joining hands with this pale upstart of a man, Hartwell refused to get in the way. He came here to find a blackmailer, and it seemed he had. All he needed was the documentation, and a bit of time to draw up the papers, and he would leave. He would file his complaint and have the authorities take care of Mrs. Durham.

Hopefully, by the grace of all that was good and mighty in the world, Mary would forgive him the act of placing her sole living family member in the gaol. She would break her engagement with Steele, citing complaints that he was a bit vain, and entertain the idea of getting to know Hartwell a little better. She would laugh at the antics of his nephew, and share a disbelieving glance at the not-so-entertaining antics of his socialite sister.

Also, he would completely heal so it would look as if he had never been scarred in the first place.

Also, Hartwell was kidding himself, and he knew it.

"And what do you intend to do then?" Hartwell said. He sighed and rubbed his aching forehead. "Seeing that you have offered for her hand and I'm obviously not going to challenge you?"

"To be honest, I rather thought you were going to fight me. I hadn't gotten past that point."

"If Mary accepts your hand, there's absolutely no way I could ever marry her," Hartwell muttered. He liked to think of himself as a good man. He wasn't so good as to think he could marry a woman dumb enough to actually want to marry Steele. He cleared his throat and raised his voice so Steele could hear him.

"So now that you know I'm not about to fight you, what is your plan?"

"Well," Steele said, "I suppose I ought to handle this blackmailing issue, now that you mention it." His expression darkened, and then, after studying the brooding Hartwell, brightened.

"No. I will not take care of this for you. You got yourself into this mess, you can get yourself out. I've the information I need."

"You're not leaving!" Steele cried, following as Hartwell threw open the library door. "You would leave me with this madwoman?"

Hartwell rounded on Steele, flattening him against the hallway wall. The wire-hung paintings swayed overhead. "Don't you ever call Mary that to her face."

"I'm speaking of Mrs. Dur—what do you know?"

Just then a pain shot up Hartwell's spine and landed at the space between his eyes. He clutched his forehead, stumbling into the staircase banister with a gasp. "Nothing," he managed. For the love of all that was painful, Trentwood must not have liked him assuming Steele had been referring to Mary! "I don't know what you're talking about."

"Hartwell! I insist you tell me what you know!"

"I must get some sleep if I'm to return to London in the morning." Jamming the pads of his fingers against his temples, Hartwell staggered up the staircase, ignoring Steele's shrieks that he return and answer his questions.

Hartwell fell into his bedroom and kicked the door shut. He heard a squeak through the wall. Far too human-sounding to be a mouse. Belatedly, he remembered Mary shared a wall with him, and felt some remorse. But the pain wasn't going away, and he was going to have to do something about it if he wanted to be able to open his eyes without searing pain ripping through his skull.

"All right, Trentwood," Hartwell said through gritted teeth, "show yourself!"

"I'm not entirely certain I can, but can you hear me all right?"

Hartwell's mouth dropped open. He sat on the floor, not knowing what else to do.

"Oh. Excellent. Apparently you can."

THIRTY-ONE

IN WHICH STEELE DISCOVERS

STEELE REMAINED AT THE foot of the staircase, unsure he wanted to follow Hartwell and continue insisting that his questions be answered. It was that scar of his; Steele just couldn't get past it, and had no idea how Mary could laugh with such gruesome features.

Mary.

With a low groan Steele buried his face in his hands. He had proposed to the woman, knowing she had waited for those words to come from his mouth for a year. A year! And now he was bound to her until she gave her response. Well, that was what he wanted, wasn't it? A way to distract Mary, to take her mind off Hartwell and her dead father? To remove those harmful influences?

It bothered him that he didn't know why he cared about such things, but he did, and such caring had made him do the unthinkable: propose to a woman he hardly knew.

"Idiot," he breathed, tapping his temples with the heels of his hands. "Stupid idiotic emotional fool."

"I beg your pardon, sir?"

Steele jumped. "Where have you been?" he asked when he realized it was Pomeroy who had spoken. He straightened his tie and waistcoat self-consciously; the tussle with Hartwell had no likely put permanent creases into his slacks, but there was nothing to be done about it.

"I was in the kitchen with Mrs. Beeton, sir," Pomeroy said, as if all butlers lowered themselves to the position of kitchen maid to help the cook do the dishes.

To be sure, Pomeroy's hands were red and wrinkled from sitting in water for the past hour, and Steele winced. He never went near the kitchens at home, he avoided any and all servants until he needed them. That was the right thing to do, the proper thing. It was unnatural, the way Pomeroy appeared at his whim and left the same way. It was disgusting the way Mary so obviously depended upon him to keep the house in order.

"How long have you been with this family?" Steele asked, smoothing his moustache.

"Since before Miss Trentwood's birth, sir," Pomeroy said.

Steele sighed inwardly. Hartwell was right about one thing: he was far too transparent. He might never make it as a true barrister. With a single question he had put Pomeroy on edge, and who knew what he would get out of the surly butler now.

"If I'm to understand correctly, sir," Pomeroy said, taking a step closer to Steele, "you have proposed to Miss Trentwood."

There was a hesitation in Steele's nod.

"If you're not serious about her, you ought to call it off, sir, pardon my saying so. Miss Trentwood's too much work for the likes of you, pardon my saying it."

Steele gaped at Pomeroy. "What?"

"Sir," Pomeroy said, his tone gaining a sense of urgency, "you must understand one thing: Miss Trentwood thinks she is haunted by her father."

Scoffing, Steele waved his hand at such nonsense. "Don't be ridiculous, Miss Trentwood has been acting rather oddly last I saw her, of course, and rightly so, given her father's death, but to say she's mad!" Steele caught his breath. Mad? No, Pomeroy hadn't used that word, but perhaps that was what Hartwell had meant by his misplaced assumption. Just what did these rascals know?

Pomeroy shook his head. "That's the worst of it, sir, Miss Trentwood's not mad, but she certainly thinks she's being haunted."

"I don't see a difference."

A creak on the stairway above them made both men look up to find Mrs. Durham watching them with an odd smile. "So you think my niece is a bit confused as well, Mr. Steele?" she said.

Steele inhaled. Neither Hartwell nor Mary was around to stop him. He could go ahead with his plan. He needn't fear marriage to Mary if the blackmailing stopped. "Mrs. Durham, I'd like a word with you, if you please." He held out his hand as she descended.

"You'd be wise to not confide secrets in this one," Pomeroy muttered, sidling away.

Lip curling, Steele shrugged away the uneasy feeling that lurked in the pit of his stomach. What could the butler know, anyway?

"What is it you wish to speak to me about, Mr. Steele?" Mrs. Durham asked, wrapped in her heavy, fur-lined Bernhardt mantle though it was actually rather balmy out. Her eyes kept darting around, but Steele didn't notice due to the late hour of day. The sun had set, and they walked with a lantern to guide them in their circuit around the manor house.

"Mrs. Durham, you know me to be a simple man, I hope."

She tittered. "Has Mr. Hartwell been at you, Mr. Steele? You are by no means simple. I think you a highly educated man entirely deserving of my bookish niece!"

If she could have seen his face clearly, Mrs. Durham was certain she would have seen the blond man turn red, if the annoyed embarrassment in his tone was any indication.

"No, Mrs. Durham, I mean to say that I am a frank man. I dislike dissembling and have no talent for it, so I'd like to get to the point."

Mrs. Durham's eyes narrowed in the darkness. They were approaching the dreaded stone staircase, now crumbled shambles, if she remembered correctly. "And I'm not one to appreciate dissembling, Mr. Steele."

He puffed a sigh into the cool air. "Mrs. Durham, I know that you are blackmailing Mr. Hartwell's sister."

"Oh?" Mrs. Durham said, moving in the direction of the staircase. She could walk this path in her sleep, she knew it so well, having traversed it so many times in daylight, and far too many in darkness. She heard Steele stumble on a slippery rock and bite back an oath behind her. She smiled. "I'm not entirely certain I understand what you mean," she called over her shoulder.

"Mrs. Durham, you know exactly what I mean. Now—wait!"

Deftly lifting her skirts, Mrs. Durham sped into the over-grown brush that was more of the Minotaur's labyrinth than the garden her sister had once loved to tend. If she turned right just then, she could hide in a cranny of the brush, and Steele would run past her. Which he did. She stepped into the broken pathway, following his frenzied chase in her own leisurely fashion. How long would it take him to realize she was no longer his quarry, but his predator?

"Mrs. Durham," Steele roared, "show yourself."

Not long enough, it seemed. "Come, come," Mrs. Durham said, near enough for him to hear her voice, but not near enough for him to determine where her voice came from. "You are being quite silly, Mr. Steele."

"Mrs. Durham, I've come to ask you to stop blackmailing Lady Kirkham. I'm determined to… to marry Miss Trentwood and it's quite appalling to think I might be related to a blackmailer. Surely you understand. Surely we can come to an arrangement."

"Of course we can," Mrs. Durham said softly.

Steele spun on his heel, but not in time to prevent a large rock from knocking him unconscious into the bushes. He fell with a hard thud on the cold ground, the lantern falling from his hand. It rolled in an arc, landing at Mrs. Durham's hem as she knelt beside him. He had a pulse, which was good, but it wasn't the strongest ever, which was even better.

"I think this arrangement shall work nicely for both of us," she said, lifting the lantern as a dark liquid trickled from his forehead. "You need some rest, Mr. Steele. You have had quite a day."

Thirty-Two

In which Hartwell realizes

THE PAIN IN HARTWELL'S head was beginning to abate, thank goodness. He wasn't certain how much longer he could have withstood the way the room would occasionally brighten as though lightning had struck, or the high-pitched squealing in his ear, or the nausea that made him want to gouge out his stomach.

He remained sitting on the floor because that felt the safest place to be. If he crawled into bed, he might fall asleep given everything that had happened earlier, and now was not the time to sleep.

Lest he should forget, he had a ghost in his bedroom. A ghost whose presence caused those unfortunate symptoms he no longer suffered. Was hearing the ghost's voice worth the lost pain? Most certainly. Was not suffering from the pain worth the thought that he might have lost his mind? Well, that was questionable.

"I sympathize with you, my boy. You've no idea what I must have thought when I first realized I was of a spectral-sort. Imagine how poor Mary felt, seeing me crawl from the grave moments after having me placed there!"

Hartwell shivered. Trentwood's voice was deep and seemed to have a constant undercurrent of amusement that made one wonder if he was making fun of them. There was a hollowness behind his words, though, which made it sound as if he were in an empty chamber, or a music hall with poor acoustics. Was that what it was like for a ghost? Standing alone in an empty music hall with only a person or two as one's audience?

The nausea was returning. Hartwell placed a steadying hand at his abdomen and swallowed away the bile taste that crowded his mouth. "You are dead, are you not?"

"Oh yes, most certainly."

The voice was coming from the vicinity of the window, so Hartwell shifted around to face it. "Might I ask why, exactly, you're haunting your daughter?"

"She's in danger."

"From Mrs. Durham?"

"Of course."

There was something in Trentwood's tone that caused Hartwell to pause and tilt his head. What else could be threatening Mary? Hartwell catalogued everything he had learned about Mary in what little time he had known her:

1. She was not insane, but

2. She most definitely thought she was haunted.

3. Given the circumstances, Hartwell tended to agree with her.

4. And then there was still that unfortunate business of her aunt blackmailing his sister.

5. Though he still hadn't figured out why.

Was Mrs. Durham's reason for blackmailing his sister the reason why Mary was in danger? And if Mary was in danger, who else was in danger?

"You have to understand something, son," Trentwood said, this time his voice sounding much nearer, as though the ghost had walked toward Hartwell while he thought. "Ophelia's been a jealous woman her entire life. Jealous, and possessive, and more than a bit obsessive."

Hartwell pictured Mrs. Durham with her idiotic dog. He had to agree with Trentwood about the possessive and obsessive part.

"She had a happy marriage starting out, but I suspect things went a bit sour when they realized she couldn't bear children. Mr. Durham was very keen on that, understandably."

Mr. Durham, Trentwood had said, and though Hartwell knew it was quite right for Mrs. Durham's husband to be named Mr. Durham, it irked him that he hadn't made the connection earlier. Mr. Durham couldn't have been the very same man who often paid visits to his sister, could he?

"The man was a doctor, of sorts, who could cure female ailments. That's how Ophelia met him in the first place. She was suffering from hysterics in the days before my marriage to her twin, and they called Durham in to provide treatment."

A smirk formed at the corner of Hartwell's mouth. Treatment for hysterics from a doctor, Trentwood said. He knew better than most that such treatments tended to be of a physical stimulation. The sort that seemed to increase the woman's hysterics before she'd fall into a languorous sleep; upon waking, she'd feel refreshed and giddy from the experience.

Yes, he knew such treatments, and understood how Mrs. Durham could have latched her affections upon such a man. Hadn't his sister done the same?

"Anyway, when Durham couldn't cure his wife, he turned elsewhere for affections, I suspect."

"Yes, to my sister, no doubt," Hartwell muttered.

"What was that?"

Hartwell jumped and scrambled closer to the door. Trentwood's voice had come from a space just beside him. "I don't suppose you've ever thought of carrying a sort of ghostly bell with you, to let others know where you are."

Trentwood laughed from a safe distance away. "You know my daughter suggested the very same? Perhaps I ought to invest in one. You wouldn't happen to know a ghostly bell procurer, eh?"

An annoyed blush spread across Hartwell's cheeks. "Well put."

Clearing his throat, Trentwood said, "So then. I suppose perhaps we both know why your sister is the victim of Ophelia's blackmail."

Hartwell's nod was curt.

"Might I ask you a question, son?"

With a deep inhale, Hartwell closed his eyes and nodded. He knew what was coming. It was the inevitable question that polite society refused to ask but always wondered. Perhaps being a ghost freed one from such dogma. Hartwell opened his eyes. Rather refreshing, these two Trentwoods: they spoke their mind regardless of polite society.

"What happened to your face?"

A knock at the door prevented Hartwell from answering. He frowned as he watched the doorknob turn. He scrambled to his feet when Mary, clothed in a nightgown and deep red dressing robe, padded into the room barefoot. Her hair was tousled and hastily pulled back with a ribbon. Her eyes were bloodshot, and her hands trembled a little. But her hazel eyes snapped with lucidity, intelligence, and a bit of ferociousness.

"Mary, what on earth?" Hartwell said. He couldn't take his eyes off her feet. He never would have guessed she had delicate, pretty toes, but she did. The realization absolutely flabbergasted him. He couldn't remember the last time he had seen any woman's foot free of its stocking. He couldn't remember the last time he had seen a woman with tousled hair and bloodshot eyes.

He couldn't remember the last time he had wanted to kiss someone so badly.

"Indeed, Mary, how improper," Trentwood snapped.

Hartwell paled. Trentwood couldn't read thoughts, could he? Hartwell cleared his throat.

Mary ran her fingers through her tangled hair impatiently. "I don't know how I'm supposed to get any sleep with the two of you gabbing at all hours of the night!" She shut the door. "Since it's obvious the two of you are such good friends, I thought I might as well join the conversation and learn a bit in the meantime."

Hartwell backed away when Mary turned on him.

"So then, Alex, what did happen to your face?"

THIRTY-THREE

IN WHCH HARTWELL CONFIDES

HE HADN'T THOUGHT FOR years about how his eye had come to be warped. He had been too busy dealing with the results and the reactions of the people around him. It had been simple enough, really, quite mundane, in fact. Hartwell was fairly certain Mary and Trentwood would be bored by the narrative, but he shrugged and crossed his arms over his chest as he leaned against the bedpost. "It looks far more glamorous than it seems."

Mary pulled up the skirts of her red robe and nightgown to pad over to the chair at the writing desk.

Hartwell caught a glimpse of her ankle with a small smile. For a woman who seemed so proper all of the time, she was incredibly wanton when sleep-deprived. He couldn't see any other reason why Mary would have burst into the room hardly dressed just to make herself comfortable for a story about his eye.

"Do tell," she said, yawning behind her hand. She leaned down to arrange her skirts so he couldn't see a speck of flesh. Pity. "I don't see how anything that caused the skin around your eye to be pulled tight could be anything but glamorous."

"She has a pert mouth when she's sleepy, doesn't she?" Hartwell said.

"Her mother was worse," Trentwood muttered.

Mary's eyes narrowed. "I don't think I like this, you two talking to one another."

Hartwell shrugged. "Well, like I said, it isn't glamorous, just an accident between siblings, one who has a penchant for dramatics."

"So you did that to yourself?" Mary's tone was deadpan.

"No, Mary, my sister did it to me five years ago, are you going to let me tell the story or not?" Hartwell snapped. "I was asking for a cup of tea and she was having one of her fits and she threw the entire teapot at my head. It was one of Mother's favorites, very delicate bone china, absolutely shattered into shards against my thick skull, cutting my face and making me as I am today."

He glared at Mary and wondered where Trentwood had gone. He waited for her to voice her apologies for being so rude, or for Trentwood to admonish her into doing so. Instead, he watched her study his face, a wrinkle in her brow.

"Yes, what is it?" he said, gruffly.

"Does it still hurt?" Mary asked.

What an odd question. Did it still hurt? It had been years ago; of course it didn't still hurt. Sometimes, perhaps, it hurt emotionally, not that he would ever admit such a thing.

There was something so appalling about knowing that his sister had thrown glass at his face because he had teased her about, well, who even knows what? To this day, she had never apologized for it. Her husband had entered the parlor and scolded her for hours while the surgeon stitched his face back together, but she never budged.

This was the sister Hartwell fought to protect. It still boggled his mind that he went to such lengths for a woman who only wanted him when she absolutely needed him. But unlike dear Florence, pardon, Lady Kirkham, family meant something to Hartwell, and he was damned if he was going to let his nephew be victim to his mother's stupidity.

"Sometimes it does, but not in the way you think," Hartwell said, finally. He stiffened when Mary rose with the obvious intent to cross the room to meet him.

"Might I?" she said.

"Might you what?" He wanted to hear her say it.

She cleared her throat and averted her gaze for a second before her curiosity got the better of her, and she admitted, "Might I touch it? It looks quite painful, but you say otherwise."

"And your father?"

Waving her hand as she crossed the room, she said in an offhand manner, "He comes and goes when he chooses. He left as soon as you said how you got the scar. His attention span is very short these days."

"Doesn't it bother you that he's here?"

"Not so much anymore," she mused, raising her fingers near to his face.

She hesitated, and Hartwell could feel how close she was to touching him. He held his breath, noting the way she studied his skin carefully, as if it were a piece of fine embroidery. And perhaps it was, in a way. He, in turn, made note of a little dimple in her chin and a dusting of light freckles across her nose. Her dark hair had highlights of red and blonde, and the white ribbon that held her loose hair from her face was tied in a simple bow.

That was Mary: practical, simple, elegant. She read books that made his head spin and argued logic until he could do nothing but smile, caught in his own game. She was pretty without meaning to be, and inquisitive to the point of annoyance.

And yet she just stood there, not touching his face even though she had said that was what she wanted to do. Hartwell winced. She wasn't looking at his scarred eye anymore, she was looking at him. Really looking at him. As if she could see straight into his mind. And perhaps she could, with Trentwood's help.

"Where is your father?" Hartwell said, his voice rasping. That had been dangerously close to an actual crack in his voice, something he hadn't done since he was in school.

Mary shrugged, redirecting her attention to his scar. She ran her fingers along the smoothed skin with feathering strokes. Hartwell shivered and closed his eyes. "Do you know, I've never done anything like this."

"Touch a man's face?"

She was quiet for a second too long. Hartwell opened his eyes in time to see her stand on tiptoe and brush her lips against the corner of his mouth. She was warm, and sweet, and he ached to be free of his responsibilities to his sister so he could do as he wanted.

"I've decided to marry Jasper."

Hartwell nodded, even though she wasn't making sense.

"Father will leave if I marry Jasper. He's always hated Jasper."

"Don't you think it might be better if you were to leave on good terms with, er, a ghost?"

"I don't know how," Mary said, throwing her hands in the air. She stepped back from him so she could pace the length of the room. "He keeps telling me I haven't asked the right questions, that I need to make decisions for myself, and he's only here to guide me but how am I to know when I need his guidance?"

"When did he appear to you?"

"The day of his funeral. Aunt Durham was with me, but she didn't see him. No one has seen or heard him until you came."

"Lucky me."

Mary spun on her heel. "I wonder if I married you, I wonder if he would leave on good terms then?"

Hartwell's mouth dropped open. She was teasing him. She had to be.

"But then," Mary continued, frowning as she resumed pacing, "that would mean you would have to propose, which you haven't."

"No, I haven't." All right, she wasn't teasing him, but perhaps she wasn't entirely serious, either.

"And I'm not the sort to beg."

"You've never seemed the sort."

"Why haven't you proposed?" Mary said, stopping again. "If only to spite Jasper? I've seen the way the two of you bicker. You don't like him; you could have countered his offer just to make him angry the way you have before."

"And use you as a toy in a child's argument? Thank you, no. I handle my matters differently. You will make your decision without any knowledge of what I think about it. You have one father in your life, you certainly don't need two." Hartwell shuddered at the thought. "And the last thing I want is to be likened to your father."

Mary smiled at that. "You are similar to him, though. My father was always smiling when my mother was alive. Smiling and making her laugh. They laughed a lot together."

"That sounds like a happy marriage."

Her smile turned shaky, and Hartwell kicked himself mentally for obviously triggering a painful memory. "Alex, I don't know what to do. I don't know if Jasper is the man I thought he was a year ago. I don't know if I'm the same woman I was a year ago."

"I'd wager to say he isn't, and you aren't, by virtue of life happening in the time between."

"Is my aunt really a blackmailer?"

Hartwell shook his head, trying to keep up with Mary's disjointed conversation. "There is evidence to suggest it, yes."

"Does Jasper know?" she whispered.

Hartwell hesitated. He had gone this far, telling her that Mrs. Durham was suspected, and there was evidence to support it.

Might as well tell her all and be done with it. He hadn't liked the squirming feeling that had teased the back of his mind while keeping secrets from her. Hartwell nodded. "Steele found the evidence."

Mary's sigh marked the deflation of her spirit. Her shoulders slumped, and her expression crumpled. The woman had withstood the death of both her parents, Hartwell's invasion of her home, Steele's insinuations, and oh yes, the presence of her ghostly father. Yet when faced with the idea that her ridiculous aunt was the cause of all her troubles? That was when she decided to fall apart? For that was what it seemed to Hartwell. She hugged herself, trembling.

"Why would she?" Mary said. "You're lying."

"Why on earth would I? What can I gain of it?"

"I don't know, I've thought it irregular from the start that you, a well-known London barrister, would come all the way out here to silence some country blackmailer, if that were even the case!"

"Mary, you saw the letters."

"You could have written them."

"They were in a woman's hand."

"Your sister could have written them." Mary flailed her hands as she spoke, an indication of her roughshod emotions. "This entire thing could be a ruse to blackmail me!"

Hartwell sighed. "You're beginning to sound paranoid."

"My father is haunting me, I don't think I can get more paranoid than this!"

With his eyes narrowed, Hartwell crossed his arms over his chest. "All right then, why would I want to blackmail you?"

She waved away his question. "Why would my aunt want to blackmail your sister?"

He winced.

"You have no reason?"

"None you would like to hear."

"Alexander Hartwell, might I remind you, I am being haunted by my father," Mary ground out. "I think I can handle whatever it is you don't wish to tell me."

With a mocking bow, Hartwell said, "A thousand pardons, I simply wished to protect your delicacy, but I see I was mistaken."

"You were indeed," she retorted, "do I look as though I'm concerned with delicacies at the moment?"

In truth, she did not. Mary was livid, but looked delightful dressed only in that scandalous red robe and pristine white nightgown. She had no idea what she was doing, what dangers she invited by standing barefoot in his bedroom, her hair tumbling over her shoulder, her eyes snapping at him in annoyance.

Why was it that at the moments she was most displeased with him, he was most pleased with her? Very inopportune.

"I think your uncle had a *tendre* with my sister." Hartwell kept his voice flat, mimicking impartiality though he seethed at the idea his sister had brought this upon herself. All that work, all that detection, for what? To discover his sister deserved it?

Suddenly, a chill ran down Hartwell's back. Who was the father of his nephew?

Both Sir Kirkham and Mr. Durham were towheaded, with bright, laughing eyes. Mr. Durham was rather more thin and scholarly-seeming than Kirkham, but that hadn't seemed to have stopped his athleticism.

"My poor aunt," Mary whispered. "To lose her husband in so many ways." It seemed too much for her. She hid her face in her hands. "And here I've been so annoyed by her ridiculous ways. For her to suffer silently!"

"Don't romanticize her," Hartwell said, his tone cold. "Mary, she's a blackmailer, and she's never silent. About anything. Except this, it seems."

Mary just stared at Hartwell. Next thing he knew, she was in his arms, crying softly into his shoulder. He gathered her close the way he would his nephew, holding her against his heart. He ran his fingers through her hair, marveling at how soft the strands were even as they tangled. He tightened his hold on her when she slowly lifted her arms to reciprocate the embrace.

"You've no idea how sorry I am it is your aunt and my sister doing this to one another," Hartwell whispered into her hair.

Mary mumbled something against his shoulder. He shifted so he could hear her better.

"Life is difficult enough without us being cruel to one another." She paused. "Will you give me time to ask my aunt to stop what she is doing? To give her the chance to see the error of her ways?"

Hartwell nodded, glad to hear how even her voice sounded. Soon he would have to let her go, despite how nice it felt to have her in his arms. Soon she would regain her sense of propriety. She would blush and not look him in the eye. Soon they would have to go their separate ways, perhaps never to see one another again.

Mary tried to step away from Hartwell, but his arm stiffened, preventing her from moving. She made the mistake of frowning up at him, of turning her hazel eyes at him.

When she had kissed him, it had been curious, chaste, innocent. When he kissed her, there was of course a hint of curiosity, as there must always be with a first kiss.

Yet it was blended with a touch of sadness, a whisper of goodbye, a breath of passion, a pull of desperation. He cradled her face in his hands gently, giving her the option to leave him. She did not. The kiss deepened into a proper goodbye. Breathless and heady. They fell away from one another gasping.

"That," he began.

"Was," she agreed.

"Completely inappropriate!" Trentwood snapped.

Mary leaped away from Hartwell, bashing her elbow against the corner of the washing table.

"Oh, don't try to play the innocent, Marianne Ryan Trentwood, I saw everything. You'll have to marry him now. You know that, of course."

Hartwell rubbed his forehead. The headache, it seemed, was returning. Or perhaps it was simply an indication that Trentwood's opinion of him was falling, no, plummeting. "With all due respect, it's impolite to spy, sir."

A gust of wind that must have been Trentwood shoved Hartwell onto the bed and pinned him there. "It's impolite to be seducing a man's daughter before his very eyes!"

"He wasn't seducing me," Mary said, though her tone seemed to wonder if that was exactly what Hartwell was doing, and it only took Trentwood's saying it for her to realize it.

"I wasn't seducing her," Hartwell said firmly. He repeated himself for emphasis. "I was saying goodbye."

"Goodbye?" The Trentwoods said in unison.

"I will take the morning train to London. You asked me, Mary, to give you time to work on Mrs. Durham, so I shall. Think of it as my wedding present to you." Hartwell refused to look at Mary. He didn't want to know which emotion held her captive: disappointment, anger, or betrayal.

"So you'd seduce my daughter in your bedroom at an unholy hour of night and then leave her?" If Trentwood had been alive and visible, Hartwell imagined every vein in his body would have stood in relief against the surface of his skin, he sounded so outraged.

"As I said before: I won't influence your daughter's decision. She must decide for herself whether Steele is her match. Unlike some people, I don't play games with the lives of others."

"You watch your tongue, boy, or I will possess you and walk you right off a cliff!" Trentwood said.

"Father!" Mary breathed, wringing her hands, "You wouldn't dare! Think of what people would say. They might call me a witch!"

Almost immediately the pressure that kept Hartwell plastered to his bed lifted. With a weak cough, he rolled to his side. "Thank you, sir, for not killing me."

To Hartwell's surprise, he heard Trentwood chuckle. "And you call my daughter an odd duck."

That seemed to wake Mary out of her stupor. "Just how often do you watch us?"

"The more appropriate question, Marianne, would be how often do I not watch you?"

Mary shivered as the clock in the hall struck five.

"So then," Hartwell said, "what do we do now?"

"Do you intend to press charges against my aunt?" Mary said.

Hartwell nodded, holding her gaze with his own.

"She's my aunt. She's the only family I have. If you press charges, I will have no one, Alex."

"You will have Jasper," he reminded her.

Mary backed up to the bedroom door. "I will have no one," she said. "Please, give me time." She left him alone, as it were, and he listened to her pad to her bedroom and shut the door. Hartwell heard her crawl into bed, the wooden frame creaking beneath her as she settled under her blankets. He wondered how long, on average, it took her to fall asleep. Was she an insomniac?

There was one final question Hartwell had for Trentwood, and he knew the ghost was still nearby because his head ached something fierce. "If you can possess someone, why not possess Mrs. Durham and be done with it?"

"You think I haven't tried?" Trentwood's voice was low, borderline depressed. "You think I haven't tried possessing everyone in the house just to see if I could? You're the only one."

Hardly comforting. "Why is that?"

"I daresay because you are the sanest one in the house. Ophelia, in comparison, is the least. I can't read her thoughts, access her dreams, nothing. She is a painting to me. I watch her, I wonder about her, I know nothing of her, only what I know from her past. She is dangerous, Alexander Hartwell. Don't let her get my child."

Hartwell's headache lifted, an inconsequential relief when compared to the fear he had to swallow upon hearing Trentwood's threatening tones. "Of course, sir."

THIRTY-FOUR

IN WHICH MRS. DURHAM GIGGLES

IT HAD OCCURRED TO Mrs. Durham as she dragged an unconscious Steele out of sight that perhaps she was walking down a path she would regret. She allowed the thought to occur to her, allowed it to bounce around in her mind, and then dismissed it with nary a sigh.

Of course this was a path she regretted taking. She had regretted this path the moment she knew she couldn't have children all those years ago. It was the same moment Henry's eyes had deadened; the same moment his caresses became rough scrapes and prods. She was no longer his wife. She had become his medical test subject.

She had submitted, of course, because she had loved him.

Mrs. Durham let Steele's head bounce against a loose rock just because she could. A low moan escaped his lips, but he did not wake.

Henry had claimed he did such experiments because he cared for her, he wanted to have a child with her, he wanted to see his family name continue. How was Mrs. Durham to know he was performing experiments of another kind with other women? Women such as the lovely Lady Kirkham?

With a low grunt, she tossed Steele's feet behind a bush, retrieved the lantern, and studied her handiwork. The bleeding had stopped, thankfully. Mrs. Durham abhorred the messy stuff. His fancy London clothes were forever ruined, no doubt, and he lay in the weeds and mud, head lolled to the side, mouth slack. In fact, Steele would have made a very convincing inebriated beggar.

Mrs. Durham squinted at the manor house, following a line of sight. Steele was nowhere to be seen, as far as she could tell. She wiped her hands on her skirts. Hiding Steele away had been a far dirtier job than poisoning her husband, but someone had to do it.

It had been too easy, discovering her husband's betrayal. Henry had gotten lazy about keeping his infidelity a secret. How could he have thought she had missed those smoldering looks across the table when Lady Kirkham deigned to dine with them, being that she was "such an old friend," and all that? How quickly Lady Kirkham had forgotten she had been the friend of the long-dead Mrs. Trentwood, and not Mrs. Durham.

How had Henry not seen, not felt, the way Mrs. Durham's heart shattered every time he made an excuse to escort Lady Kirkham home, though she had her servants and private carriage. It had been the *way* Henry had handed Lady Kirkham into the carriage, the *way* his hand had lingered at the small of her back, the *way* he had caressed her hand, which had heightened Mrs. Durham's alarm.

Mrs. Durham had recognized those gestures. Those gestures had belonged to her.

But that had been months ago, before Henry had died. She wiped a traitorous tear from her eye. And now to figure out how, exactly, to explain Steele's disappearance.

"You don't think this is going to work, do you, Ophelia?" a man's voice said.

Mrs. Durham twitched. "Henry?" she said, swinging the lantern around to catch sight of whomever it was who spoke.

"You need to let the past be, Ophelia," the voice said.

The voice didn't belong to Henry. Henry's voice was higher, more manic. Or was that simply her memory of his death, when he had begged for relief from the effects of the poison? Mrs. Durham set her mouth into a thin line.

"I cannot stop," she said.

"Then I will stop you," came the disembodied reply. The voice was familiar, but she couldn't place it. Not that it mattered. Her plan was foolproof.

A high-pitched giggle escaped her lips. "Try, if you like."

Mrs. Durham returned to the manor house, depositing the lantern to the front table. She climbed the stair to her bedroom, rather, her sister's bedroom, peeling her gloves from her hands finger by finger.

As she pulled her nightgown over her head, Mrs. Durham wondered about the last letter she had sent. Hopefully it had reached Lady Kirkham in time. Hopefully Lady Kirkham was so distraught by the contents, she was packing her bags at that very moment to journey to Compton Beauchamp.

Mrs. Durham smiled. She was well on her way to achieving her goal. Her movements slowing from fatigue, she said her prayers, climbed into bed, and fell into a peaceful slumber.

The following morning, Mrs. Durham arrived at the breakfast table to find Mary eating alone, looking more dejected than usual. Her hair was pulled back haphazardly, and her bleary eyes betrayed the fact that she had gotten little sleep. She wore her customary black dress, but it was wrinkled to the point of disgrace.

Mary was odd, but never careless. Something was amiss.

"Where are our guests?" Mrs. Durham asked as if she hadn't any idea, and helped herself to a plate of bacon and toast.

Mary slurped her coffee, no doubt because she knew it would make Mrs. Durham's toes curl. So gauche. So uncivilized. Henry used to do the very same thing every morning, even after she scolded him.

"Alex has left for London. Apparently he has learned what he needed to learn." Mary paused to study Mrs. Durham's expression.

Mrs. Durham concentrated on seeming calm, disconnected, having only the barest interest. "How unfortunate. You shall certainly miss his company."

Mary's hands fluttered over her plate. "Yes, well. I knocked on Jasper's door, but didn't hear anything. I suppose he needs sleep."

"You know, you will have to change how you do things now," Mrs. Durham said, taking her seat at Mary's left.

Mary stopped eating to look at Mrs. Durham. "Change how I do things?"

"Yes, of course."

"Of course? No, Aunt, I don't understand you." Mary's voice was strained to the point of breaking. "What do you mean I must change things? And why must I change things now?"

"Don't take that tone of voice with me, young lady. I'm your mother's twin sister, let's not forget that. I was the one with the temper, you'll remember."

Mary nodded, her eyes wide. Mrs. Durham hoped Mary was remembering the time when she had accidentally, or so she claimed, spilled all of her expensive Parisian *eau de toilette* on the Persian rug. That rug had absorbed the scent so thoroughly, it had tormented her for months. Mr. Durham, in turn, had chided her for being so careless.

Mrs. Durham had caught Mary unawares and boxed her ears until her entire face was red, her body quivering. Mary had been eight-years-old only, but she had the tendency to tell falsehoods already. Mrs. Durham had been determined to beat the idea out of her, and to this day, she liked to congratulate herself on a job well done.

Mary was watching Mrs. Durham, waiting for an answer, the little chit.

"You're to marry Mr. Steele, are you not?" Mrs. Durham said.

"Well I, that is, I hadn't..."

"Of course you are. Let me tell you, Marianne, there are things men will say because they think they are right, and most of the time, they are. But remember this, Marianne, above all things: you have only one family. Your husband has no call to be loyal to you, unless he makes the choice."

Mary's mouth sagged open.

"He will tell you lies, about your family especially, in the hopes you will turn on them."

"This is hardly the sort of thing a newly engaged woman wants to hear, Aunt Ophelia."

Mrs. Durham pointed her knife at Mary. "You listen when I speak to you."

At this point, Mary rose from her seat, apparently done with her half-eaten plate of food. "I think I'd like to check on Jasper after all. Pray excuse me."

Ah yes, Mrs. Durham thought with a wry frown, *go down one path expecting Mary to follow, and she will always do the opposite.* Oh well. That was the benefit of being older, wiser, more clever... she could always readjust. "Are you certain he is in his bedroom? I thought I saw him taking a walk earlier."

"Really?" Mary said, frowning as she left to peer out of the library window. "I can't see him. Do you know which direction he was taking?"

Mrs. Durham made a show of seeming hesitant by looking askance at Mary and stuttering over her words. "To be sure, I hadn't thought of it at the time, but it did seem as though he was walking to Compton Beauchamp. Now that I think about it, he had a satchel with him."

Mary's laugh was shaky. "Whatever are you talking about?"

Really, it was too easy. "We had been talking last night about families, and the topic of Mr. Hartwell's unfortunate business with his sister came up, and Mr. Steele, or so it appeared to me, was so disturbed by the news that it seems he has returned to London to help Mr. Hartwell."

Mrs. Durham watched Mary closely to determine what she knew. Those two meddling men had done their part in ruining her plans by appearing and asking questions. She had no idea why Hartwell would leave. He seemed as stubborn as anyone she knew, including herself, which was a feat. Mrs. Durham wouldn't mourn the loss of his presence.

But Mary seemed distressed. Far too distressed that Hartwell had left. And there was no way she could know that Steele was in her garden, nursing a head wound. Mrs. Durham had checked on him as soon as she had dressed, making sure to tie his hands and feet together before he woke.

In fact, Steele had roused mere minutes after Mrs. Durham had completed her final knot, just as she was tying a piece of cloth over his mouth. He was very alive, and very angry. Thank goodness he had been too weak to do more than thrash about on the ground, no doubt slinging insults at her through the cloth that gagged him.

Young men had no respect for their elders these days. It really was such a tragedy.

With this knowledge in mind, Mrs. Durham wondered just what it was that had Mary so upset. What had Hartwell said to her before he left?

Petit-Ange scurried along the floor at the hem of Mrs. Durham's dress. Mrs. Durham scooped him up so she could rub her frustration into the spot behind his ears. Mary knew something. She had to. Mary kept glancing at her with a slight frown puckering her brow. And she kept opening her mouth as if she wanted to say something, but thought better of it.

And what about the way she kept looking to the garden, as if she knew, impossibly, that Steele lay there, his pulse growing weaker, his moans getting softer?

What was Mrs. Durham to do? She had plans, plans that she would not allow to be spoiled by the likes of Mary, of all people.

One way or another, the Kirkham baby was going to be hers.

THIRTY-FIVE

IN WHICH HARTWELL DEPARTS

THE WEATHER WAS BALMY, a bit misty but pleasant, as Hartwell walked the half-mile to Compton Beauchamp. He had his satchel in hand, his hat atop his head, and was doing his best to ignore Trentwood's voice, who followed him the entire way.

"You can't be serious about leaving my daughter," was how Trentwood notified Hartwell to his presence.

Hartwell jumped, almost dropping his satchel in a puddle of mud. He scrambled, catching it just in time though he had to fall to his knees in the puddle. "Really, Mr. Trentwood, this is getting to be ridiculous."

"Yes, yes, you and Mary seem to think I ought to carry a bell with me. Ought I clear my throat before speaking?"

Eyes narrowed, Hartwell stood and brushed off what mud he could. "That would help, I'm sure."

"Very well then." Trentwood cleared his throat. "You can't be serious about leaving my daughter alone with that woman."

Hartwell inhaled deeply. He counted to twenty. Calming down was his only option; he had no way to show his frustration with a ghost. Nor did he want to try showing his frustration, if the ghost had the ability to possess him, as it seemed Trentwood did.

"Mr. Trentwood, Mary isn't alone, she has Steele, and Pomeroy. Certainly they will keep an eye on Mrs. Durham."

That seemed to silence Trentwood for a while, because it was a full ten minutes before Hartwell heard anything else. In the meantime, he was able to admire the countryside, something he hadn't had a chance to do while at the manor house.

Again he was struck by the green elegance of the area. He wondered if the Browns were nearby, if they had wondered what had become of him after depositing him at the manor house. Did they think he had lost his mind, purposely entering a house whose mistress thought she was haunted?

Well, perhaps he had. That could be the only explanation for why Hartwell now thought he was haunted by the same specter.

Trentwood cleared his throat. "I wish you two would stop wondering if you're mad simply because you can speak to me," he said, sounding irritated. "It makes a man feel unimportant."

"I was just starting to enjoy the sights, Mr. Trentwood," Hartwell muttered. "You wouldn't mind coming back later, perhaps? When I'm alone in my bedroom and no one can see as though it looks like I'm talking to myself?"

"Well, son, you probably will be alone when you return to London, for there's no one there to greet you."

Hartwell stopped walking. "What's that supposed to mean?"

"You'll want to step to the side of the road in about two minutes," Trentwood said, ignoring Hartwell's question. "There's a carriage of people coming your way."

Frowning, Hartwell followed Trentwood's advice. What on earth was the ghost talking about? Hadn't Mary said that no one came to visit her? That the people who had come to her father's funeral had been people she had never met, people who hadn't bothered to help in her time of need? Who, but for Hartwell and Steele, would want to come to such a back of beyond place?

He had his answer soon enough.

A carriage careened down the road at breakneck speed. The horses frothed at the mouth, their sides heaving under the whippings of the driver. There was little luggage, so at first he thought it was some London idiot having a bit of fun down a country road.

Then the curtain of the carriage window flapped open. Hartwell saw, quite clearly, his mother and sister clinging to one another, the baby between them.

Across from them sat a fainted nursemaid, who flopped about the carriage in an almost comical fashion. Hartwell and his mother shared a moment of shocked recognition. Then the curtain flapped shut and they were gone, around a corner and down a slight hill.

He imagined the carriage shuddering along through the green lane. He thought he heard the frustrated whinnies of the horses as they were jerked to a stop, gravel and dead leaves flying up beneath their hooves as they dug the ground.

Hartwell was halfway to the manor house before he realized he had dropped his satchel along the way. The carriage was at the high wrought iron gates. The driver was arguing with his mother, saying he deserved more than his usual fare for such unusual demands to get to the manor house at the risk of his horses and his life.

Hartwell paused in his sprint to kiss his mother's cheek and gasp that he would have a word or two with her. He checked the fainted maid, righting her from her toppled position at the bottom of the carriage.

His sister was not there. He looked at the manor house and saw the upset trail of gravel that belied her flight. His sister had always been lightfooted, even as a child. He wasn't surprised that, even saddled with a baby, she managed to run to the house, probably dressed to the nines in her whale-boned bodice, smart bustle, and one of those ridiculous little hats that women wore these days.

This was one of the many times Hartwell was sad to be right. He reached the front door just in time to see his hysterical sister handing her baby to a beaming Mrs. Durham.

"Florence," he shouted, "what are you doing?"

"Don't worry, Mr. Hartwell," Mrs. Durham called to him, "everything is quite all right now that they are here."

Hartwell reached the front door, gasping for air. Everything was as he had left it not an hour ago, which made logical sense, of course. But his world had been upended.

There was the worn rug that he had ruined, when he stood there soaking wet with a shivering Mary in his arms. There was the side table with the silver salver, long-since cleaned of the results of Mary's upset stomach. There were the typical pastorals hanging by wire that decorated every manor house, and the miniatures of family long since passed.

Everything about this manor house brought Mary to his mind, even as he advanced on Mrs. Durham with his nephew in her hands.

Where was Mary? What had Mrs. Durham done to her? And where was Steele? Did neither of them know what was happening at the front of the house? Were the newly-engaged already so stupid with affection and love that they had forgotten there were bigger issues at stake? Why was no one stopping Mrs. Durham from taking the baby?

Unthinking, he reached for his nephew.

Mrs. Durham hissed—she actually hissed—at Hartwell, shielding the baby from his grasping fingers.

"Mr. Hartwell," she said, "your sister has entrusted him to me." She backed into the house, her eyes shifting from one sibling to the other. "Florence, do come in," she said, tittering, "you look positively exhausted."

"Indeed, I am," Lady Kirkham said. "Thank you for offering your home to us as a refuge, Ophelia. You've no idea how trying these times are!"

Hartwell bit the inside of his mouth to keep from screaming. What a fool his sister was. What a trusting, idiotic fool.

Thirty-Six

In Which the Family Descends

Mary sat in the library, hands resting in her lap. After a moment of staring at the locked library door, she began to tap her fingers against her skirts. Mrs. Durham had locked her in the library not five minutes ago, and she was beginning to feel rather peeved about it.

Where in the world had she gotten a key to the library in the first place? And where was Pomeroy, or her father, when Mary needed them?

With nothing better to do, she began sifting through the books, fuming all the while.

"You're going to have to change the way you do things now." She mimicked Mrs. Durham in a nasal tone, a sneer curling her lip. She shoved two books onto an inexplicably straight shelf. She backed away from the bookshelf and pivoted on her heel so she could study the library in its entirety.

All the bookshelves were righted. None of them sagged, none of them were dusty. The library looked as it had when she had first fallen in love with it as a child: well-used, yes, but orderly. Mary smiled, hugging a book to her chest.

She bit her lip to keep from laughing as she realized that everything was going to be okay. Yes, it would take time to convince her aunt to let her out, and more time to convince her to stop blackmailing Lady Kirkham. But it was time well-spent, wasn't it?

Mary jumped when Trentwood cleared his throat.

"You can't say I didn't warn you about my arriving," he said, waving a finger at her. "I distinctly cleared my throat this time."

Relief flooded Mary and she smiled. "If you were alive I would hug you. The oddest things have been happening lately."

"Odder than my existence?"

Her lips quivered. "Quite near, I should say."

"I suppose Mrs. Durham locked you in here?"

"Of course."

"Where did she get a key?"

Mary threw her hands in the air. "I wish I knew! Alex is gone, I can't seem to find Jasper—I came in here because Aunt Durham said she thought she heard his voice—and now I seem to be stuck in here." A book caught her eye, and she snatched it from the table with a squeal of delight. "This was mother's favorite! I thought it was lost."

When Trentwood appeared at her side, Mary was overwhelmed by warmth, rather than the cold which usually came along with being too near him. She glanced at him, startled to find him practically radiating golden tones.

"Your mother was an odd little thing," he murmured, staring at the worn copy of Greek mythology. "You're much like her."

Mary's brows rose. "Thank you?"

A clattering at the front door of the house made them turn.

"Now who would be visiting at this unseemly hour?" Mary mused. "Father, I don't suppose you could…" Her voice trailed off as she watched Trentwood walk through the door. She shivered. She didn't suppose she would ever get used to the sight of that.

Another clattering at the bay window made Mary turn around to see a hand waving frantically. She inched closer, thinking the hand looked a bit solid to be Trentwood's, and in any case, wouldn't he walk through the door once his curiosity about the commotion at the front door was satisfied?

Then she saw the ridiculous sight of Pomeroy hopping up and down, trying to catch a glimpse of her in the library. The bottom of the bay window was just out of his line of sight, though he was a tall man. The sight of him jumping to reach her was cheering, both because of how silly it made him seem and because it was so pleasant to know he had searched her out.

"Miss Mary, are you all right?" he said, panting, as she unlocked the window and pushed it open. His white hair was tussled by the wind and misty rain. His jacket flapped open, and she saw a pistol tucked in his waistcoat.

"Pomeroy!" Mary said, pointing at the pistol. "What on earth do you have that for? Where did you get such a thing?"

His expression, having brightened upon seeing she was not hurt, turned grim. "Mr. Steele is missing, Miss Mary, and I think your aunt has something to do with it."

Mary narrowed her eyes and brushed back a lock of hair that had fallen from her haphazard chignon. "Explain yourself. My aunt is distraught, yes, and perhaps even a blackmailer. But she wouldn't hurt anyone."

Unbidden came the memory of her aunt boxing her ears after spilling a favorite perfume. And the way she used to carry on, screaming at Mary after her mother had died for being a spoiled brat. But those were isolated incidences, weren't they?

Those moments had been when Mary had deserved a sort of schooling. Surely they hadn't been the result of a hidden mean streak in her aunt.

Pomeroy waited in the rain while Mary thought. When she looked at him, her expression troubled, he said, "Mrs. Durham and Mr. Steele left for a walk to talk privately. I checked his bedroom this morning, Miss Mary. He did not sleep in his bed."

Mary's breath caught in her throat. It was as Mrs. Durham had said. Steele had left her.

Something in her expression must have betrayed her, for Pomeroy rushed, "His belongings are still in the room. He hasn't left the manor house, I don't think."

At that moment, Trentwood returned. "You will never guess who has come. Oh good, Pomeroy found you."

Mary heard Hartwell's voice shouting, and she whirled around. "What's going on out there?"

"It seems Hartwell's sister has deigned to grace our humble home," Trentwood said.

"A carriage of ladies arrived at the front gate this morning," Pomeroy said, "bringing with them a baby and a fainted nursemaid. They must be relations of Mr. Hartwell, for he was chasing them down. By foot!" Pomeroy grinned, looking most impressed. "The man has gumption, Miss Mary."

Mary looked from Trentwood, who stood at the still-locked library door, to Pomeroy. "Well, I must get out there. If Lady Kirkham is here, who knows what Aunt Ophelia will do? I assume Alex told you, Pomeroy, that my aunt has been blackmailing her."

Pomeroy shifted his weight uncomfortably. "I might have known a thing or two about it, yes. I might have found some drafted letters and placed them so Mr. Steele could find them."

"Pomeroy," Mary breathed. "You knew all along? And you didn't tell me?" Her voice rose to a shriek.

He winced. "You were grieving, and the master made it quite clear before he died that I was to distract you. Make certain that you didn't wallow, as it were."

Oh, now that was rich.

Her dearly departed father hadn't wanted her to wallow, and so he instructed his trusted servant to distract her. No doubt that was why, upon seeing Hartwell, Pomeroy had insisted Hartwell retrieve her that first day she had attempted to escape to Wayland's Smithy. No doubt that was why Pomeroy had agreed to both Hartwell and Steele staying, though they hadn't the room, and no doubt made his chores all the more difficult for having to look after more people.

How kind of her father to not want her to wallow after his death. How unkind of him, then, to haunt her! How was she supposed to avoid wallowing if he was always there to remind her he was gone?

Mary's hands began to shake. The blood in her head roared through her veins. Her shoulders stiffened, and she felt her eye begin to twitch. For a moment, she thought she would have trouble breathing, but then she realized, not only was she breathing, she was gulping down air, trying to calm down.

"Miss Mary?" Pomeroy said, hesitant.

"Did you know, Pomeroy," Mary said, glaring at Trentwood, "that my father is haunting me?"

A pregnant pause from Pomeroy. "I know you think you are being haunted."

"Oh no," Mary snapped, pointing at him, "do not make me out to be mad, Pomeroy. My father is most definitely haunting me. He is standing right here with me. Go on, Father, show him. Do something so he knows you're here."

Trentwood was frowning at Mary, as though for the first time since his death he couldn't read her thoughts. Which seemed about right, for Mary couldn't read her own thoughts; she was so angry she could hardly put two words together without spitting.

"What are you about?" Trentwood said.

"Show him."

Wary, Trentwood lifted a pillow from a chair and threw it out the window at Pomeroy's head. It was a familiar motion to both Mary and Pomeroy; it was the motion most favored by

Trentwood as he lay dying in bed. It was one of the few ways he could voice his frustration in those last days.

Pomeroy stumbled back from the house, his face ashen, the pillow forgotten in the mud at his feet.

"So you see, Pomeroy, I am not mad. My father haunts me."

Pomeroy nodded.

"Now would you be so kind as to help me out of here? I would risk jumping from the window myself, but I'm not entirely dressed for the occasion," Mary said, motioning to her stiff, high-necked bodice and layers upon layers of skirts complete with bustle.

Apparently too shaken to speak, Pomeroy returned to the window and held out his arms for Mary.

"And what shall I do?" Trentwood said, watching as Mary dragged a chair to the window so she could climb over the ledge.

"Find Jasper for me. He's here somewhere, and he might be hurt. And then make certain my aunt doesn't hurt anyone else, if she has a mind to." Mary clung to the sides of the window, her knuckles white. She hadn't done anything so unladylike since she had been too young to be considered a lady. How she hoped Pomeroy would catch her, or at the very least, break her fall.

"You aren't really going to jump from the window!" Trentwood said, rushing to her side. "You could break your neck!"

The wind burst into the library, fluttering the pages of books not tucked into the shelves. It whipped Mary's hair free from the few bobby pins she had in place. She shook her head, freeing her eyes from her mess of dark hair. Her skirts tugged at her legs, cajoling her to jump. Her hazel eyes met Trentwood's pale ones.

"If you're so concerned, be a good ghost and make sure I don't break my neck." With that, she dropped from the window ledge. The library fell silent.

Across the room, the doorknob began to turn.

THIRTY-SEVEN

IN WHICH NERVES ARE TESTED

A FAMILIAR CLEARING OF the throat made Hartwell groan inwardly. *Really, Trentwood, you have the most awful timing.*

"Sorry, my boy, can't seem to help it," Trentwood replied, in far too cheerful a manner.

Didn't Trentwood realize his daughter was missing, his sister-in-law a blackmailer, and possibly worse? Where was everyone, anyway? Hartwell still hadn't seen Pomeroy or Steele yet, and that knowledge was grating on his nerves.

"Mary is in the library," Trentwood said. "And of course Ophelia's the blackmailer. Who do you think put it into Pomeroy's head that he ought to make the letters obvious to Steele? Or, better yet, who do you think put it into your mother's head that you ought to come to Compton Beauchamp in the first place?"

"You knew the entire time?" Hartwell hissed.

Lady Kirkham and Mrs. Durham, who were cooing over the baby, stopped to stare at Hartwell.

"Knew what, Alex?" Lady Kirkham said, frowning prettily. She did everything prettily, all the more to annoy Hartwell. Or so he felt. She had her pretty blonde curls with her pretty blue eyes, her pretty blushing cheeks, and her pretty delicate bone structure. He had been the uglier child even before she had mangled his face. Being around her made him feel ugly. Made him want to act ugly.

"Now's not the time, son, rein yourself in," Trentwood warned. "Ophelia's got your nephew, and no matter how much you dislike your sister, you care about the boy."

Hartwell grimaced. "You knew," he faltered, shoving his anger aside to address Lady Kirkham's question without arousing Mrs. Durham's suspicion. What could he say? "You knew where to find me? To find us?"

Lady Kirkham laughed her tinkling laugh. Hartwell had once heard one of her suitors liken it to the sound of diamonds falling. Hartwell had liked the analogy. Diamonds were hard, unforgiving, and entirely too perfect for the everyday.

"Of course I knew where to find you, Alex," Lady Kirkham said, sharing a look with Mrs. Durham that showed just how little she thought of her brother. "I gave you the address, didn't I, then?"

"So you did," Hartwell said between stiff lips. He waited until Mrs. Durham had shifted her wary gaze from him back to the restless baby in her arms before attempting to address Trentwood again. *Where is Mary?*

"Locked in the library," Trentwood said. "Mrs. Durham saw the way she wasn't believing her folderol about Steele leaving last night and convinced her to step into the library."

How did she get a key to Mary's library?

"I can't read her," Trentwood admitted. "She's terrifying."

Which was rather terrifying for Hartwell to hear from a ghost.

"Her thoughts are erratic. She hardly knows herself, and so I can't know her, or guess her intentions."

Hartwell frowned at the way Lady Kirkham was encouraging Mrs. Durham to play with the baby's adorable little fingers and funny little toes. How had his sister come to think of this manor house, of all the places in the world she could have escaped to—Scotland, Ireland, Italy! For the love of all that was holy, why didn't she skip off to Italy?

No, Italy would have made sense, and sense had never been his sister's strong point. She could have gone somewhere safe, as he had insisted in his written replies. Instead, she came to the very place she ought to have avoided. Hartwell had half a mind to leave Lady Kirkham to her fate with Mrs. Durham. He had half a mind to go back to London and pummel Sir Kirkham for giving his sister so much god-forsaken freedom.

Hartwell felt as though he stood in the very center of a massive storm that threatened to destroy everything he loved.

So much for Mary's plea that Hartwell allow her the opportunity to stop her aunt. So much for any chance they could have had together. Mary being who she was, she would of course feel guilty if Steele had been hurt by Mrs. Durham.

She would accept Steele's marriage proposal as an apology, of all things. And even if she didn't, Mary would never entertain feelings for a man who had no qualms in persecuting her aunt in order to protect his family.

Why did Mary have to be so blindly loyal? To the likes of Steele and Mrs. Durham, of all people?

Focus man, Mrs. Durham has your nephew.

Hartwell knew he could get the baby away from Mrs. Durham. That is, he hoped he could, without hurting the babe or his sister in the process. A plan formed. Hartwell would retrieve the baby, somehow, and get his sister out of harm's reach. He would take his family back to London, away from this mad manor house.

At which point, Hartwell would bring Mrs. Durham to trial for attempted kidnapping, and several counts of blackmail, and send her to the gaol. Or Bedlam. That would be more fitting.

Which meant that unless Mary cared for him, more than he thought she did, she would marry Steele, and he would never see her again. It would have to take a very great amount of affection, bordering on love, in fact, for a woman to forgive a man for sending her only relative to a life of misery for the rest of her days.

The ghostly voice belonging to Trentwood had been silent for longer than was to Hartwell's liking. He shook his head, realizing he had trailed Mrs. Durham and Lady Kirkham unconsciously as they wandered toward the library. Perhaps Mary could help them. Perhaps Trentwood could send Mary the message that they were approaching the library. Perhaps she could grab the baby from Mrs. Durham and flee.

That was a lot of coincidences upon which to rely, but Hartwell was tired. He was beyond tired, he was exhausted. One didn't just bounce back from gabbing all night with a ghost and his daughter, then walk a mile, only to sprint back propelled by horror.

Trentwood, where have you gone? If thought voices could sound annoyed, Hartwell figured his was the very definition. *Send Mary the message that we're approaching her.*

With quite the embarrassed sound of clearing his throat, Trentwood admitted, "I can't."

Hartwell looked in the direction of the mirror sharply, where Trentwood's voice came from. *Why not?*

"She's jumped."

"Jumped?" Hartwell cried.

Lady Kirkham glared at him. "Alex, really. You're beginning to embarrass me." She turned to Mrs. Durham, who planted a sickly sweet smile on her pudgy face. "Please tell me he hasn't been doing this the entire time he's been here."

"Oh no," Mrs. Durham simpered, "he's been the definition of a gentleman."

A most unladylike snort escaped Lady Kirkham's lips. After all, she was only the wife of a knight and was allowed an uncouth moment or two. "There's no need to tell falsehoods on my behalf, Ophelia. We both know my brother's never been gentlemanly."

Hartwell itched to respond to his sister's jibes, but was too panicked by Trentwood's terse responses.

What do you mean, she jumped?

"She's determined to rescue Steele," Trentwood spat, "good little fool that she is. Pomeroy told her Steele didn't sleep in his bed last night, and thinks something's happened to him. Something has, of course, but why she feels she needs to save him is beyond me. Jumped right from the bay window into Pomeroy's arms, and they're off searching the gardens for him."

Bile rose in Hartwell's throat as he remembered, clearly, the odd fairy tale Mary told him that day they walked together. She had found her prince to save, then.

Thirty-Eight

In Which We Meet the Babe

The baby's weight in her arms made Mrs. Durham sigh with relief. This was what she had been hoping, wishing, praying for these last months of planning and plotting. This little bit of fifteen pounds that relied on her not dropping it to the floor for its survival. The baby was warm against her breast, and the little white frills that edged his dress seemed to tickle his cheek as he slept.

Mrs. Durham hadn't seen the baby's eyes yet, but she knew the color, just as well as she had known the color of her husband's eyes. This was Henry's child. She knew it. He had the same wrinkle in his brow as he shifted in his sleep, the same way he puckered his lips in earnest concentration. His lovely blond hair shone in the sunlight that streamed through the still-open door, which Hartwell had so rudely slammed open in his pursuit.

"Dear Mr. Hartwell," Mrs. Durham said, blinking dazedly at him, "would you be so kind as to shut the door? The baby will catch cold." She lifted her shoulder to shelter the baby from a breeze that blew through the hallway.

"Indeed, Alex!" Lady Kirkham said, "How could you be so careless? The baby!"

Hartwell spun on his heel and slammed the door shut, rattling the old hinges. He watched the door rather warily for a moment as if he expected it to crumble.

Mrs. Durham bit back a snicker. "Your brother is rough with my sister's home," she said in a spiteful aside to Lady Kirkham. "Do you know he wasn't here more than five minutes when he ruined my dearly departed sister's bell pull? It was the last piece of embroidery Gertrude had worked before her untimely death. Mary was quite inconsolable."

Lady Kirkham shook her head, tsking at her brother.

Hartwell, to his credit, colored and would not meet their eyes.

The baby's little fist grabbed Mrs. Durham's probing finger and she cooed with delight. "What is the little darling's name?"

"Henry, naturally," Lady Kirkham said.

Mrs. Durham reeled back as though snapping free from a tow line. She clutched little Henry to her chest.

"Ophelia," Lady Kirkham said with a nervous chuckle, "you'll smother him."

Her eyes mere slits, Mrs. Durham backed toward the library. "His name is Henry, you say?" Hartwell advanced, and Mrs. Durham's eyes flickered from brother to sister. "Did you hear, Mr. Hartwell? Your sister named him Henry. That was my husband's name, you know. It's a fine name. A strong name." She yanked the little white bonnet off of Henry's curls and rubbed her hand against them. "His curls, so like my Henry's."

"Mrs. Durham," Hartwell said. He had his hand out to her. He sounded as if he was in a cave somewhere. "Mrs. Durham, you must give me the baby now."

"I don't see why," she replied, holding little Henry closer. "He's mine now."

That grabbed Lady Kirkham's attention right quick. "Whatever do you mean? Hand me my child at once, Ophelia."

Mrs. Durham giggled. "Your child? Your child? You mean my child. You gave him to me."

Lady Kirkham swallowed. "I did no such thing."

"You handed him to me," Mrs. Durham insisted, frowning, "and told me to take care of him. He's my Henry. He's my Henry's little Henry. Isn't that right, Mr. Hartwell?"

Hartwell flinched when the baby cried out, having sensed the rising tension in the close, dark hallway.

"Everyone thought I was so stupid, Mr. Hartwell. They thought I wouldn't see how they looked at one another. It truly was a wonder. Did they not realize I could see when she touched the back of his neck? When he spoke to her, his eyes plastered on her lips? The way they stood and sat beside one another, always claiming to be friends?" Mrs. Durham threw her words at Lady Kirkham like daggers, and every one landed with deadly accuracy.

Lady Kirkham staggered back, crashing into the stairwell. "What does she mean? What does she mean?"

"You're a fool if you think I'm giving up my husband's child," Mrs. Durham said. "By rights, it should have been my child. He was my husband, Florence! And you, you were supposed to be my friend."

Her voice broke on the cursed word.

"But you never were, were you? You and my sister, always laughing, having fun, being the flirty fun women I never could be, though I tried so hard, so very hard." Tears streamed down her face. The baby began to cry in her arms. "See how little Henry cries for his father?"

Mrs. Durham's expression hardened.

"Don't cry, my darling. We'll see your papa soon."

THIRTY-NINE

IN WHICH MARY SCRAMBLES

MARY BLINKED AND COUGHED. Pomeroy had broken her fall, to be sure, but not nearly as smoothly as she had hoped. She had tripped on her skirts when she jumped from the window ledge and swallowed a shriek when she went flying at Pomeroy, rather than landing in his outstretched arms. The two of them crashed to the ground with muffled groans.

They lay there, breathing taking up all their concentration.

"Satisfied?" Trentwood said, looming over Mary as she blinked at the cloudy sky. He crossed his arms over his chest, one of his brows raised in amused annoyance.

With a groan, Mary rolled off Pomeroy and crawled to the side of the manor house, where she could pull herself upright. She tested her right ankle, which felt a bit tender.

Pomeroy sat up, rubbing the back of his head. "Oh," he said weakly, looking at the sticky red mess he saw on his fingers.

Mary inhaled sharply. The side of Pomeroy's white head was turning a dark red color. Blood trickled sluggishly from where he had hit a rock in just the right way. She had hurt Pomeroy. All because she had been too stubborn to ask her father for help.

She had to stop the bleeding. She had to get cloth to staunch the blood flow. But she hadn't anything other than what she wore, and she couldn't very well take off her clothing.

"A man's life could be on the line, Marianne," Trentwood snapped, startling Mary from her panicked ruminations. He joined her at the wall, glaring at her dazed expression. "Seems you got the wind and your wits knocked out of you. Stay still."

"What? I—what are you doing?" she gasped as he reached beneath her skirt. A second later she heard a loud ripping noise, and he held half of her petticoat. Her cheeks turned bright red. "You could have asked, at the very least!"

"Lecture me later, Mary," Trentwood said, wrapping the torn fabric around his hand so it made a small wad that he could press against Pomeroy's head. "Tell Pomeroy to put his hand where the cloth is. You need to find Steele."

Mary licked her lips. Pomeroy stared at her, eyes wide, mouth slack from terror. She couldn't really leave him alone with her father, could she? Certainly not when he was so obviously afraid of this invisible hand pressing fabric against his head.

"Mary," Trentwood shouted, "Steele is in the garden and he's hurt. Wake up!"

Jumping, Mary rushed to Pomeroy's side. Yes, right. Now was the time to act. She put her hand where Trentwood's was and felt a chill run the length of her arm. She gritted her teeth and ignored the sensation. "Pomeroy, dear, I need you to hold this."

His pupils were beginning to dilate.

"Pomeroy, I'm going to walk you to the door, and have Mrs. Beeton let you in, and then I'm off to find Jasper, do you understand me?"

Pomeroy's eyes rolled up, trying to see the back of his head where Mary's hand pushed the fabric into his wound. "Your father," he said.

Mary ripped another length of her petticoat so she could tie the wad of fabric in place. "Yes. He's here," she grunted, tugging Pomeroy's arm. She used her entire body weight to leverage him to standing. She ducked beneath his arm to support his falling weight and stumbled along the uneven ground to the kitchen door. "He won't let anything happen to you."

Pomeroy chuckled. "More so than what already has? You always were one to get into scrapes, Miss Mary, but you never hurt anyone else before."

Mouth dropping open, Mary was saved from replying when the door flew open to reveal Mrs. Beeton staring at them with a dripping soup ladle in her hand. A part of Mary recognized the liquid as beef stew, the sort they had been having for two days now, and her stomach turned. When her mother was alive, meals repeated by the month, not the day.

"Miss?" Mrs. Beeton said.

Mary cleared her throat. "Do help Pomeroy, Mrs. Beeton. We've had a slight accident, and I'm off to find Mr. Steele." She deposited the slumping Pomeroy to the nearest chair with Mrs. Beeton's help. She instructed Mrs. Beeton not to enter the main house, for there was something afoot and she didn't want to see anyone else hurt.

Mrs. Beeton was already busy bandaging Pomeroy's head and forcing a glass of whiskey down his throat. "Of course, Miss. Is it Mrs. Durham, Miss? Pomeroy had been telling me he didn't think she was aright."

That comment sent Mary running in the direction of the garden. That was three people, now, warning her about her aunt, and nothing good came of anything said in threes, or so her mother had told her when she was young. She held her skirts high, almost to her knees, as she bounded down the tumbling rock stairs to the overgrown garden.

"Jasper?" she cried. Where was Trentwood when she needed him? What was it he had said? Steele was in the garden. Which garden? The garden, of course, the one they never had to mention by name. The one in which her mother had died.

Mary pressed her lips together as her brows furrowed with determination. This was not to be Steele's last moment on earth, not if she had anything to do with it.

Winding her way through brambles, half-dead rose bushes, and mud puddles, Mary couldn't find Steele. Perspiration beaded on her nose, though it was cold enough she could see her breath in the air. She tripped on a gnarly tree root. Too winded to cry out, she fell on her knees and the palms of her hands, scraping them against dead brambles along the path.

Mary stayed there on the ground, trying to catch her breath. If she didn't slow down, she wouldn't be any use to Steele if she found him. Not if. When. When she found him. She closed her eyes. She gulped air and winced at how it scraped its way down her throat. When she opened her eyes, she realized there was something odd about the mud puddle she had just barely avoided.

It was smaller than the others, and darker, more ominous. It looked like dried blood. "Jasper?" She heard a stifled moan from the other side of the hedge.

Mary crawled around the corner to find Steele propped against a Grecian pedestal, hands and feet tied together, mouth bound. His impeccable hair was matted to the side of his head with the same dried blood that had alerted her to his presence. His eyes were dull as they watched her untie him, and he was shivering uncontrollably.

"How long has she kept you here?" Mary asked, fearing his answer. He threw his arms around her, hugging her tightly.

Mary knew it was from relief at being found, and wanted to reciprocate. He had been through an awful night, if she understood things correctly. Somehow her aunt had cajoled him outside to the garden, the same way she had been cajoled to the library.

"I'm glad I found you," Mary whispered.

Who knew what could have happened if she hadn't found Steele? He shook in her arms. It was almost as if he was holding onto her in order to steady himself.

Mary waited for the rush of affection, relief, passion to overcome her. She waited, and it did not come. Instead, her thoughts returned to the manor house, where Hartwell and his family were with her dangerous aunt.

"Jasper," she said, pulling away from him, "we need to go inside. Now."

FORTY

IN WHICH MARY SCREAMS

HARTWELL FOLLOWED MRS. DURHAM into the library, his eyes not leaving baby Henry. The window in the back of the room was gaping open, leading Hartwell to believe that, yes, Mary had indeed jumped in order to save Steele. He only hoped Mary had landed safely. Perhaps that was why he felt Trentwood's presence. Trentwood knew Mary was safe and so had come to protect him. Yes, that was what Hartwell chose to believe, rather than the nausea-inducing suspicion that Mary had snapped her neck.

Hartwell shook his head. He would find out if Mary was all right after making certain Mrs. Durham no longer had her hands on his nephew. One thing at a time.

"Make her give me my baby back!" Lady Kirkham's smooth voice adopted a dreadful tone that raked across Hartwell's nerves.

"Quiet, Florence," he snapped, "you never care about that baby until he makes you the center of attention, so you can stop with the doting mother act!"

She drew herself up to her full height, which was very nearly Hartwell's height. "How dare you speak to me in such a manner! I am a lady of the realm!"

He rolled his eyes. Enough was enough. "You're the wife of a knight; stop putting on airs you've no right to." Lady of the realm. What nonsense, when it only lasted as long as her husband's life and wouldn't be passed on to his children. Ridiculous.

Lady Kirkham's eyes bugged out and her lips slammed shut as if she had just realized she had swallowed her tongue. Hartwell wished she had. Then he wouldn't have to hear her babble on about how her marriage had pulled the Hartwell name up from the mere, recently-displaced, landed family they were.

"Children, are you bickering again?" came Dame Hartwell's cheerful tones from the hallway. "I always thought you two would grow out of such childishness, but I suppose not." She sauntered into the library, patting Lady Kirkham's cheek along the way.

Dame Hartwell was a small woman, with delicate features and a propensity to smile. Her insignificant stature and overall pleasantness belied the iron pole she had for a spine, and the way her voice could cut through a humid day like a pail of ice water. She wore a gray suit for traveling, which complemented her soft tones nicely: her blue eyes snapped, her gray hair gleamed.

Mrs. Durham had backed up to the open window, where the wind blew fiercely through the sole access point to the interior of the house. She clung to baby Henry, madness alight in her eyes.

"Alexander," Dame Hartwell said, "I told you there was danger in Compton Beauchamp, and you were to put a stop to it."

Hartwell's mouth dropped open. "Excuse me? You said no such thing!"

"I did, I said exactly what Mr. Trentwood asked me to, and yet here we are, with Mrs. Durham—it is Mrs. Durham, isn't it?—with my grandson." Dame Hartwell's clipped London tones seemed to wake Mrs. Durham out of her trance.

"Your grandson?" Mrs. Durham said.

"And my nephew," Hartwell chimed in, much to the apparent annoyance of his mother, who glared at him.

"But he's my son," Mrs. Durham murmured, dabbing a bit of spittle away from Henry's mouth. "He's my little Henry."

Dame Hartwell shook her head. "He's our little Henry. Yours and ours. We neither of us want to see him hurt."

Hartwell closed his eyes against the sight of Mrs. Durham backing ever closer to the open window. When he opened his eyes, she was pulling herself up onto the ledge. He jumped forward, arms out to catch her as she wobbled while finding her balance.

"Henry and I," Mrs. Durham warbled, "are going to visit his father now."

"What do you mean? What can she mean? Alex!" Lady Kirkham cried.

Hartwell's back was to his sister as he and his mother advanced slowly on Mrs. Durham. He imagined Lady Kirkham wringing her hands, tears streaming, being her usual useless self. He allowed the uncharitable thought of mucus dripping from her nose, just because it pleased him in that way of feuding siblings.

Trentwood?

"Right here, my boy," Trentwood said, just to his left.

"So glad you've returned, Mr. Trentwood! I was beginning to think I had imagined you," Dame Hartwell said warmly, though her eyes also never left Mrs. Durham and Henry.

Mrs. Durham's eyes danced from Hartwell to his mother and back. "What are you on about? Mr. Trentwood is dead, as dead as my Henry." She lost her concentration, and though she clenched the side of the window, began to fall backward.

Hartwell heard screams from his mother and sister. He saw the baby flying through the air. He winced at the thud of a body landing five feet to the ground. At the crash of a skull hitting an unfortunately placed rock. Or fortunately, depending on one's perspective.

The sound of Mary, screaming.

FORTY-ONE

IN WHICH MARY MOURNS

LATER, HARTWELL REALIZED TRENTWOOD had snatched the baby from Mrs. Durham's flailing arms, which was how little Henry came to be in Hartwell's hands. He stood in the library, staring at that open window, hearing Mary screaming outside.

"Why would she jump?" Mary kept sobbing.

Hartwell, with a squirming Henry in his arms, moved his right foot and then his left until he stood at the window, staring down at Mary. She rocked back and forth, Mrs. Durham's lifeless body in her arms.

Steele leaned against the manor house, resting his elbows on his knees, his forehead in the palms of his hands. He watched Mary, unblinking.

Mary must have felt Hartwell watching her. She looked up. Her eyes were bloodshot, her hair completely free of any binding or bobby pin. Her hands looked scratched and bloodied, her skirts a tangled mess. The accusations in her flooded eyes made Hartwell step away from the window.

Mary buried her face in the crook between Mrs. Durham's snapped neck and shoulder.

"You should probably go," Trentwood said.

Hartwell's nod was small. He closed his eyes against a tear that threatened to fall, handed Henry to his mother, and walked away.

FORTY-TWO

IN WHICH FAREWELLS ARE SAID

UNLIKE TRENTWOOD'S FUNERAL, ONLY Mary, Pomeroy, and Mrs. Beeton stood to watch Mrs. Durham's casket lowered into its grave. The sun hid behind storm clouds. The casket made a dull thud that sounded far too much like how Mary imagined it must have sounded when her aunt cracked her head against the very same rock that caused Pomeroy to walk around with his head bandaged for days.

Why hadn't she moved that awful rock?

"You shouldn't be doing that," Trentwood said, appearing at Mary's side.

They were burying Mrs. Durham at the family plot, on the other side of her twin's grave. It seemed appropriate that the two people Mrs. Trentwood had loved, her husband and her twin, should flank her in life and death.

"Pomeroy," Mary said, her voice dull, "would you be so kind as to leave me, for a moment?"

"I don't know if I should," he said, inching his fingers along the brim of his hat in his hands. He kept looking at Trentwood's grave, as if the man himself would crawl from it.

Mary's smile was a bit wry. Poor Pomeroy, if he only knew Trentwood had already done that. "Go on, I will be perfectly fine. Watch me from the window, if you like. I won't go anywhere."

Pomeroy's eyes narrowed as if he knew she was lying to him. But another glance at Trentwood's not-yet-level grave made up his mind for him. He placed his hat on his head, tipped it to Mary, and left her alone with Trentwood.

Waiting until Pomeroy was out of hearing, Mary said in flat tones, "What is it I shouldn't be doing?"

"You know very well. Mary, you can't keep blaming yourself for situations that are out of your control. You did not kill your mother, migraines did. You did not kill me, my stubbornness did. And you definitely did not kill your aunt, her madness did."

Mary sighed, nodding. "I know."

That seemed to startle Trentwood. "What?"

"Father, I'm right where I began two months ago after your death. I'm alone, I have no money, I have no friends, and now I don't even have family." She lifted her black netted veil, the very same one she had worn to his funeral, and looked him in the eye. "I haven't been sleeping, trying to decide what I'm to do. I have nowhere to go, I haven't the education to be a governess, and I don't want to leave home. But I can't see another way out of it."

"You have your inheritance," he reminded her.

Mary waved her hand at him. "Money isn't going to solve my problems."

"Well, it won't hurt," he retorted. He inhaled, sighed, and looked at Mrs. Durham's grave. "It's probably better this way, for her, at least. She got to hold her husband's child. That's all she really wanted, it seems."

"Yes," Mary said, "hold him, and kill him, and kill herself. Or have you forgotten already?"

Trentwood pulled out his pocket watch, swinging it from its gold chain. "So morbid," he muttered.

"My mother's sense of humor," Mary said, gesturing at her mother's grave.

"Indeed."

They stood there, staring at the gravesite.

"You know," Trentwood mused, "I haven't been here since I was buried."

Mary looked up at him, squinting. What was he about to say? She bit the side of her cheek when she saw his expression. He was going to leave her. Just when she didn't want him to, he was going to leave her.

"I can't stay like this forever," he said as explanation.

"You wouldn't have to," Mary said. "Only until I die."

Trentwood chuckled at that. "I'd like to, my girl, but you've no need of me anymore. You're out of danger, and you've gotten a bit of your spirit back, and you've found affection, if you're brave enough to accept it."

Mary frowned. Steele had been very quick to leave after a day of sleep, eating what was left of her food stores, and the regaining of his senses. With him, she was sure, went his proposal of marriage. Funny that she didn't miss him all that much.

"I could have told you marrying Steele would have been a mistake," Trentwood said, "but you were sure to have married him then, just to spite me."

"I was going to marry him if he would have me."

"Yes, because you thought it would chase me away."

Mary frowned at him.

"Marrying a stupid man won't make me leave your life." Trentwood grinned at her. "I would have haunted him until he lost his mind, or you came to your senses, whichever came first."

Mary crossed her arms over her chest and glared.

"Why don't you take a holiday from this dreary place for a while? Why not go to the city, enjoy a play or two? See the queen's jubilee? You can come back in the summer and begin repairing the house then, when it's a bit nicer out."

To be sure, this was a miserable spring. Raining every day since Mrs. Durham's death a week ago, with no sign of the weather improving in the slightest. Mary turned her face upward to the raindrops that were starting to fall.

She inhaled the fresh air and exhaled slowly. She released the tension in her shoulders. She let her hands drop to her sides. In this unguarded moment, her heart peeked out from behind the walls she had erected to suggest a small, simple thought.

Mary's eyes popped open.

Trentwood nodded. "It's about time, young miss."

He leaned over to kiss her forehead, and with everything else she had seen, Mary knew she was not imagining the feathery feel of his lips, the peppermint on his breath, the suggestion of whiskers on his cheek. She shivered and closed her eyes. His lips left her, and with them, the sensation of his presence.

"Sleep well," Mary whispered, sinking to touch the foot of his grave. She was alone and knew that was how it would be unless she did something about it. It was as her mother said. All women have a prince who needed rescuing. "Give my love to Mama."

FORTY-THREE

IN WHICH MARY PURSUES

EN ROUTE TO LONDON, JUNE 1887

THE TRAIN RIDE HAD Mary on edge even more than she expect-ed. It rocketed through the countryside, bringing her closer to London than she had ever thought possible. Having never been on a train before, the sights and smells were almost too much.

She wanted to vomit from the overpowering stench of soot and overripe bodies, all on their way to the golden jubilee of their Regina Victoria. She was crowded in with the other upper middle class, and there was no way around it. She couldn't ask for a private carriage because she hadn't the money or the status to facilitate such a demand.

So Mary sat with Pomeroy at her side for she had insisted he stay with her, trying to figure out what she was going to do once she got to London. The crowds, she had read in the papers, were immense, unimaginable. Apparently they stretched to the limits of sight, preparing to hail their glorious Queen Victoria as she traveled the distance from Westminster to Buckingham.

Mary told herself that was why she couldn't keep any food down. She was worried for the queen.

So many people fighting to catch a glimpse of the little woman was sure to frighten her. So easy for someone with ill will to get close enough to harm her.

Mary shook her head. What a silly thing to think. The queen was surrounded by her adoring subjects; who would want to, or dare to, hurt her on such a momentous occasion?

The train slowed to a halt far before Mary had grown accustomed to the odd rhythm. It had been smoother than horse-drawn, yet her stomach felt as though it was spinning.

The noise in London was overwhelming. All of civilization had convened on London, and they were happy about it for some reason. There were placards and walking bands, paper boys and constables. Hails between friends. Raucous laughter. Claps on the shoulder and invitations home for a drink before the queen's parade tomorrow.

With Pomeroy's help, Mary stepped from the train and was handed into a carriage, where the world was, thankfully, quieter.

"Where to, Miss?" the driver said.

Mary looked at Pomeroy. Pomeroy rattled off some London address with a knowing smile at her and settled into his seat. How he knew the address she wanted, she had no idea. But there were a great many things about Pomeroy that Mary didn't know. It seemed it would always be that way.

Mary closed her eyes, the comforting familiarity of a horse-drawn carriage lulling her to sleep. She paid no mind to the shouts and cries and whinnies around her, the sounds that made up London life. She was far too exhausted, and she needed her energy to do what she meant to do.

Pomeroy shook Mary's shoulder. "We've arrived."

"Hmm?" Mary said, blinking sleepily. "Arrived? Arrived where?" She allowed Pomeroy to take her hand and help her from the carriage. They stood before an austere red brick building, a brass name plate with the name "Hartwell, Barrister" etched on it.

Mary licked her lips. She nodded.

Pomeroy opened the door for her, and she swept inside to find Steele filing a ledger away in one of at least fifteen tall bookcases.

"How do you do, Jasper?" Mary said.

He spun on his heel, dropping his papers. He blanched at the sight of her, backing into the bookcase behind him and disrupting even more papers.

With a tight smile, Mary inched into the room, not wanting to step on the papers Steele continued to drop and jostle out of place.

"Steele," Hartwell shouted from the back room, "what the devil are you doing out there?"

Steele managed a garbled grunt of a reply.

"How many times have I told you, that—ah. Oh. Hello," Hartwell said, emerging from the back room with his sleeves rolled up past his elbows, his hair a mess, his scarred face looking particularly awful in the harsh afternoon sunlight. He stared at Mary as if she were a ghost. A seemingly welcome one, if his broad smile meant anything.

Mary caught her breath. Before Hartwell could respond to her appearing in his office, she stepped forward, holding a careworn letter. "My father's will stated that I need to provide a key to retrieve my inheritance, but I haven't any key."

Hartwell nodded. "Yes," he said slowly, looking as if he had difficulty wrapping his mind around the vision of her standing before him. They had not seen one another for almost three months. It stood to reason he would be rather befuddled, to say the least, especially since the last time they had spoken, her aunt had been alive, and she had been haunted.

"What are my options, then, to retrieve my inheritance, paltry though it must be, without the key?" Mary hoped Hartwell smiled because she looked well. She had, with Pomeroy and Mrs. Beeton's help, slowly put the manor house to rights. They had gone on walks, and she had regained some of her walker's coloring. She had picked up reading again, and laughing. She was a member of her little community again, and the local farmers had welcomed her with warm arms.

Just as she hoped Hartwell would do now.

Hartwell frowned, not at Mary but at her necklace. Her mother's pendant. He crossed the room and lifted the pendant, turning it from side-to-side in his fingers.

"Your father said, or rather, his ghost said—"

"Ghost?" Steele shrieked.

"—it was your mother's key you needed," Hartwell finished over Steele's interruption.

Mary nodded, holding her breath. She didn't care about the inheritance, and she needed to tell him that. It wasn't the inheritance she came to retrieve. It was him. Hartwell. Her Hartwell, with his laughing eyes and mangled face and intense love for his nephew. He had said only she could make up her mind about Steele's offer, and his unspoken, but, she hoped, implied one.

Without a word, Mary turned around so Hartwell could unclasp the necklace from her neck. Her smile was hesitant as Hartwell looked at her. She couldn't read his expression, but his eyes, his dark, laughing eyes, said all she needed to hear.

Her necklace in hand, Hartwell pulled her close, hugging her. "I'm so sorry about your aunt."

Mary pulled away just enough to look him in the eye. His arms were strong, steady, safe. Warm. She felt warm and right, standing there in his arms with Steele and Pomeroy trying to pretend they weren't gawking. She smiled at Hartwell. He smiled in return.

"What are your plans?" he whispered.

Mary pressed her lips against Hartwell's as her answer. She felt him smile as the kiss deepened. Her arms wrapped around his neck, his arms around her waist. They clung to one another, feeling as though they were the only two persons in the room. It was Steele's scandalized "Ahem!" which made them pull away from one another, laughing, breathless.

Pomeroy leaned against the doorjamb, grinning.

"You'll have to marry him now, you know that, of course," she thought she heard Trentwood say.

Mary leaned her head onto Hartwell's shoulder.

Yes. I suppose I shall.

Mary didn't know how much inheritance she had. She didn't know if her pendant was the key to the lock box. She wasn't sure if she could live in London with the noise and pollution, or if Hartwell would be willing to come home with her to Compton Beauchamp. But all that was insignificant to the feeling of standing in Hartwell's arms, knowing he had cared for her even when he had thought she was mad, and she for him even though the world thought he was grotesque.

It was more than enough for Mary. And in the end, that was, she remembered her mother saying, the point of such fairy tales.

The story, her mother had always said, came to an end when the heroine thought nothing better could happen to her.

Message from the Author

I hope you had as much fun reading this as I had writing it. If you liked this book, please consider writing a review at one of the locations below. As an independent author, your reviews and word-of-mouth are key to the success of this book and my writing career.

Website https://worderella.com
BookBub https://worderella.com/bookbub
Goodreads https://worderella.com/goodreads

Acknowledgements

No one makes a book alone, and anyone who tells you that is lying. I have a huge list of people to thank, so bear with me!

I owe a great debt of thanks and a series of hugs to the following people for contributing to and supporting this endeavor…

Thank you to my family for listening when I went on a happy-writer-rant about some plot development I had discovered. And for not putting me on medication when I admitted I had characters in my head and they were telling me to write their story.

Thank you to the people who have been with me since this book was called Trentwood's Orphan and was about breach of promise: Graham Carter, Jill Daher-Twersky, Susannah Jane, Joe Murphy, and The Ohio State University library system.

Thank you to my editor, Cindy Sherwood, for helping this book be as good as it could be!

Thank you to my Kickstarter peeps that helped make this book financially possible! Kickstarter is a website that allows creative projects to accept funding pledges from anyone with a credit card. Thank you, everyone, for believing in me and Haunting Miss Trentwood (alphabetical):

Adrienne Dye, Allison Cooke, Andrew Selig, Angie Nelson, Ava Misseldine, Bobak Kechavarzi, Brandon Stephens, Brittani White, Caitlin Boyle, Caitlin O'Sullivan, Casey M Addy, Cathy Windle, Chris Basham, Cindy Gildersleeve, Ebiji Akah,

Erica LeMaster, Evangeline Holland, Geoffrey Stetson, Guy Jacks, Hailey Anderson, Heiko Maiwand, Jackie Akah, Jacqueline Abreo, James M Turner, Jay Steele, Jennifer Center, Jeremy Center, John Wayne Hill, Julie Hoopes, Kate Logan, Mark Kroll, Linda Jackson, Lorelei Kelly, Lynn S. Dombrowski, Matt Edwards, Moe Rafiuddin, Nikki Lemon, Nina Onesti, Robert J. McCarter, Robert Kariuki, Susannah Jane, Suzy Turner, and William Malinowski.

And thank you to everyone else who supported my 2010 Kickstarter project. You know who you are! If you don't, check out my website to find your name.

Become a VIP

If you would like to be contacted when I release a new work, subscribe to my newsletter or become a patron of my community, the Cozy Coterie. Cozy Coterie patrons receive discounts from my store, including exclusive editions.

Newsletter https://worderella.com/vip
Cozy Coterie https://worderella.com/cozycoterie

TITLES BY BELINDA KROLL

HESITANT MEDIUMS

Haunting Miss Trentwood
Miss Preston's Predicament (story)
An Inconvenient Séance (story)
A Spirited Engagement

OTHER TITLES

The Last April
Catching the Rose

Beatrice Learns to Dance
as Binaebi Akah

Miss Preston's Predicament

A Hesitant Mediums story

*It was a truth universally ignored, most principally by the dowager
Dame Hartwell, that ghosts and gatherings did not mix.*

In this short story, the fashionable and eccentric dowager Dame
Hartwell has lured the reclusive Miss Tessa Preston to attend her
drawing room séance. If Dame Hartwell can't convince Miss
Preston, her former protégé, to return as her medium-in-res-
idence, she doesn't know how she will protect her son and
his new fiancée from the brewing storm of malcontent spirits
surrounding them.

MISS PRESTON'S PREDICAMENT is a short story be-
tween novels. It is a standalone referencing characters and events
from the cozy Victorian fantasy romance, HAUNTING MISS
TRENTWOOD, the first in the Hesitant Mediums series.

An Inconvenient Séance

A Hesitant Mediums story

It was a truth universally ignored that sons abhorred being sent to séances in search of a wife.

In this short story, Jasper Steele has had enough of ghosts to last him a lifetime, so why is he attending a séance? Mostly to appease his mother, who worries about his head and his heart after his summer in the English countryside getting rejected by Mary Trentwood.

Eloise Carterprice has never been one to let a good opportunity escape her, so it's only natural that her ghost appears during the latest séance hosted by her mother. Will Jasper find a bit of romance? Will Eloise have her bit of fun? Read on, dear Reader, read on!

This is a short story bridge between HAUNTING MISS TRENTWOOD and A SPIRITED ENGAGEMENT. It is a companion story to "Miss Preston's Predicament."

A Spirited Engagement
Book 2 of the Hesitant Mediums

*It was a truth universally acknowledged that ghost brides
are annoying romantic rivals.*

Making her reluctant return to London after a ten-year absence,
Tessa Preston cannot hide her dismay at her employer's friendliness with Jasper Steele, the man who chased her away. To make
matters more annoying, he's haunted by a *most insistent* ghost
bride.

Determined to prove her indifference to the charming Jasper,
Tessa realizes the entitled ghost demanding his attention may
not be all she seems. Meanwhile, unaware of Tessa's enmity,
Jasper is delighted to have a second chance at her affections,
and will let nothing, not even her cold stares, dampen his
enthusiasm.

A SPIRITED ENGAGEMENT is a standalone romantic fantasy featuring characters from the cozy Victorian fantasy romance, HAUNTING MISS TRENTWOOD, the first in the
Hesitant Mediums series.

ABOUT THE AUTHOR

Belinda Kroll writes sweet and cozy Victorian fantasy and fiction. Think Jane Austen-lite vocabulary meets modern sass. She is a user experience design professional, hobbyist photographer, and lindy hopper.

Kroll is obsessed with eyeglasses, Korean dramas, home renovation and cooking shows, and petting every dog that allows her to do so. She has a line of stationery for writers, readers, and creatives at Bright Bird Press. She lives with her family in Ohio.

Website https://worderella.com
Instagram https://instagram.com/worderella
Patron community https://worderella.com/cozycoterie
Bright Bird Press stationery https://brightbirdpress.com

www.ingramcontent.com/pod-product-compliance
Lightning Source LLC
Chambersburg PA
CBHW050249110726
47898CB00007B/2333